Frances Cashel Hoey

The Lover's Creed

Vol. II

Frances Cashel Hoey

The Lover's Creed
Vol. II

ISBN/EAN: 9783337053284

Printed in Europe, USA, Canada, Australia, Japan

Cover: Foto ©Andreas Hilbeck / pixelio.de

More available books at **www.hansebooks.com**

𝔄 𝔑𝔬𝔳𝔢𝔩

BY

MRS CASHEL HOEY

AUTHOR OF

' THE QUESTION OF CAIN ' ' THE BLOSSOMING OF AN ALOE ' ' NO SIGN ' ETC.

'ONE, AND ONE ONLY, IS THE LOVER'S CREED'

OLIVER WENDELL HOLMES

IN THREE VOLUMES—VOL. II.

London

CHATTO & WINDUS, PICCADILLY

1884

LONDON : PRINTED BY
SPOTTISWOODE AND CO., NEW-STREET SQUARE
AND PARLIAMENT STREET

THE LOVER'S CREED.

CHAPTER XII.

A WRENCH.

' FATHER, you cannot mean it.!'

'I don't often say what I don't mean. You will find this is not one of the times I have wasted breath. Let me have no nonsense; I never was in less of a humour to put up with it.'

Mavis glanced from her father to his wife. Mrs. Wynn sat speechless, pale, and terrified. This way of taking his announcement angered Wynn more than any she could have adopted. He shouted at her—

'Why the devil don't you speak?' then

moved a step or two nearer to the poor woman, who shrank from his approach. She did, however, manage to stammer out—

'Was this your business all those weeks?'

'Yes, it was. What, you guessed I had some business out of the common, did you? You are not such a fool as you look. This was my business, and a troublesome job, too; you may be sure I did not want to make it more troublesome, by bringing you into it a bit sooner than I could help.'

'You might have told us, father,' said Mavis, emboldened by the terror which the idea of being taken away from England had for her. 'This concerns us as much as you.'

'Us! What? You and my wife! A precious pair, always ready to set yourselves against me. And my business is as much yours as mine, is it?'

'Yes, father. I think it is. This means that we shall have to go to the other side of the world, and leave—leave——'

'Leave your airs and your rubbish, your psalm-singing and your parson; all you've got to leave that I know of. There isn't much to complain of in that, and it would not make any difference if there was. You've got to do what I bid you; I don't care a d—n what you think about it.'

Mavis made a struggle for composure. She felt the uselessness of resistance; the truth of her father's remorseless words was not to be disputed. As for her own suffering under them, she said to herself, as she so often had occasion to say :—' This shall be for by-and-by; there is something else to do now.' She seated herself by Mrs. Wynn's side, took her hand into her own cool, firm clasp, and said submissively :—

' Let us know your wishes, father. You cannot wonder that we are surprised and frightened; but if you will explain this decision that you have come to, we will do what you please.'

'I should hope so,' said Wynn, with a sneer. 'But perhaps you'll just speak for yourself, Mavis. You take a deal too much upon you. My wife has a tongue, I suppose.'

True tyrant that he was, he could not brook the silence of his victim; he wanted to hear her complain.

Mrs. Wynn said feebly—

'Of course, Wynn, whatever you choose must be done. I am not very strong, and I am so used to being always in the same place that I am frightened; but it must be as you like. Only, I never thought you would give up the farm. I thought you always liked a farmer's life.'

She was talking on in her nervousness; he stopped her with a short laugh. This did not reassure her. Farmer Wynn's womankind had as much reason to dread his laugh as his frown. On the present occasion, however, it meant a revulsion towards comparative good humour.

'So I did, and so I do; but there's a better

life than a farmer's in England. The life of a ettler in Australia, where the crops are gold, is quite another story. Money makes money there, and I've a mind to die a rich man— after I've lived a rich man for a good long spell.'

'Is my uncle a rich man?' asked Mavis.

'I've no doubt he is; but Lewis Wynn always said little, and so had little to mend. He has never told me what he's worth. He has told me that Melbourne's the place for a man to go to who wants to make money quickly, and enjoy it before he's too old to enjoy anything. What he has done I can do, for he started with next to nothing, and I have not done so bad with what I had when I began life.'

The farmer chuckled, and stuck his hands deep into his pockets. Neither his wife nor Mavis had ever previously heard him admit so much. Each was wise enough to make no comment and to ask no question.

'My brother has no children,' continued Wynn, 'and whatever he's got to leave had better come to me than go to strangers. He thinks well of my going out there, so I'm going.'

'Was it only because you did not want to be troubled with our regrets that you have kept this from Sarah and me until now?' asked Mavis, gravely.

'Do you want a better reason? I don't care how you take it now; the business is done, and you will have enough to do to get your own gear ready. But while I had the arrangements with the Squire to make, and Reckitts to see and settle with, I did not fancy a couple of whingeing, whining women to bother me.'

'Then you knew this would be bad news to us, father? You knew that we should grieve at leaving our home?'

'I thought it likely, and I did not see the good of giving you more time than I need to grieve, as you call it—that is, to grumble at me, and call me names to the neighbours.'

' Are we going to my uncle's house?' asked Mavis, abandoning the personal part of the discussion without any protest against her father's last sentence.

' Perhaps so; I do not know; I have not made up my mind yet. But it is no affair of yours where we are going; you will be comfortable and well off, and you won't have more to do for it there than you have here, if that's a recommendation to you.'

' My uncle lives in Melbourne?' asked Mavis. ' Has his house any name?'

' What the devil is that to you?' snarled Wynn. ' If you can't ask more sensible questions than that, ask none. You had better attend to what I am going to say, both of you, for I shan't fancy repeating it. Reckitts is coming in for good in ten days from to-morrow, and he takes over the whole concern. The Squire has agreed to all he asks; the transfer of the lease will be made then. I've got the new lease—that's it that came to-day—and I shall remain here until near the time of sailing.'

'Does the Squire know?' asked Mrs. Wynn, timidly.

Mavis listened breathlessly for the answer, for she thought: 'If he does, he may have mentioned it in writing to Jack, as a bit of news about the estate, and Jack will have learned it, not from me, and be miserable.'

'Of course he knows, you fool. Who should know if not my landlord, Reckitts's landlord that's to be? He has known it as long as myself, and he gave me a lot of useful information. The Squire isn't what they call a stirring man, but he knows one that is when he sees him; and he is not likely to stand in anybody's light, though people do say he has stood in his own. Things ain't going well with the Squire. It would be a good job for him if he wasn't a gentleman, as mustn't grime his

hands with any dirtier work than the handlin'
of old books, for then he could come out to
Australia, too, and soon put his affairs all
straight.'

Mrs. Wynn was too much stupefied by the
prospect before her to feel curiosity about the
affairs of Squire Bassett, or any other indi-
vidual. Mavis was too conscious of her own
secret to venture to express what she felt.
Repeating his chuckle, and re-shoving his
hands into his pockets, Farmer Wynn aban-
doned that branch of the subject, and began in
his most dictatorial style upon another.

'Everything is done, except the getting
of your clothes for the voyage. I shall take
you out as first-class passengers in a good
ship, the " British Queen," from 'Liverpool.
The passages are taken ; you and Mavis will
have a cabin to yourselves. If you are not
comfortable it will be your own fault. How
soon can she be got ready to leave here ? '

Wynn addressed Mavis, and made re-

ference to his wife as if she had been a
bundle.

'To leave here! for Melbourne?'

'For Liverpool!' Wynn shouted the words
at Mavis, and his coarse face reddened with
anger. 'You are as big a fool as she is. You
will have to get the things you want in Liverpool. I suppose you'll have the sense to know
what they are. I'll find a hundred pounds
between you.'

'Are we to take all our things away with
us?'

'Certainly,' answered the farmer, with the
sneer and the short laugh that always hurt
Mavis like the stroke of a whip. 'You don't
suppose you're going to the other side of the
world to stay a week or two, do you?'

'My books, and music?'

'Oh yes; your tools can be packed up;
perhaps you'll find some use for them out
there.'

'I will implore him to let me stay in

England, and be a governess,' thought Mavis;
but the pressure of her stepmother's hand
restrained her as the words were on her lips.
She remembered the promise she had made to
herself; the wan and frightened face by her
side suggested a vision of what Mrs. Wynn's
life would be, on the ocean, and in a strange
land, without her. No; she would never
leave her.

'Do you know where that sister of yours is
to be found in Liverpool?' said Wynn to his
wife.

'She lives at 108, Cecil Street, in lodgings.'

'When did you last hear from her?'

'Two months ago.'

'Write and tell her you are coming to
Liverpool with Mavis, and that you want her
to take lodgings for you; perhaps there may
be rooms in the house she lives in.'

It was characteristic of Wynn to ignore the
existence of his wife's sister until her services
happened to be required for his convenience,

and then to take them for granted; but Mrs. Wynn did not observe this. A faint pleasure stirred her at the prospect of seeing her sister once more.

'I suppose you can be ready to start in three days. You may set about buying your things as soon as you get there. Your sister— what's her name, Jane—will put you in the way of that. You will stay there until I join you.'

Mrs. Wynn again grasped Mavis's hand, but she did not hazard any appeal. It was the dread of going to a distant land, not the pain of leaving Fieldflower Farm, that oppressed her so terribly. The abode of her tyrant could have no charm, no tie, for her; it was pure physical terror that had laid hold of her.

'Mind what I have said, and take care you don't give me any more trouble.'

With these words Wynn left the room.

'Oh, Mavis, what are we to do? It is the cruellest thing that ever was done! And to

do it in this secret, sudden way! to be all this
time settling with that man, and we never to
have a hint of what was before us! If it had
not been for the Dame's Parlour we might
have guessed, and found out; but I did think
it was the old furniture that brought him here.'

'I might have guessed nearer the truth, as
near at least as father's giving up the farm,'
said Mavis, 'when I had to copy the inventory,
but I never thought more of that. It does
seem cruel indeed, and useless, too, for he has
no great occasion for more gain than comes in
his way here. However, after all, he has a
right to do with his life what he likes, and if
he had but told us sooner——! Sarah, do
you dread the idea of leaving this place so
very much? You have told me you did not
care for it, or for anything—how should you?
Perhaps the new life in a new country may be
better.'

'No, no; nothing will ever be better. He
will take himself with him wherever he goes;

and wherever I go, there's no peace for me. Oh, Mavis, I may as well tell you now what I have been thinking these months past; it is that I shall not be alive much longer—and I wish, I do wish, I could die here quietly. I am not able for it, my dear; indeed I am not able for it.'

'I know you are not,' said Mavis, sadly. 'I fear you have been weaker lately than you have admitted. I don't wonder you should dread a long voyage, and an unknown land at the end of it.'

'I shall never live to get to the end of it, and I have always had a dread of the sea. I was never on it; but I have seen ships, and the people that come off them, at Liverpool, and I know what suffering there is for weak people at sea. Think, Mavis, of being shut down in a storm, in your narrow berth—why, it must always be like a coffin, with the lid taken off, but kept close over your head all the time—think of lying there, listening to the

wind, and the sea, the shouting and trampling,
and being so ill that you could not care what
happened to you, if only it was not just the
very thing you have got to bear for weeks and
weeks.'

Mrs. Wynn's eyes searched her stepdaughter's face with anxious and pitiful crav-
ing, and Mavis measured the poor woman's
terror of the impending change, by the fact
that it had roused her to such an effort of
imagination.

'My father does not know, he cannot
realise, the woful thing it is to you,' she said.
'I will go to him and tell him. You said nothing; you took it too quietly; you made no
fight.'

'Of course I didn't, it would have been no
good. Things would be only made worse for
me; they always were when I attempted to
cross him or to object. I never do anything
of the kind now. And you must not, Mavis;
you must not indeed. We have only got to

submit, my dear; all is settled and done; he
will never go back upon it. I'm more sorry
for you than for myself. It must soon be over
for me, anyhow; only now I shall be put
down into the sea, and have no grave. That
won't really matter, you know, only I have a
shrinking from it. I should like to lie in the
quiet ground, in my own country. But that is
only a fancy. You'll get to the other side of
the world all right; but oh, how will you bear
it when you're there? And what will Mr.
Jack say?'

'I don't know. He will be shocked, of
course. It is dreadful to think that I shall
be so far away from him when the war is over
and he comes home. Think, Sarah'—here
Mavis relaxed the restraint she had put upon
herself and burst into tears—'think of all the
time that I shall be in that horrible ship, with
no possibility of hearing from him. Think,
only think, that *anything* may happen, and
I not know it, while we are going to the

other side of the world. Oh, what shall I do? what shall I do? Why, Sarah, it must be months before J can get a letter from him in Australia?'

' Yes, I suppose so.'

Beyond a feeble assent Mrs. Wynn could not go. The deadlock was so hopeless that she had neither suggestion nor consolation to offer.

' He will come to me there,' said Mavis, ' when the war is over; but this will make everything so much harder.'

' Yes, dear, yes; I see that.' These words, repeated several times, were all Mrs. Wynn could utter, while Mavis gave way to the fit of weeping that seemed to relieve her.

But Mavis soon recovered herself, and then she proceeded to discuss the active side of the position whose passive side was so formidable to them both. The time allowed them was very short; there was much to be done, and Mavis was relieved to find that she was able slightly to divert Mrs. Wynn's mind from her sad forebodings by keeping before her the prospect of a meeting with her sister. This was something near to grasp at. It was Mavis who wrote to Miss Price; and it was due to her skilful management that Mrs. Wynn got through the last few days at Fieldflower Farm with but little bad language from her husband, and without any actual ill-usage.

On what Mavis suffered it would be useless to dwell. Amid all the hurry of their departure, she contrived to make farewell visits to the Parsonage, to Bassett, and to the general shop in the village. At the latter place she learned that the approaching departure of the Wynns had excited some curiosity, but little concern. She herself was almost a stranger —people in those parts took a good while to recognise new comers—her stepmother was too generally esteemed 'a poor creature' to be regarded as a loss, and nobody liked Wynn well enough to regret him seriously. Williams

noted with businesslike indifference her directions that letters for her, marked 'to be kept
till called for,' were to be forwarded to the
care of Miss Price, 108 Cecil Street, Liverpool.

Mavis knew that (in so far as anything was
certain) she should see Bassett again, when
Jack had come to the other side of the world
to seek her, and taken her home; but the
neighbours to whom she said farewell knew
nothing of this, and their apathy was chilling
and painful. That Melbourne was a long way
off, and that she would see a deal of the world,
were the commonplaces to which her friends
restricted themselves.

Early on a beautiful day in May, Mavis
made her farewell visit to the Parsonage, and
there at least she did not meet with indifference.
Mrs. Colvin liked her. She understood Wynn's
character, and she felt for his wife and
daughter the sound and discerning compassion
that the happy wife of an amiable man was
bound to feel. Mrs. Colvin was not altogether

sorry that Mavis had to go to Australia, for, although her notions of the Colonies were as vague as most people's in those days, she had an idea that marriage under prosperous conditions was more likely to come in the girl's way there than here. She was less concerned personally, because she would have had to part with Mavis under any circumstances.

Change had set in at peaceful and monotonous Bassett; it was busy at Fieldflower Farm; some dimly understood trouble was overhanging the house on the hill, and the Parsonage was shortly to have a new occupant. Mr. Colvin had been appointed to a foreign chaplaincy, and the coming month would see the family settled in an Italian city. Mr. Colvin's successor was already named, and had come down from London to inspect his future abode. Mr. Gale was a shy man, academical of aspect, a bachelor, a student, and he knew no more about music than he knew about millinery. Mrs. Colvin foresaw that the choir-

singing would speedily come to an end.
Mavis left the house more than ever heavy-
hearted; it would all be so different when Jack
came home.

The last of the three visits was a sharp
trial to Mavis. Mrs. Wynn accompanied her
to Bassett, and they were received by Miss
Nestle with her usual self-possession. At the
House there was no external mark of change;
whatever the Squire had communicated to the
head of the executive there, remained a secret.
Let who would guess at or talk of Mr.
Bassett's affairs, it should not be in Miss
Nestle's hearing. Nevertheless, Mavis discerned
trouble in the faithful woman's face, and that
quality in herself which responded to this
reticence made her honour Miss Nestle for it;
although it could not be denied that there was
a lack of sympathy with her visitors on the
part of the latter. If Jack had given Mavis a
hint that he suspected Miss Nestle of suspecting
him, she would have been to some extent pre-

pared for the satisfaction with which the good spinster regarded the departure of the Wynns, and for her manner of viewing an undertaking whose mere suddenness and reversal of long-existing conditions would formerly have incurred disapproval.

Only that there was no fire in Miss Nestle's own parlour, and that the rich odour of the hawthorn blossoms came floating in through an open window, telling of the advance of the season, all was just as it had been on the memorable day when Trotty Veck introduced his master to that master's Fate. The furniture of Miss Nestle's room was polished to the same pitch of perfection, the invariable work-box and key-basket occupied the same spot. On the hearth-rug lay Trotty Veck, who had been solemnly confided by Jack to Miss Nestle's care, and was growing much too fat for his own good in consequence of her more zealous than judicious discharge of the trust. Trotty greeted the visitors with

the faithful friendliness of his nature and his
race. Mavis took him up and hugged him.
Miss Nestle's eye fell upon her as she did this,
with anything but an approving expression.

'I am sure this is an excellent thing for
you all,' said Miss Nestle to Mrs. Wynn, with
brisk cheerfulness. 'You will be quite strong
and well out there, and Mavis will be sure to
get a good husband. It is a capital idea of
Farmer Wynn's ; a capital idea. Of course
the Squire approves of it.'

'I believe he does,' said Mrs. Wynn, rue-
fully, while Mavis bent over Trotty Veck, and
kept silence.

'The Squire is always interested in the
welfare of Bassett people, when they are
deserving. I have heard him say that's a
fine country you're going to.'

Miss Nestle's manner was patronising, and
her tone was unusually grand. Her secret
knowledge of the change in the Squire's fortune incited her to impress his importance

upon her hearers with additional urgency, but
they, having no insight into her motives, were
hurt by her demeanour. Mavis would have
dearly liked to ask leave to revisit the rooms
she had seen in Jack's company; but Miss
Nestle's mood was evidently unpropitious, and
she refrained from the request. The leave-
taking over, Mrs. Wynn and Mavis agreed that
they did not know what to make of Miss
Nestle.

'She seemed quite glad to get rid of us,' said
Mrs. Wynn. 'I am sure we never did her
any harm, or gave her any offence. It was
odd too that she never mentioned Mr. Jack's
name. Formerly she was always talking of
him. I wonder what she would say if she
knew that you will be mistress at the House
some day.'

Mavis smiled, very sadly.

'She would be shocked. That would indeed be not knowing my place, and not keeping
in it. I never think about that part of the

future. At all events we may be sure that the
story they are telling in the village is not true.
The Squire is not going to leave Bassett.
Miss Nestle was too cheerful for that.'

The last day Mavis Wynn was to pass in
the place which, though not dear to her in the
sense of a happy home, had the sacred associations of her love to render it precious, was a
serene and beautiful one. By incessant exertion in the preparations for departure, Mavis
secured time to visit the swan's nest and the
turret-bower, also to linger a while at the window in the Dame's Parlour, and look her last
on the fields and the river. She had bravely
held at bay the dread of all that lay before her
while her head and her hands were taxed to
the utmost, and all her efforts were directed
to helping and comforting Mrs. Wynn ; but
although her faith in Jack, and her youthful
confidence in the future, were strong, she
broke down when those farewells had to be
made. The futility of the promises she had

given to her lover, the sudden shifting of the
scene of her life, the unknown to be en-
countered, the secret that she carried in
her breast, oppressive notwithstanding its
sweetness—all these combined to crush her
at the last.   Hidden by the green shelter of
the turret-bower, Mavis knelt on the spot
where she and Jack had talked of a future
which, whatever it might prove to be, could
not resemble their forecast of it, and prayed as
she had never prayed before.

*　　*　　*　　*　　*

The visitor at the Farm, so soon to be its
occupant, had seen but little of Mrs. Wynn
and Mavis.   Mr. Reckitts was a quiet elderly
man, whose ambition it had long been to
occupy a position of the precise kind that
Wynn was relinquishing.   The arrangement
suited both parties to a nicety.   Mr. Reckitts
kept himself discreetly out of the way of
the women, meeting them at meals only, and
probably did not give a thought to their senti-

ments. He was not accustomed to the society or the ways of women, and his most distinct impression in reference to Wynn's wife and daughter, was that they were lower-spirited than he should like to see them if it were any business of his.

Wynn accompanied his wife and Mavis to Chester, and saw them into the train for Liverpool. He had been tolerably civil to them both since he had signified his will—(for this they probably had to thank the stranger's presence) but he told them no more of his purposes. Mavis had not yet written the letter that was to convey the tidings of what had befallen them to Jack Bassett. Her last letter, a happy and hopeful one, had been written on the very day her father's communication was made. She decided that she would write from Liverpool when the time was close at hand for their sailing, and when she should have some more full and certain information to give to Jack.

Mrs. Wynn slept during a part of the journey, and Mavis anxiously noted the exhausted look in her face. The words 'I shall never live to get to the end of it,' and 'I shall be put down into the sea, and have no grave,' sounded in her ears again.

CHAPTER XIII.

EMANCIPATED.

' NAME of Wynn here?' asked a porter who ran along by the train as it was pulling up at the terminus.

' Yes,' said Mavis, looking out, and the next minute the sisters, who had not seen each other since Sarah Price's wedding-day, met. Jane Price was not like her sister; in her quick movements, intelligent dark eyes, and decided manner Mavis discerned a helpful character; and she was cheered by the impression, although she could not imagine how any help was to come to them from Jane Price.

' I am so glad our lodgings are not near the water,' said Mrs. Wynn, as the fly bore them well away from the shipping quarter to a steep

quiet street, with an air of provincial gentility
upon it. 'I cannot bear it. I was thinking of
that in the train, and wishing I had thought of
asking Mavis to tell you to take lodgings somewhere out (f sight of it.'

Jane Price and Mavis interchanged glances.
The sisters had not indulged in close confidences
in their rare letters, but the younger's sharp
perception had guided her to an estimate of
the lot of the elder, and this the sight of Sarah
had confirmed.

The rooms prepared for the travellers, in
the house with Jane Price, were comfortable
and orderly. Mrs. Wynn was delighted with
them, and so cheered up under the novelty and
freedom of the position that when Jane—who
had only a brief leave from her business until
evening—had left them, she proposed to go
out with Mavis, and take her to see the house
in which she had lived as a girl.

'But you will be so tired,' objected Mavis,
' if you go out after your journey.'

'Not at all; I feel too restless to stay in the house. We need not think about the things that are to be bought until to-morrow. Do let us go out after dinner.'

The street to which Mrs. Wynn and Mavis had to inquire their way was at no great distance, and they easily found it. Mrs. Wynn recognised the surgery and the bakery at the corner, and told Mavis that the former had belonged to Dr. Chad, a good friend of her mother's. They found the house : it had been newly painted, and a round table covered with an anti-macassar, with a wax apple under a glass shade forming its central ornament, stood in the parlour window, where Mrs. Price's arm-chair and family mending-basket used formerly to be.

They walked up and down on the side opposite to the house, and Mrs. Wynn told Mavis how the rooms were laid out, and how they had been divided, in her time, among the Price family, for which they were rather a tight fit. She was strangely excited for her, but happy too, it seemed to Mavis, and numerous were the reminiscences, not in the least remarkable in themselves, which she imparted to the patient listener.

Mavis was thinking how real it was to Sarah, and yet they were all gone : the father and mother, the brothers, the old home, and old life! Another home and another kind of life had just passed away also, and the unknown was again before the fond, simple-hearted, broken-spirited speaker. Was all human experience like this? Did all things come like shadows, so depart? She hated the thought, as the young always do hate it ; she wanted to cling close to the solid and lasting reality of her own love and Jack's, of their handfasted promise, and their blessed hope. She shrank from the horrid sense of slidingness and shiftingness in everything that came to her with Mrs. Wynn's trivial talk.

'It is too late to go to the new cemetery to

see their graves, to-day,' said Mrs. Wynn, when the tide of her recollections began to ebb ; ' we had better do that on Sunday, when Jane can come with us.'

They turned back, and walked up the street. As they reached the surgery at the corner, where a gig was standing, a grey-haired man, with a kind face, came out and met them on the pavement.

'Doctor Chad ! ' exclaimed Mrs. Wynn. ' Don't you know me ? I am—I mean I was —Sarah Price.'

'Why, of course I know you ! ' said Dr. Chad heartily, shaking hands, and darting, as Mavis remarked, a keen, searching look at her. ' How are you, and where are you staying ? '

Mrs. Wynn told him, and introduced Mavis, whom the doctor also favoured with a piercing glance, but of a different kind.

'You are in Liverpool for a visit only, I suppose ? '

'For three weeks,' said Mavis, 'and then we are going to Australia—to Melbourne.'

'To Melbourne! a long voyage. How is that? I understood you were settled in Cheshire. Don't tell me now, however; I am hurrying off to an appointment. I'll come and see you to-morrow, Mrs. Wynn; I should like to hear about it. You and I were old friends, you know.' He pulled out a note-book, wrote down the address, and after glancing over previous entries on the page, added: 'Eleven o'clock. Good-bye.'

'What a quick sort of man,' said Mavis, as the gig rattled away down the street, 'but how kind and clever-looking. I'm so glad he's coming to see you, Sarah; because, though he's coming as a friend, I shall ask him about you as a doctor. I had made up my mind you should see a doctor, and it's better to have this one who is a friend.'

'He won't want to be paid, I know, and I own I should like to have something to do me

good, just to make me feel a little better able
to bear it ; ' she leaned heavily on Mavis's arm,
and she was now very pale ; ' but the medicine
will have to be paid for, and your father won't
like that. He gave me very strict orders about
what we were to spend, and there's nothing
extra allowed for.'

'Leave that to me, Sarah. Whatever Dr.
Chad orders for you, you shall have.'

' It will have to be saved out of the money
for our clothes, then.'

Mrs. Wynn was so well used to her husband's meanness, that she did not attribute the
silence maintained by Mavis during the rest of
their walk to his daughter's shame and indignation.

At eleven the next day Dr. Chad called on
Mrs. Wynn, and, after a little friendly talk, he
said to Mavis that he wished to be left alone
with his old acquaintance, who did not seem to
be well.

Mavis left the room, giving the doctor a

grateful glance, and he observed to Mrs. Wynn that her stepdaughter was a nice-looking girl; adding, 'And as good as she looks, I dare say.'

On this hint Mrs. Wynn spoke, and in her homely way told her old friend what Mavis was to her. She probably did not intend to be so . outspoken; but, partly because the matter was so near her heart, and partly because Dr. Chad possessed all a physician's expertness in getting at information, she made him acquainted with the wretchedness of the home which Mavis and she had left, and revealed the misery and apprehension with which she anticipated their voyage. The doctor heard her with quiet attention.

' It feels like old days,' said she, ' to see you sitting there just as you used to sit with my poor mother in her trouble; as if your time was all your own, and you had nobody but her to think of.'

' I remember,' said Dr. Chad, ' and just now I have nobody but you to think of. Tell me more of this restlessness and sinking—since when have you suffered from them?'

With this the good doctor went into the case in his thorough fashion.

'And now,' said he, when his questions had been answered, 'I will let Miss Wynn come back to you. She is in the next room, I suppose.'

He went to the door and saw Mavis standing within the threshold of the bedroom on the other side of the passage, evidently with the purpose of intercepting him. He put a finger up in warning, called to her cheerfully to come in, and took leave, saying that he would send some medicine which would do Mrs. Wynn immediate good, and would see her again to-morrow. In the meantime she was not to fatigue herself in any way,

'But what about the shopping, Mavis?' Mrs. Wynn began nervously, so soon as Dr. Chad had closed the door; 'I'm sure I don't know how it's to be done if we don't set about

it at once.   There's that list that Jane made out
last night; it will take time and management
too, if we're to do it for the money.'

'No matter,' said Mavis, firmly; 'the first
object is to get some health and strength for
you.   Leave Jane and me to settle about the
things.'

They passed a quiet day.   Mrs. Wynn took
her medicine, and said she felt rested.   When
Jane Price came in from her work that evening,
she found her sister asleep on the sofa in the
sitting-room, and Mavis watching by her side
with a very grave face.

Jane Price bent over the sleeper for a few
moments without speaking; then asked Mavis
in a whisper to come into the adjoining room.

'Dr. Chad came straight from here to the
shop and sent for me,' said Jane; 'he was very
kind, but he said there was bad news, and I
had better hear it before I saw Sarah again, as
she must on no account be frightened or flus-
tered.   She has got something wrong with her;

it is " a dangerous form of heart disease in an
advanced stage." Those are his own very
words, so the name doesn't matter. Now,
Mavis, what is to be done? She must not be
told, because any shock might, and probably
would, kill her; and as for the voyage to
Melbourne, even if she had not such a horror
of it, that is quite impossible.'

Mavis, who had heard this without an ex-
clamation, but whose face was colourless, replied
by a question:

' Must she die of the illness in any case? '

' He did not positively say so, but I believe
that is what he means.'

' I wonder how soon? '

Jane Price gave her a sharp, not altogether
pleasant look.

' You take it easily, although you've gone
white enough. Of course Dr. Chad said nothing
about that.'

' I wonder whether he would tell me,' said
Mavis, ignoring Jane's remark, ' for a great deal

would depend on it. I mean, if my father is told she is likely to die soon, he may be induced to alter his plans; but unless the doctor can positively say she is, she will have to go.'

Although her tone was cold and hard, it was not to be mistaken for that of indifference, and Jane Price did not misjudge her. Mavis leaned against the wall, and passed her hand across her forehead.

' Do you mean to say that Sarah's husband —brute as he is—I can't help it, though he is your father—will take her away on a voyage to the other side of the world, in the state she's now in, if Dr. Chad thinks she will live long enough to be put on board the ship? I know little about him—Sarah is not one to tell much, even to her own, when it's got to be told in writing—but I did not think he was so bad as all that comes to.'

' It is better,' said Mavis, mildly, ' for you and me to talk without using hard words. They do no good, and it will be well not to

have to think of them afterwards. I mean
that my father knows little and believes less of
Sarah's state of health, and will not be turned
from his purpose easily. Jane,' she added hesi-
tatingly, and with some awe in her tone, 'I'm
afraid it would be no surprise to Sarah, but good
news, to be told that she has not long to live.
She has had a feeling of the kind lately, I know,
and a great deal of her horror of the voyage
comes from the idea that she will die at sea.'

' What a life hers must be! I thought she
looked very bad, but I don't know much about
illness, and what Dr. Chad said took me by
surprise. Perhaps you think I take it easily
too ; but I have not seen her for five years.'

' I don't think so at all,' said Mavis, gently.
' I think you are kind and good to her. And
we have got to consider her only, you know,
not our own feelings. I think I hear her stirring. We cannot make up our minds to anything to-night.'

' Except, I should say, that you ought to

write to your father and tell him what Dr. Chad's opinion is. What is the use of spending money on an outfit for a voyage she cannot take? Yes, Sarah, we are coming.'

They returned to the sitting-room and found Mrs. Wynn awake, unrefreshed by her sleep, low, and querulous. The evening wore on and she did not improve. The patient self-repression that had formerly afforded her any slender chance she ever had against her tyrant, forsook her when she had made a temporary escape from him. She now admitted that she was ill, and indulged in the luxury of complaint. It was remarkable that she made no allusion to the business that would have to be undertaken on the morrow, and that she said nothing about the approaching voyage.

In the early dawn Mavis, who shared Mrs. Wynn's room, heard her name called cautiously, and, replying that she was awake, rose from her bed and went to her step-mother.

' Have you been long awake ? ' she asked.

' Yes, a long time. Draw the blinds up, let all the light in, and sit here on the side of the bed. I have something to say to you; when I have said it I think I shall get some sleep. That's right, I love the light. Now wrap my shawl round you, and listen to me.'

With a shiver, not of cold only, Mavis seated herself on the bed, and Mrs. Wynn, drawing herself up on her pillows, said quietly:

' I have been kept awake all night by the trouble of my mind over this illness of mine.'

Mavis, startled, looked sharply at her.

' I remember Dr. Chad's ways, long ago as it is, too well to be mistaken, and I know he thinks I am very ill. Why, my dear, I could have told him that any time this year past. You know what I expected, and the only difference is that I hope I shall not have to begin the voyage at all; I hope I shall be allowed to die quietly here with you and Jane.'

' Oh, Sarah,' said Mavis, with tears, ' don't
say such things to me. Dr. Chad will cure
you, I am sure.'

' God forbid! There's no fear of that;
neither he nor any other doctor, Mavis dear.
But there's something I've been thinking of all
night; it is that you must promise me you
will not write to your father about my being
ill.'

' Dr. Chad will desire me to write to him.'

' No, he won't; he will take it for granted,
and if he should say anything I will put him off
it. Your father said nothing about wanting to
hear from us, and I may as well have what
peace I can get. Promise me that you will not
send for him, no matter what happens, and I
will be content. If I had the secure feeling
that he would not come here, I could go to
sleep now, this moment.'

There was a terribly anxious look in the
exhausted face; how wan it showed in the
growing summer dawn! Mavis, however strong

her misgiving, could not resist it. She gave the required promise, and Mrs. Wynn thanked her with a sigh of relief. Mavis laid her hand gently on her stepmother's :—

'Sarah, is it really so bad, so dreadful as this? If what you fancy was true—but, mind, Dr. Chad does not think it is—if you were really going to die, do you mean—in earnest, and thinking of it as one of your last thoughts—that you would not wish to see my father again?'

'It is not my fault,' said Mrs. Wynn, humbly; 'at least I don't think it is. I'm sure there's no revenge or malice in my heart, or anything except that I am so tired, so very, very tired; but I do not wish ever to see your father again in this world. I should be so glad to be dead before he comes to fetch us.'

The homely phrase, the matter-of-fact way of putting a truth terrible to the girl in the first flush of her youth, love, and hope, so affected Mavis that she forgot caution.

'Oh, Sarah!' she exclaimed. 'To be his

wife, his own real wife, and to feel that the best
thing would be never to see him again ! Surely
that would punish him, and make him repent,
if he knew it.'

'No, it wouldn't,' said Mrs. Wynn, with
simple conviction. 'Why should he care any
more now than he has ever cared? I am no
more to him because I shan't be here long, than
I've always been, and we've seen what he's
made of that. I don't want him to be punished,
and I hope, before his time comes, he will repent
of everything he has ever done that was wrong,
but I don't wish it to be on my account particularly. I try not to think of that; it 's been
but a few years in his life, after all, though it 's
been a long time in mine; and I only want
peace. To die in peace,' she went on, as if
speaking to herself; 'how well I know what
that means now. You will get me to do it,
won't you, Mavis?'

Her stepdaughter answered only by her
tears, but Mrs. Wynn was unmoved and

content. She said no more, and holding Mavis's hand, fell into a quiet sleep.

The days that followed were not very clear in the memory of Mavis. Dr. Chad came to the house every morning, and made no refer-ence to Wynn, so that Mavis concluded his patient had told him her wishes. Mavis and Jane would sometimes talk of the position with apprehension, and ask each other what they should do if the farmer were to arrive, and be violently angry. Jane declared that she should not care, so that he could be kept from molesting the dying woman. Mavis had none of Jane's philosophy; the mere idea of her father's coming filled her with fear.

Engrossing occupation, blending night with day, and destroying the distinctions of time, while it confused Mavis in one sense, found her active, clear, and systematic in another. No patient could be better nursed than Mrs. Wynn was, and as the inroads of fatal illness became more and more evident, the indifference and

quietude that attend a comparatively painless
malady took possession of her. She did not
inquire about anything; she betrayed no
curiosity respecting the comforts with which she
was liberally supplied; she made no reference
to past or future. Wynn might never have
existed, the projected voyage to Melbourne
might have been a long-forgotten dream, and
the room in which she lay, while the days were
lengthening into summer, might have enclosed
the whole of her existence and her consciousness,
for any sign she made.

It was within two days of the time at which
Mavis, with a sinking heart, had reckoned that
her father's arrival must be looked for, when
Mrs. Wynn, who had been lying quiet but wake-
ful since Jane had left the room for the night,
asked Mavis whether the nurse was there?

'No, we are alone. I shall stay with you
until morning.'

'I want to know,' said Mrs. Wynn, in the
old tone of anxiety that Mavis had not heard

for many days, 'where the money for all these
things comes from. Is it Jane's? Am I taking
it out of her savings?'

'No, dear,' answered Mavis, kneeling by the
bed, and placing her arm gently around her
stepmother. 'The money is not Jane's, and you
must not give a thought to it, or disturb your
dear mind about it for a moment. The money
is mine, and I never thought to prize it so much
as I do prize it for what it is doing for me now.'

'Yours?'

'Yes, mine. When Uncle Jeffrey sent for
me, it was to give me a present from my aunt.
She had put by all she could save, for years, to
make a little sum for me. She gave it to my
uncle when she was dying, and asked him to
keep it safe for me. The sum was two hundred
and fifty pounds, and when Uncle Jeffrey gave
it to me he told me my aunt's fear was that I
should not be able to bear the life at the Farm.
She knew I should have to go back there after
her death. So she wanted me to be safe, in

case I had to leave the Farm and face the
world, with some money to live on until I could
get into a way of earning. I was not to let
you know that I had this money, lest my father
should find it out. I kept it hidden in the oak
cabinet in the Dame's Parlour ; it is all in bank
notes. I soon found out how right my aunt had
been ; only for you I could not have borne it.'

'You might have gone away, where you
would have had peace, with all that money,' said
Mrs. Wynn, with quiet wonderment, ' but you
stayed for my sake ! May God reward you !
You have a great part of your reward already.'

'In Jack?' said Mavis ; ' yes, indeed I have,
if you call that a reward which I don't believe
any one in the world could deserve.'

' And now your money is going ; you are
spending it on me, to keep my last days peaceful. But, Mavis, when I am gone, what are
you to do ? '

Mavis was disconcerted by this question.
Did Mrs. Wynn take any account of time?

Did she remember the date at which they were to sail for Melbourne, and that Wynn was to join them a short time previously? She feared to put this question, lest the dread of Wynn's coming should seize upon his wife. She tried to turn the matter aside with a caress, but Mrs. Wynn was too much in earnest; she had for the moment thrown off the lethargy of her disease, and Mavis was forced to meet the difficulty. Mrs. Wynn's next words were characteristically practical :

'You were to get clothes for the voyage; have you got them?'

'No, I have not.'

'Then you are not going with him. This is what I have been thinking of all these hours, trying to settle it in my mind. Do not go with him, Mavis. I know now that it was all for my sake—and I shall soon be out of your way, and out of his reach. I have longed to say to you, don't go with him to the end of the world; only that I knew he would leave you to starve if he could not force you to obey him. But he cannot leave you to starve now, and I say to you, don't go with him.'

'Everything is changed, you know, by your illness. I need not make up my mind to anything.'

'Make up your mind, dear, and keep it made up. I am too sleepy and tired to talk any more, but I'm not afraid now. I shall not be here when he comes; my mind is at rest; no harm can come to you; there's a happy life before you. May God and man be as good to you as you have been to me! I am glad that I shall have a grave after all.' Almost with the last words Mrs. Wynn fell into a doze. Mavis continued for some time to kneel by her side, lost in thought. At length, with a deep sigh, the sleeper awoke, and made an attempt to turn towards the wall. Mavis aided her, arranging the pillows and coverlet afresh, and giving her some water, which she drank with ease, holding the glass herself. Then

Mavis took her seat in a wicker chair, for a long watch, to be relieved by the nurse at five in the morning.

The stillness deepened, and as it grew the wakefulness of Mavis increased. There was nothing to be done; the patient was tranquil, to all appearance free from suffering ; time and circumstance combined to make the solemn time one of reflection and memory. Of all the thoughts that oppressed Mavis in those hours, the saddest one was the impossibility of feeling regret. This woman, dying in the middle term of life, who loved her and whom she loved, was so absolutely tired of existence, that Mavis could not be sorry for her. There was natural awe, a natural shrinking from the sight of death, the fear that when the deliverer came there might be a struggle ; but there was no regret. Mavis felt what she had said to herself about her own young mother : ‘ David Wynn's wife could only be glad to die.’

A letter to Jack, half written, lay in a table

drawer near at hand.   Mavis finding the night
so quiet, and the patient continuing to sleep,
carefully shaded the light, and added a sheet to
the record of her life which she had been keeping from day to day.   An occasional twitch of
the limbs broke the quiet of the sleeper, but
more and more rarely; and at each Mavis
would closely observe and soothe her with a
word and a touch.   The dawn was breaking
when, after a long interval during which there
had been perfect quiet, Mavis put away her
writing and extinguished the candle.

Mrs. Wynn was always anxious to have the
daylight let into her room as early as possible,
so Mavis drew up the window blinds, and looked
out, with a shiver, at the new day.   It was
coming up, golden, red, and glorious, over the
commonplace scene; the silent houses in the
steep, grey, middle-class street had a roseate
glow upon them, and there was a twittering of
unseen birds in the air.

Presently she went round to the side of the

bed near the wall, and looked intently at the sleeper. Surely there was a change in the worn and sunken face! The habitual look of exhaustion was no longer there; an aspect of peace and restored youth had replaced it. The half-closed eyelids and the slightly-inclined brow were smooth; the thin white cheek rested easily upon one hand. Mavis bent hastily and touched the other; it was chilly; it gave no answering pressure. In an instant she had flown across the passage and called Jane and the nurse.

'She's gone off very quiet, poor dear,' said the latter; 'and what a good thing that is! It isn't often so, I do assure you.'

It was over. Over, the life of obscure martyrdom, with no crown, no palm branch, and no chance of enrolment in the ranks of any glorious army. Over, the reign and rule of the tyrant whom there was none to punish and few to condemn. Over, the mean misery that has its counterpart in the lives of many women.

CHAPTER XIV.

A CRISIS.

FARMER WYNN was free from sentimental regrets on taking leave of Fieldflower Farm. He
had made a tolerably good thing of it; he
intended to make a much better thing of the
years that lay before him. As for any one
part of the world having a superior claim over
any other on the consideration of a sensible
man, except upon the ground that there was
more money to be made in it, he would with
equal sincerity have scouted such an idea and
despised the promulgator of it. His personal
preparations were made. The round car was
to perform its last journey in his service on
the day after that on which this story returns to
Fieldflower Farm. The beady eyes of Reuben

were rounder, blacker, and brighter than ever,
with the double satisfaction of getting rid of
his old master for good, and being himself
retained on the establishment under the new
one. Everything was going exactly as David
Wynn desired. He had heard nothing of the
women; but that did not trouble him. He
was sure of their obedience to his orders; they
would be all right.

The old house had probably never looked
more picturesque and peaceful than on the last
day its former owner was to pass beneath its
roof. The sunshine, the scents, the sounds
of the May-time all made the scene beautiful.

There was an unusual stir, a coming and
going of workmen about the place, and Mr.
Reckitts—presently to be known as Farmer
Reckitts—was out with his late entertainer,
now his guest, for the greater part of the afternoon, superintending certain proceedings which
would have astonished Mavis not a little. A

covered van drawn by two sturdy horses had
twice made its appearance at the Farm during
the day, and its contents, consisting of household furniture, had been conveyed from the
Farm-side to the Dame's Parlour-side. For
several days previously the ancient rooms had
been in the hands of cleaners, and fires had
been kept burning on the hearths.

What, besides a new master, was coming to
the old house ?

The movement was external as well as
internal. The green sward on the Dame's
Parlour-side, with its islands of flower bed
stretching down to the river, and its narrow
gravel path, bordered by sweet herbs backed
with plants, and marked here and there by
strange foreign shells and honeycombed stones
from far-off sea-coasts, was also in the hands
of strangers. Two gardeners and a weeding
woman were at work at different points of the
venerable expanse that replaced the ancient
moat, and in a shady corner stood a trim cart

drawn by a prosperous donkey, no other than
the Squire's own Jacob.

What did these things portend ? Only a
further development of the era of change that
had set in at peaceful Bassett. The Squire,
forced by circumstances to leave his ancestral
home, had determined not to separate himself
from his old friends and associations. This, a
man of less proud simplicity of character might
have done ; but he would stay in the place where
he could still see the soulless things he had
loved so well, and the humble people among
whom his later life had been passed, and to
which his son might one day return, to fill the
position that he himself had imperilled and
lost. The project formed by Wynn, and imparted by him to Mr. Bassett on the morrow of
Mr. Dexter's mission of evil tidings, adapted
itself admirably to the Squire's plan. This
latter had been formed in his mind before
Jack's departure, but he had not given his son
a hint of it. The Squire's new tenant at Field-

flower Farm was a single man, whose small household might be as separate from that of his landlord, resident on the premises, as the Dame's Parlour-side from the Farm-side. The strange, solemn, sunny old rooms, with their traditional memories of his own family, had always had an attraction for the Squire.

The bargain, an advantageous one for Reckitts, was readily made, and the approaching departure of Farmer Wynn was a signal of preparation for the installation of Squire Bassett and Miss Nestle.

How often had the thoughts of Mavis turned to those deserted rooms, and her memory faithfully rehearsed the scenes that they had witnessed! How often had her fancy retrodden the river-side path, and renewed her vain promise to her lover that there she would every day recall to mind that she was his, while the river ran and the wind blew. She had thought of the rooms in solitude, dismantled, shut up, neglected, and of the river-side path trodden by strangers. Of the thing that was going to happen she had not the most distant idea, while, tossed on a sea of conflicting emotion, with her head and heart full of the past, she awaited, by the side of the dead woman—who looked so unspeakably peaceful—the dreaded coming of her father.

Magnetic messages (the word telegram was of later use) were rare in country parts in 1854, and when one addressed to Wynn arrived at Fieldflower Farm, he swore at the bearer and at the expense before he opened the despatch. For a moment he did not seize the sense of the laconic contents : 'My sister died this morning.' Whose sister? What was this to him? He twisted the large flimsy sheet impatiently in his hands, but the uncertainty was over almost with the thought. It was Jane Price's sister, his sickly, tiresome, cowardly wife, who was dead. He was alone when the message was brought to him by Reuben, and though the boy was bursting with curiosity, and also with ardent

hope that, like most intelligence which costs
money, the news was bad, he did not dare to
linger or watch his former master.   With a
black frown, but no other sign of emotion,
Wynn turned away from the house and took
the path towards the weir.

A frown as black was on David Wynn's
face when, on the following day, he entered the
room in which his daughter and Jane Price
were sitting side by side on the hard little sofa,
with the blinds drawn down.   Mavis stood up,
trembling, but Jane Price kept her seat and
also her unmoved countenance.   She did not
care (to use her professional phrase) ' a button '
for Farmer Wynn, and she meant to let him see
that.   It might do him good, she charitably
argued, to be brought in contact, even so late
in the day as it was now, with one woman
whom he could not bully.

' Father ! '

Mavis advanced to him, but he roughly

put her aside, strode up to the sofa, and said insolently :

'You are Jane Price, I suppose? Is this your message? Is it true?'

'It is my message, and it is quite true that my sister, your unfortunate wife, is dead. If you want to know anything more from me, you will have to keep a civil tongue in your head, and to mend your manners.'

Wynn glared at her, in mingled rage and amazement ; but Jane Price calmly went on with the running together of two lengths of black crape. Her face was serious, as befitted the circumstances, but it bore no signs of acute grief. The sincerity of the woman was as marked as her self-possession. Mavis, ghastly with fatigue and agitation, shrank into a corner by the chimney-piece, and hid her face in her hands.

'What did she die of? Why was I not told she was ill?'

' The doctor who attended her will tell you
in Latin what she died of,' answered Jane Price
sternly, and looking him straight in the face :
' I will tell you in English. She died of your
ill-treatment, she died of fear, she died of the
life you had led her, she died of what you threat-
ened her with. You were not told, because she
earnestly begged that we would not tell you,
and because I was determined she should die in
peace, out of sight and hearing of you. She
has died in peace, and my concern in the
matter is ended.'

' Who is this doctor?' demanded Wynn,
with an oath ; 'he shall answer for this. As
for you, you jade——'

' Father! father!' entreated Mavis, ' pray,
pray don't say such things! Think of her
lying there, so close to us, so white and quiet,
and do not insult her in death.'

This appeal did not touch Wynn's heart,
but it shook his nerves. He had a craven fear
of death, and the image of it, brought by the

words of Mavis to his coarse material mind, in
the person of the poor woman whom he had
ill-treated and despised, was abhorrent to him.

' Come here ' ! He took Mavis roughly by
the right arm, forced her to stand before him,
but let his voice drop almost to a whisper (as
though the closed ears could catch its tones !)
although he was conscious of the cold contempt
with which Jane marked that he did so.

' Tell me, if you can, without any of your
cursed rigmarole, how this has happened? '

Mavis, striving with her sobs, and quivering
under the cruel grasp of his hand, was trying
to answer him, when the door opened and
Dr. Chad entered the room. Jane rose,
and Wynn instinctively loosed his hold of
Mavis.

' This is Doctor Chad,' said Jane ; ' he will
tell you anything you want to know, and you
can make what arrangements you please.
Come, Mavis.'

' One moment,' said Dr. Chad, following

Jane to the door, ' you had better give me that
key.'

She reluctantly placed the key of the death-
chamber in his hand, and took Mavis away.

The interview between Wynn and Dr. Chad
was a very brief one.   The farmer left the house
without requiring to see Mavis again.   The
doctor sent for Jane to come to him alone, and
she found him looking both sad and indignant.

' He's gone?'

' Yes, he's gone; and first, here is the key.
He declined seeing the poor thing—he was
plainly frightened, but he said he did not see
the good of it, and hated corpses.'

' I am so glad.'

' Well, as you care about it so much, so am
I.   The man is a curious creature ; I never
came across a meaner or more odious one.   He
was going to bluster and bully ; but he dropped
that tone very quickly, when he found I knew
all about him, and would be prepared to justify
my professional conduct in the case.   I had

only to hint at certain discoveries I had made
—there, there, don't cry, she is safe from him
now—and he sneaked as abjectly as he had
blustered boldly.'

'What is he going to do?'

'He is going to give her a proper funeral.
I have promised to choose the ground. I know
your parents' grave; it shall be close by, if
possible. The funeral must take place on
Saturday morning, early, for he and his
daughter have to go on board the "British
Queen" in the afternoon. He said he presumed her preparations were all made.'

'Mavis is quite ready.'

'He will not come here in the interval.'

'I am glad of that.'

'He will send a carriage for his daughter
and her luggage in good time. She will have
to go to his hotel. You must prepare her
for all this, poor girl! I undertook that for
you.'

'I will see to all that concerns Mavis.'

'Well, then, I must leave you. Try and get her to lie down, and sleep, if you can. I shall see her to-morrow.'

Dr. Chad kept his promises ; the inevitable business was all well and duly done; but he did not see Mavis on the following day. She had begged, Jane said, that she might not be disturbed.

The funeral, attended only by Wynn and Dr. Chad, took place at the appointed hour. In due time afterwards a carriage, with a servant from the Railway Hotel on the box with the driver, drew up at 108 Cecil Street, where the blinds were up again. The maid who opened the door was directed to inform Miss Wynn that she must be quick, as her luggage was to be sent on board at once.

The maid took a letter off a table in the hall, and handed it to the servant from the hotel.

'Miss Wynn ain't been here this two days,' she said. 'She left this letter to be kept till

sent for by her pa.   So you'd best take it to
him.'

Half an hour later the same carriage
stopped at 108 Cecil Street.   Wynn jumped
out and knocked furiously at the door.   On
this occasion it was opened by Jane Price.
She looked composedly into his face—it was
livid.

' Where is my daughter ? ' he stammered,
but without crossing the threshold.

' I don't know.   If I did know, I would
not tell you.   She has escaped you, like your
other victim, my sister.   You'll have to do
without a victim for a while, David Wynn.'

She moved the door to close it; but he
put out his strong hand and held it back, while
he said in a tone of fury that made Jane turn
pale in spite of her triumph :—

' When you see her next, give her my
curse ! '

CHAPTER XV.

TEMPERED WIND.

THIRTY years ago the Euston Road enjoyed the distinction of being the chosen home of artists in tombstones, manufacturers of metallic monstrosities for the adornment of gardens and the correction of smoky chimneys, and agencies for providing governesses for school and family consumption. The deep - set three - storied houses, with their narrow windows, had a gloomy look, for the gardens were mostly occupied by plaster images, stone monuments, and terrible creations in lead and zinc ; where this was not the case, the horticultural art was a good deal neglected, and the rockery, with a preponderance of oyster shell, had been cultivated to the exclusion of the higher ideal.

The wire blinds of the ground-floor windows of a certain dull clean house in the Euston Road were inscribed in white paint with the words, ' Governesses' Agency and Registry Office ; ' while a board hoisted on poles above the entrance gate bore the inscription, ' Home for Governesses.'

On a day in early summer, Miss Metge, the ' Principal ' of this Agency and Home, was more than usually occupied with the morning's letters. The routine of her work was not generally of an interesting kind, although it sometimes brought her in contact with remarkable scenes of life's history. Its nature was monotonous, and its tendency was depressing. Without sharing the views of the sentimental novelists of a bygone day, respecting the charms, the virtues, and the woes of governesses, and the hard-heartedness and hauteur of employers, Miss Metge was constantly faced by the fact that toil, loneliness, exile from home, at the time of life when life is fairest, and, to the fortunate, most promising, fall to the lot of a sadly large number of young English women who are very ill-fitted to bear those trials. In some instances, however, she was led to commiserate the employers of these young women fully as much as she pitied themselves, and to regard the difficulties of the position as pretty equally divided. A case in point was in Miss Metge's mind at this moment, while she was entering the names and addresses of the writers of a number of letters just received in a long book with initialled pages. She had selected two letters, and placed them under a paper-weight, for separate consideration.

Miss Metge was a short, solid-looking woman of forty-five, with a pale complexion, thin, smooth dark hair, a broad sensible forehead, eyes which, although light in colour, were remarkably penetrating, a clear voice, and a quiet, business-like manner. She was invariably dressed in a black silk gown, with

cambric frills at the neck and wrists, a small
three-cornered black gauze shawl of unknown
antiquity, and a contemporaneous pair of cob-
web-like lace mittens. Her occupation was a
humble one, and not lucrative; but it never
occurred to anybody to doubt that Miss Metge
was a gentlewoman. The front parlour, which
she used as an office, and where she passed
several hours every day, seated behind the wire
blind, and intent on the business of the agency,
was plainly furnished, but scrupulously clean,
and arranged with a peculiar precision and
handiness. Miss Nestle would have regarded
Miss Metge with esteem, recognising in her
orderly papers, accurately kept books, and
calmly-superintending aspect, evidences of a
spirit akin to that which presided over the
Museum.

Presently Miss Metge rose, and, taking with
her some of her papers, went into a back
parlour, communicating with the front room.
There she remained a short time, and return-

ing, applied herself to the two letters which she had laid aside.

She was still occupied with these documents when the clang of the gate apprised her that some one was coming. Looking over the top of the blind she saw a lady approaching the house, attended by a grey-haired manservant in a very sober livery, that yet had not an English look about it.

'She is early,' said Miss Metge, as she replaced one of the letters under the bronze hand on the table, put the other in her pocket, and went out to meet the visitor at the hall door.

'You got my note, Mary?' said the visitor, after they had exchanged cordial greetings.

'Yes; this morning.'

'I came early, to catch you before your busy time. Can we talk here without interruption?'

'For the present, yes.'

They were in the front room, and the lady looked about her curiously.

' How tidy it all is,' she said ; ' I think I could tell any room that had been arranged by you. And here are the old properties, too '— she pointed to a timepiece on the mantelshelf, and a Boule inkstand, much too handsome for the rest of the office-table furniture. ' Do you remember when we used to call you "Line and Plummet"?'

' I remember,' said Miss Metge. The visitor's mood changed ; she sighed as she took the chair Miss Metge placed for her, and her face became downcast.

This lady was one who could hardly have been unremarked anywhere; her stately beauty and grace had been gently dealt with by the hand of time, although she was fully forty years old. She was tall, slender, and in her rich but sombre attire there was a peculiar individuality, while eccentricity was avoided as successfully as subservience to fashion. The regularity of her features and their pensive beauty were lighted up by the fire of her dark and piercing eyes. These eyes looked out from under the level dark eyebrows with directness and investigating force that might have been embarrassing, if the woman who possessed this penetrating regard had not been endowed with tact, taste, and a somewhat weary and disdainful indifference towards other people and their business; for they said plainly that there would be little use in trying to keep from her anything she cared to discover. Yet were they not hard or aggressive, but simply seeing, will-directed, and beautiful. Rich chestnut locks had once shaded those dark eyes, and dropped vine-like tendrils on the smooth brow and fair neck, but in that single respect the change wrought by time was strange and startling. The hair, laid plain upon the temples and braided in a heavy coil at the back of the head, was of a gleaming silver whiteness, which contrasted with the complexion, still soft and carnation-tinted. Abundant as of old, and glossy as the white

hair of English women seldom is, not a thread
in it but was of snow. Something in the face
at once lofty and absent, a look as of one
who has lived much apart, and taken little
heed of the small things and the everyday
events of life, displaced at times by a flash
of rapid perception and keen sensibility; such
were the characteristics of the face which Miss
Metge perused with the solicitude of an old
and unaltered affection.

'I have no good news for you, Mary. On
the one point which we have agreed never to
discuss unless there is something positive to tell,
we need not speak, for there is nothing. Everything remains as when I last wrote to you.'

'Then you have really come about this
matter?' asked Miss Metge, laying her fingers
on the paper-weight for emphasis.

'Yes, dear friend. I must have come to
London on purpose to see you about this; but
I also had to see my publisher about a book.'

'Another book? How hard you work,

Dorothea! And is it still a dead secret, or has it become an open one?'

'It is still a secret. In my secluded Breton home I am quite unsuspected, and in the world of letters here nobody knows, and nobody cares to know, who it is that, under the name of " Ignota," gives them a novel now and then, into which she has woven the threads of her own life, and poured the trouble of her own heart. My publisher and yourself are the sole possessors of the secret of my authorship.'

'And I should not have known it,' said Miss Metge, with a smile, 'had you been able to keep the old familiar scenes and the one ideal character out of your first story. They betrayed you at once to me.'

'Naturally. I do not count that as betrayal. But they never could betray me to him. He knew nothing of the old familiar scenes, and in the ideal character he would not recognise a portrait. I am safe there.'

'I wish with all my heart you were not

safe. I believe it was all a disastrous mistake, and would be remedied if you were understood.'

'Never, never now,' said the lady, hurriedly, and putting out her hands with a distressful gesture. 'All hopes of the kind have entirely vanished. They have never been more than shadows. Did I not say that we would not talk of this? I am here for a few days only. I have my old rooms. You must come to me, Mary, and we will go to see a play, and hear an opera. So much revival of the old times will do us good. Now let us talk only of what I have written to you about.'

The business side of Miss Metge's character asserted itself at once. She shifted her chair round to the office-table, and opened her notebook. The visitor laid her hand on Miss Metge's wrist.

'Wait a minute, Mary,' she said, 'before you refer to your candidates. You do not doubt, I hope, that I gave Miss Litton a fair trial? You don't think it was a caprice that made me part with her?'

'Not at all. You treated her with unusual liberality. It is just one of those very common cases of a person cheerfully undertaking a post for which she is totally unfit. How often, do you suppose, do I meet with that kind of thing?'

'Constantly, no doubt. Miss Litton's singing was atrocious, and her French—well, it was not French at all, simply; and besides, there was a more serious objection. She brought no intelligence, no interest, to bear on the position, and it needs both. There was no helpfulness in her, and she could never have been made to believe that she was less than perfect in any way. I used to be amused, even when I was most disconcerted, by her self-assertion. Her " recommendations " were made to do duty for everything, and she found it impossible to believe that my requirements could be other than those of Lady Mary Dunning or the Countess of Kyrle.'

'That question of recommendations is a very important one,' said Miss Metge ; 'and yet I have sometimes found it does not turn out so ill to take a little risk. I am very glad you have applied to me in person this time; it will be more satisfactory for you to see for yourself what I can do for you, and whether there is any one among the applicants here whose looks you like. Looks go a good way with you, I fancy—indeed, I know. That was one reason why I sent you Miss Litton. She is nice looking.'

'Very ; but Sybil never took to her, and then, of course, there was no use in going on with the thing. I should like the young lady to be nice looking, Mary, and—and as unlike Miss Litton as possible.'

Miss Metge smiled. There was not a little archness in her serious eyes as she said : 'You are just as impressionable as ever, I see, and it is as much a question of your " taking to " the companion as it is of Sybil's.'

The visitor laughed. The sound was a musical one, the voice fresh and flexible.

' I'm afraid you're right, Mary, and that I am still to be caught by the eye and the ear. But what I am saying is not so silly as it sounds, for the whole thing turns on the effect on Sybil. Tell me, do you think you have any one on your books who, possessing the one indispensable accomplishment, music, has exceptional intelligence, and is a sympathetic person? I may be asking more than you can know about any of the ladies who put their names on your books, and tender their recommendations in evidence; but I thought it possible there might be somebody staying at the Home.'

Miss Metge's reply was arrested by sounds from the adjoining room; a delicious ripple of music from a piano of fine tone, touched by masterly fingers, and then the first notes of an Italian song, rich, thrilling, exquisitely pure and true. The effect upon Miss Metge's visitor was remarkable. She raised her head; her nostrils expanded ; the eagerness in her face was like that which sculptors have lent to the Hunting Diana. She half rose from her chair, but Miss Metge, touching her arm, enjoined quiet and silence with a look. They both listened intently, the visitor with all the delight of one who, being athirst, drinks of some delicious beverage. With the ·first break in the song she whispered to Miss Metge :—

'Who is it? How came she there?'

'A young lady staying in the Home. She thinks I am alone, as there was no knock at the door when you came in.'

'She won't leave off, will she?'

'Not if she does not find out that there's some one here.'

They kept silence while the delicious music came rolling towards them, and tears of the keenest pleasure stood in the eyes of Miss Metge's visitor. The singer was in a variable mood. There was none of the set form of 'practising' about her revelry in sound that morning; in full and assured freedom she poured forth song after song. Miss Metge's visitor became more and more entranced, until, as the last strains of the sweet, powerful voice were dying away, she had forgotten Miss Metge's presence, and was far off in a world now rarely visited by her fancy.

'That is the end of it,' whispered Miss Metge, as she pointed to the timepiece. 'She will be going now. I can't let them use the piano in agency hours.'

They heard the closing of the instrument, and the next moment a young lady, very plainly dressed in mourning, entered the room by the folding door. On seeing the stranger she paused, embarrassed, and said, glancing at some papers in her hand—

'I beg your pardon; I did not know you were engaged. I came to bring you back these letters.'

The stranger, in whose eyes the tears of emotion which the young singer had awakened

were still glittering, looked at her eagerly,
unconscious of the intensity of her own gaze.

' Thank you, Miss Warne,' said Miss Metge.
' Is there anything you would care to look
after among them ? '

' I think not. I am afraid '—here she
glanced towards the visitor—' I have been
disturbing you very much. I went upstairs to
get my music after you brought me the letters,
and I did not know there was any one in this
room.'

' It is from us an apology is due,' said the
stranger, with a gracious bow, and a smile
that fell like a sunbeam on the girl. ' We have
been enjoying stolen sweets, indeed. I have
not had so rare a treat for many a day, and I
thank you for it most heartily.'

' You are very kind. I am happy to have
pleased you with my singing.'

She laid the papers on the table and left
the room.

' Who is she ? What is she ? Where did

she come from ?   What is she looking for ? '
The stranger asked these questions all in a
breath.   But Miss Metge did not immediately
answer any of them.   She asked a question
instead :—

'What do you think of her looks ? '

' I think they are only less charming than
her voice, and I have heard but two or three
in all my time that have given me so much
pleasure.   Come, Mary, do tell me who she is.'

'Her name is Margaret Warne.   She is
living here for the present.   I will tell you
what I know about her.   She has been in
my mind in connection with this business of
yours.

' This is, as you know, an institution of the
semi-charitable, semi-self-supporting kind, and
my interest in it is not speculative.   I am paid
a salary.   The Home can accommodate twenty,
and it is generally full.   A donation of five
pounds gives the right to recommend an in-
mate.   The Home has an excellent character,

and is scrupulously administered. I do what I can to enliven it for these poor young women, many of whom return to it several times. About ten days ago I had a note from an old friend of mine, Dr. Chad, of Liverpool; merely a line, asking me whether by any good chance I had a vacancy, as there was a young lady whom he was anxious to recommend. I had a vacancy. By return of post Dr. Chad forwarded his subscription of five pounds, and the formal recommendation of Miss Warne, who arrived twenty-four hours later. I liked her looks and her manners, but I am so well used to seeing young people in the raw-recruit stage of their training for the long life-campaign, that I perceived at once she knew nothing about what she was undertaking, and also that she had recently undergone some severe nervous strain or shock. When it came to the formalities, the entering of her name and requirements on the books, I discovered that she did not know what salary to ask, that

she was not prepared to find she could not
remain here for more than one month without
looking for employment, although she might
remain for three if waiting for an engagement,
and that Dr. Chad was her only reference.
The latter discovery was an awkward one for
me. I had slightly strained my powers. If
the question were ever raised I might be cen-
sured on this ground. I said nothing to Miss
Warne on any of these points, but cheered her
up as well as I could, and especially advised
her to work diligently at her music. I give
them all the same advice,' added Miss Metge,
with a queer little smile ; ' and highly disin-
terested it is, for its results to myself are awful.
Then I wrote, very frankly, to Dr. Chad,
stating my dilemma. He took his time about
replying, and I received his answer and your
note by the same post this morning. I should
like to read to you what he says.'

'One moment, Mary. Does Miss Warne
wish to go out as a governess?'

'Either as governess or companion to a lady. Of course I thought of her for you so soon as I had read your note; but there are objections, and it is just the sort of thing I could not have proposed to you by letter. Dr. Chad writes :—

'" I understand your meaning perfectly, and had foreseen this difficulty; but I cannot remove it. I admit that there is a story in Miss Warne's life ; that painful circumstances have left her in an isolated position, and that she has no one but myself to refer to. Moreover, I know that, although you will have no difficulty in taking my word for her, it is a very different matter for you to place her in a position of trust on the sole strength of my word. I have so much knowledge of the facts as enables me to assure you that Miss Warne is blameless in the family affairs that have come to an unfortunate conclusion, and that she has conducted herself admirably in an exceptionally trying position. Any lady accepting her services would have to do so with no clearer knowledge than this—a very difficult condition, as I have explained to her more fully than her own inexperience enabled her to perceive, and one which I know no one so likely as yourself to be able to arrange. I hope you will take to the poor girl; she interests me. She comes of very respectable people. So much I am free to tell you; but, with the exception of myself and one humbler friend, she is alone in the world."

'Now,' continued Miss Metge, 'I have observed Miss Warne closely for the few days she has been here. I like her altogether. Her music you can pronounce upon. Of her education I don't pretend to know much; her speech, manners, and behaviour are those of a gentlewoman; she has the quiet ways and the thoughtful look of one who has already had a good deal taken out of her by life. She is strictly reserved; not the smallest indication of her history has she afforded me; but in that

reserve there is nothing furtive, nothing under-
hand. Indeed, I have observed with pleasure
the ease and trustfulness with which she takes
it for granted that she will be neither questioned nor entrapped. I have been thinking
anxiously over the chances for her. I do not
know of anything I should like to put her into,
even if the obstacle could be got over. The
question is—could you, being pleased with her,
and having my word for the value of Dr.
Chad's recommendation, overlook the story in
her life that is not to be told?'

Tears sprang to the eyes of the stranger as
she answered :—

'A story in her life, poor child! And can
I overlook it? Mary, what a question! Is
there no story in my own?'

'That is not the point. This is the matter
of engaging a companion for Sybil—a position
of exceptional trust. You have the assurance
that the circumstances are not to Miss Warne's
disadvantage——'

'Ah! if as much could be said for myself!'
broke in the visitor, impatiently. 'Go on,
go on.'

Miss Metge went on, with a deprecatory
shake of her head: 'You have to consider
whether you could be reconciled to knowing so
very little about her.'

'I do not think I should grumble because
the poor girl kept her affairs to herself, and I
am sure Sybil would get on with her. No, no;
this is *not* one of my impulses, and it is *not*
running away with me. I have not lost the art
of reading your face, you see. Besides, what
did you say about its being well sometimes to
take a little risk? Look at her sweet serene
face, my dear Mary; why, she is the very picture of goodness!'

'And not the least like Miss Litton?'

'And not the least like Miss Litton.'

'Then you would like to entertain the idea
seriously, and to see Miss Warne about it?'

'I should, indeed. On my side I don't

think there can be any difficulty; but perhaps she might not like the sort of life I have to offer.'

'Judging from what she has said to me, I should think she would regard the proposal as a special providence. There goes the bell. Office work is beginning. Will you see Miss Warne now, or take a day to think over it?'

'I will see her to-day, if she doesn't mind.'

'Then come in here, and I will send for her.'

Miss Metge introduced the visitor to the back parlour—a clean, dull room—and went herself to prepare her client for the interview. She returned in a few minutes, accompanied by the young lady, and saying that she was waited for by a person who had an appointment with her, but would see her friend again, withdrew. Miss Warne was very pale, and nervous beyond disguise.

'Miss Metge has told you,' began the lady; then, after a quick glance at her, she said, with a complete change of tone, and taking the girl's hand with familiar kindness: 'My dear, you look quite ill. I shall take you out for a drive, to begin with. We can talk much better in the carriage. Run away and put your bonnet on, and be quick.'

The stranger's carriage was a handsome brougham; the horses stepped together to perfection; the rapid, even motion was a delightful sensation to Miss Warne, who had been suffering from want of air and exercise. A pretty tinge of colour came into her face, an embarrassed pleasure showed itself very becomingly, as, with a few words in reference to the day and the sunshine, the elder lady endeavoured to put her at her ease. As the carriage passed the 'Out' gate of Euston Station, an elderly gentleman, who had been seeing a friend off by a forenoon train on the London and North-Western line, was standing on the pavement, with a shabby black bag in his hand, having just hailed a hansom.

The gentleman with the black bag was Mr. Dexter. The friend with whom he had just parted was the Squire.

'He did not see me,' said Miss Warne, as if to herself, and her companion fancied her tone was one of regret.

'A friend of yours? Shall I stop the carriage?'

'Oh no, thank you,' said Miss Warne; 'it is only a gentleman who was very kind to me once when I was travelling alone.'

CHAPTER XVI.

MAVIS TO JACK.

'I was obliged abruptly to close my letter, partly written while I was sitting by the side of poor Sarah in her last hours, and in which I told you of her death, and my own resolution. Still, I am not afraid that it will have vexed you or made you uneasy, dearest Jack, because I was able to tell you that I had found a friend. Now I am going on with my story. I shall not, however, tell it in the journalising way of the big packet that I posted at Liverpool on the day of poor Sarah's funeral; the same day I had looked forward to with horror as the first of the voyage which she dreaded with so fatal a fear.

'I remember you said, when we went up to the top of the tower, that you liked to be able to make a picture in your mind of each place in which I should be likely to pass any of the time of your absence. We little thought, then, your fancy was to have a wider sphere than the Farm. Now, before I tell you anything that has befallen me since the close of my last letter, I will try to describe the place in which I am writing to you, on an evening that is beautiful, even in London, and in the Euston Road. All this side of the town is strange to me : my uncle and aunt lived at Chelsea, near the river. The house is large, dull, quiet, and what in London they call clean. I have a good-sized front room, up two long flights of stairs. I can see a good deal of sky overhead, a long strip of grassplat, with brown shrubs between it and the wall of the next garden on both sides. A couple of trees, with brown leaves making a push for life, stand sentinel at the iron gate ; on the other side of the street there is a long line of tall dull houses. Exactly opposite is a sculptor's yard, filled with marble monuments and

plaster images. There are two windows in my
room, with brown curtains, and there is a good
deal of brown in the carpet ; but everything is
very neat. What do you think stands in the
middle of the little table, close up to the window, at which I am writing? You would
never guess! Then I will tell you. It is the
china bowl from the Dame's Parlour that used
to hold the flowers you brought me from
Bassett. I packed it up in my trunk—I have
all the flowers too—when I thought I was
going to the other side of the world. I am
safe and comfortable here, but I am very sad.
There are several governesses in the Home, all
waiting for re-employment. Some of them are
quite young, others are so far on in life that it
is woeful they should still be obliged to go on
earning a livelihood among strangers. Dearest
Jack, if that which seems to be my lot here
were really my lot, how hard it would be to
bear! How blessed and dear is the truth,
notwithstanding all that I have suffered, and

the long time it may be until you come for me!

'The lady at the head of the Home is a kind and clever woman ; she likes me, I think, and she is almost as fond of hearing me sing as some one to whom I wish—oh how I wish !— I could sing the music that I have been learning here. For I have been going to your church, Jack, the Catholic church in Moorfields, and there I have been struck with great amazement.

'But I am straying from my subject, as though I were talking to you, not writing only. Miss Metge has been very kind in her quiet way of conveying to me that she is satisfied with my meagre account of myself, and trusts me. She evinces interest in me, but no curiosity. I believe that I am writing on like this, while my head and my heart are filled with thoughts and heavy anxieties, just because I am almost afraid to take up my story where I dropped it, so keenly did I suffer in forming the resolution to

remain in England. I know you will not blame
me for saying but little to you of my father;
it is better that only what is absolutely necessary should be said, even between you and me.
What I know about him is only that he sailed
for Melbourne by the " British Queen," on the
appointed day, a few hours after poor Sarah's
funeral. A respectable lodging had been taken
for me at Bootle, and the address was, at her
own request, not given to Jane Price, until she
had ascertained that my father had sailed.
The rooms were taken by a friend of Jane's,
and two days before the funeral I left the
house in which Sarah died. When Jane knew
that my father was gone, she told the truth
to Dr. Chad, and asked him for his advice.
I don't think he was angry with her or with
me, but he naturally took the matter very
seriously. Neither he nor Jane knew the real
position in which I was left, and it was no
wonder he should ask her whether she had
found it so easy to make out life for herself,

without help, as she seemed so light-hearted about my having to do the same? She said, she had not found it at all easy; but nothing could ever be so bad as my having to undergo what had killed her sister; and after all, if there was nothing else to be done, she could get me into the millinery room in the shop she is in.

'Jane told me this when she came to see me in the evening; she told me also that Dr. Chad had said it would be a pity I should do no more than that, with the good education I had received, and the musical gifts I possess. Jane stayed with me that night. I went to Liverpool with her in the morning, and she left me at Dr. Chad's surgery. He was very kind, sorry for my loneliness, and so perplexed about me that I longed to tell him I was not, although a most unhappy girl in some respects, the forlorn being he believed me to be. You remember, dearest Jack, how I longed to tell poor Sarah that day when you understood it all so quickly, without my having to explain, and allowed me to give her the consolation that to the last she clung to. When the end was very near, she said to me words of most uncalled-for gratitude, and spoke of you as my " reward "—as if anything I had ever done, or ever could do, were worthy of such a re-compense as the love that is your free gift to poor me.

'You will like Dr. Chad when you know him. He is so quick, intelligent, and sym-pathetic. I have a picture in my mind of our going together to see him, and of his surprise, and quick piercing look at me, when he learns where the courage and serenity he praised me for during Sarah's illness, had their source and origin. I was free to tell him that I had money, and of course that made things easier than if I had been in pressing need ; but he pointed out to me that I must be very saving. I found he took a most serious view of my father's probable line of action, and I conclude

that he had heard a great deal from poor
Sarah, or guessed at it himself, for he said he
felt bound to advise me to leave my father
entirely out of my calculations for the future;
that he believed the step I had taken to be an
irrevocable one, and that I should never hear
of my father again. I cannot quite think this;
he may not care to know anything about me
now, but it will be different when you have
come home, and I can tell him how happy
my life is going to be. At least I will try
to think that he will be glad. I suppose if
I were to address a letter for him to the Post
Office, Melbourne, it would reach him, because
I am sure, even from the little he said about
my uncle Lewis, that he is well known in
the colony. I will, however, do nothing until
I hear from you.

‘ Dr. Chad not only thought that I ought
to apply myself to some regular employment,
but that I ought to do so at once, before any
more of my money was spent ; and he spoke

to me of a friend of his in London, Miss Metge, the lady who is at the head of this house. Amy Silcote's having married and gone to live in Scotland, as I told you in my last letter, has deprived me of the only acquaintance I had here; but as I must be among strangers in any case until you come back, it does not really signify much.   Of course I was always thinking in all things of what you would like and approve, and although I felt frightened for a while, because we are both so young, and so far apart, I soon cheered up, remembering that after the words you made me say that day nothing can really harm us.   But it came into my mind that as I had to go among strangers for the time of your absence, and had to do so without being able to wait for your opinion and sanction, it would be well to use another name.   Dr. Chad agrees with me in this, and he has recommended me to Miss Metge by my mother's name, Margaret Warne.   I found Jane Price very anxious on this point : she said several times that it was important to place myself quite out of my father's reach ; and as I could not tell her why I do not feel this so strongly as she does, I thought it best to acquiesce quietly. She is a good kind woman, but oh, so practical ! I suppose this comes of her loneliness and hard work since her parents' death. She has been very kind to me, and I can see that she feels and fears for me in the unknown world that lies before me. This made me wish *that she could know*; and yet I doubt whether she would understand, if she did know ; for she would think chiefly about the difficulties and the distance. I think of them too, but they cannot silence the hymn of thanksgiving that my heart is always singing.

'I need not say more about my stay at Bootle, or my journey up to London. Miss Metge met me at the station. The Home is almost always full : the vacancy when Dr. Chad applied on my behalf was fortunate.

Of course I principally rely on my singing in seeking an engagement as companion to a lady. I should prefer that to being a governess. You must not mind this, dearest Jack, though I cannot expect you to like it; you must only think of the great misery we have escaped; you must only try to fancy what it would have been to come home, and then have to seek me at the far end of the world!

'I am working hard at my music; there is a good piano in the back parlour—though probably inferior to Miss Nestle's "beautiful piece of rosewood"—and I have the use of it, when Miss Metge is alone in the front parlour, which is her office. She likes to hear me sing. Nothing has come in my way as yet, and as I have never been companion to anybody—except poor Sarah—there may be some difficulty and delay; but I have so much to think of always, that the time does not hang heavily upon my hands. Miss Metge has a great regard for

Dr. Chad; she will take pains to place me well on account of his recommendation. We go out together in the evening, when she has time for a walk, and she is a wise and pleasant companion. In one sense she is as practical as Jane Price herself; but she is a gentle-woman, and very well informed. We talk much of the War, and the Eastern countries, and she has explained to me a great deal that I knew nothing about. We read Mr. Russell's wonderful letters to the " Times," and it is delightful when I find something in them that you have already told me. I understand the various " arms " of the Service now, and I am familiar with the generals' names, and the relative positions of the allied armies.

'I have a song about the English and French flags: each verse ends with—

"While their united standards wave
O'er a united host."

A French lady residing here is very disdainful about this sentiment; she sniffs expres-

sively when the others ask me for "The
United Standards." I feel sure she is secretly
longing for a signal disgrace to befall "our"
side. She is a strong Legitimist, and the
success and prosperity of France are no causes
of joy to her, because they are Imperial success
and prosperity. That, Mr. Jack, is a sound
feminine notion of politics: party first, and
the rest nowhere. I have learned a good deal
about a good many things since I have been
here.

' All the ladies in the Home are educated
persons, and as we are strangers to each
other, although we are thrown into a certain
amount of daily companionship, we do not
talk of our own affairs or those of other
people. There is some really good conversation, led and fed by Miss Metge. Our reading
yesterday was the "Times" letter, dated
May 11—the same day on which you wrote to
me—in which the arrival of the Duke of
Cambridge and Marshal St. Arnaud at Galli-

poli is announced, and Mr. Russell describes
the review of the French troops. We were a
party of quiet women, each of us with her
private unshared troubles; the scene of the
allied camps and their life was distant and
strange to us; but the subject took hold of us
all, not of me only, whose heart is at Gallipoli.
There is a grey haired young woman here, a
Miss Rivers; her nerves are quite worn down
by two years' work with some dreadful little
girls, whose mamma would have it that each of
them possessed a special gift, which was to be
cultivated by the governess, but not considered
in the governess's salary; well, even she cared
to hear of that brilliant sight. How delighted
you will all be when these letters go out to
Gallipoli again, and you can follow the details
of what you have seen *en masse!*

'Mr. Russell gives such hearty and generous
praise to the French troops. I wonder whether
you too have been struck with their gallant
bearing, and " the ready, dashing, serviceable

look about the men, that justified the remark of one of the captains, ' We are ready as we stand to go on to St. Petersburg this instant ? ' " What strange people the natives of the place must be !   After reading of so imposing a spectacle as that grand review and sham fight, with 20,000 troops upon the opposing ridges of hills, the valley full of guns, the columns extending upwards of eight miles, and wondering where *you* were, and from what point *you* saw it, it has a singular effect to read that " Gallipoli, with its fifteen thousand inhabitants, sent not a soul to gaze upon the splendid spectacle ; " and that " while there are six or seven French men-of war anchored in their waters, while frigates and steamers and line-of-battle ships are passing up and down in continuous streams, waking up the echoes of the Dardanelles with endless salutes, not a being ever comes down to glance at the scene."

' Our poor home-bound imagination was strongly stirred, very strongly, as we sat sew-

ing, with our work-boxes before us, and Miss
Metge read aloud to us that brilliant description of the great gathering of foreign warriors,
of the indifferent Greeks, the imperturbable
Turks, the English soldiery who " assisted " in
large numbers, and the fine cortège which Mr.
Russell describes as " a wonderful vision of
prancing horses and gorgeous caparisons, of
gold and silver lace, of hussar, dragoon, artillery, rifle, zouave, spahi, lancer, of officers of
all arms." If there was not to be any fighting, all this would be as delightful to read as a
fairy tale ; but when I think of what it is they
are preparing for with all this gorgeousness
and grandeur, it makes me tremble. Nevertheless, I try to remember what you said about
what you expected of me, and to be something like your ideal.

'Your dear and precious letter was sent on to
me here by Jane Price. The sight of it made me
quiver. The mingled joy and fear in which I
constantly live seem to be doubled when I see

your handwriting, and the date makes me realise—as, I am sure, the dates in my letters make you realise—how widely we are parted, at what a distance each is following the track of the other's life. I like that young Frenchman you mention. I am glad you let him talk to you of his mother. You and I can understand him, because neither of us ever knew what it was to have a mother. I am sure he is a fine young fellow, though not a big blue-eyed curly-haired hero like—some one. Tell me his name in your next letter.

'Almost the worst part of leaving the Farm was the impossibility of my doing as you especially desired, with respect to the Squire. I told you of the visit poor Sarah and I paid Miss Nestle, and the dear, dear behaviour of Trotty Veck; but I did not tell you how sorry I was that 1 could not see the Squire. I suppose I must have seen him when I was a very small child, but never since; and when I knew that we were going away, I had a hope that he might come back

to Bassett within the few intervening days, and
that I might chance to meet him. I think if
he had come back, I should have invented
some pretext to find myself in his presence ;
but his return was not even talked of. It
gives me a very lonely feeling to think that my
Jack's father would not know me, and I
should not know him, if we were to meet in
this big city ; and yet, no matter when or
where we might meet, we should be thinking
of the same person, the same place, the same
circumstances ; we should be full of the same
hopes and the same fears. The ridiculous
rumour of which I told you in my last, was
the latest so-called intelligence when we were
leaving the Farm.

'How delightful it would be if Russia would
give up and give in, and you could all
come quietly home again! You will quite
believe that you are very angry with me when
you read that sentence ; no doubt it is foolish
and ignorant ; but I think it is a sentiment

shared by most women, and that in reality
we do not care a bit the more for you because
you are heroes. I do not mean that we are
not proud and happy that you do your duty,
but that is a different sort of feeling. I don't
think I want you, now, to look like one of the
splendid officers in "Tom Burke of Ours"—
but at first, when you brought me the book, I
did think a good deal about it; that was before
you had become all the world to me. Now,
whatever you do, wherever you are, you will
be always the same to me; and though I cannot keep my promise to think of our betrothal
vow every day by the river-side at the Farm,
and to renew it while the river shall run and the
wind shall blow, I think of it here every day
and all day, and I renew it with my first waking
thoughts when my eyes open in the morning.

' I wonder how the Bassett woods are looking now, and whether any one at the Farm cares
for the view from the turret-bower, or likes to
look out of the window of the Dame's Parlour

across the river and over the fields? I do not
know who is there. Among them may be a
girl like myself, and her happy fate may be
coming to her also over those fields and across
that same river. I wonder, if there is a girl
there, whether she ever tries, as I did, to re-
people the Dame's Parlour-side, in her fancy,
and to think out the lives of those who were in
these rooms before her, in the old and the later
times? When I used to have such fancies, how
much astonished I should have been if I had
seen a vision of myself as I am now—all alone
in London, and waiting to go I know not
whither, among strangers! How much more
astonished if in a vision I had seen you!

'I leave my letter until to-morrow. Good-
night, dearest Jack.

* * * * *

'I resume very late my daily delight of
writing to you. A strange thing has happened
to-day. A lady has engaged me as companion
to her daughter, after having heard me sing and

seen me only once. I did not know there was any one in the front room with Miss Metge; I was playing and singing in the back-parlour. The lady, who had come to the Home to enquire about a companion for her daughter, took a fancy to my voice, and then, it seems to me, Miss Metge having told her how much, or, rather, how little, she knew about me, she sent for me, and we had a private interview. She asked me whether I would mind going out of England, and said she was quite satisfied with what she had heard, and that she did not require any recommendation beyond that of Dr. Chad. It is very strange and fortunate that what Miss Metge feared would be a great difficulty should be so easily set aside. She took me out in her carriage, and explained everything to me. I cannot imagine anything of the kind more desirable than the position she offers me.

'First, dearest Jack, I must tell you what she is like. She is not old at all, but her hair is quite white and beautifully glossy; she has dark grey eyes, and a fresh complexion; her figure is tall and stately; her manner is graceful, sweet, and simple. I felt that I could be perfectly at ease with her, although it would be impossible not to be respectful also, and always conscious when with her of my own youth and insignificance. She has a remarkably considering face; as though she thought a great deal, and very deeply. Two or three times while we were out she seemed to be carried away from the time and place by her thoughts, and would rouse herself with a kind smile, and ask me something about myself. But this was not until we had talked over the matter, and come to an agreement. Her great anxiety is about her daughter, whether she will like me and I shall like her. The chief requisite is that the young lady's companion should play and sing well; for she is extremely fond of music. " My wish is," she said, " that you should find a happy home with us, for as long a time as it suits you to remain. Two young girls like yourself and my daughter, on an equality in every respect, as I should wish you to be, ought to be able to settle down into your own and each other's ways, and to be happy together. At least," she added, touching my hand lightly, " I think she may be quite happy, and you as nearly so as the fact that you are not with your own kin, and have a life-history apart from those around you, would permit you to be under any circumstances. Don't imagine that I overlook or underrate that difference." Having said this, she gave the conversation such a turn that I could not think she was expecting me to answer, and began to talk of the country around her house—a château, near Quimperlé, —and of the journey to Brittany.

‘ I wondered whether I should be expected to teach or study with the young lady, who is about my own age; but I found there are to be no lessons; nothing but general companionship, and music. I am glad I am going to

Brittany. I have read and heard a great deal about that loyal and faithful province of France. My uncle had a number of books that treated of Brittany ; he liked the wild mournful music of the Bretons too. He used to say it was the only French music that had any soul in it.

'The lady's daughter is not at home. During her mother's absence she is staying on a visit with a neighbour, a French lady. I am to be sent over to my new abode under escort of an English maid, and the old French man-servant, who is what my uncle would have called "quite a character," profoundly respect-ful to his mistress, but almost fatherly in his ways, and evidently incapable of having an interest apart from hers. His name is Grégoire, and he reminds me of stories that I have read about the faithfulness of old family servants in the French Revolution time.

'The lady has to remain in London a little longer, on business. She said that she should like her daughter to make my acquaintance with as little delay as possible, and, if I did not mind, she wished my engagement to date from the actual day. I agreed to this, of course, and she took me back to the Home. I felt rather confused, but very thankful for such an unhoped-for way out of my difficulties. I hope you will be pleased, dearest Jack. Is it not strange how soon and how completely all the face of one's life may change without one's own agency? When I think of the day that first brought you before my eyes—how short a time ago !—how my life seemed all fixed and dark, and how in every respect it is totally changed, I am bewildered.

'I should be frightened by the feeling that one is so helpless with respect to one's own fate, only that mine has been so much more than merciful, so beneficent, in giving me to you. It seems so long ago since the time when I used to steal away to the Dame's Parlour and take breath, as a swimmer in the sea takes breath to meet the on-coming wave.

I feel as though it must have been in another life, in a different world, that I had only one friend, and would have been thankful at any moment to look at her in her coffin. Until I hear that you are satisfied I shall not be content; but I do think I have done the best I could under the circumstances. There is something so sweet and kind in the lady's manner that I feel sure I shall not be lonely or unhappy in her house. I wonder, dearest Jack, whether if she proved to be very kind to me, and that her daughter liked me, and we got on well together, you would allow me to tell her my true story? But, of course, it is absurd even to put such a thing before you, when I have no more than a first impression to go upon.

'Miss Metge is greatly pleased, and has said a great deal to me about the lady, who is an old friend of hers. She feels convinced that I shall be very happy, and that I shall suit the position. I hope so.

'I had thought of posting this to-morrow, but on consideration I will keep it over until I have more of my story to tell you. I was unfortunately forced to make my last letter so gloomy, that I want this one to reassure and cheer you as much as possible. I am to leave London on the day after to-morrow. The English maid is to come in the morning, to help me to get ready for the journey. We are to rest two nights on the way. I have not yet told you that the lady's name is Vivian. Her daughter, Sybil, is her only child. Madame Vivian is half French; her mother was a Frenchwoman. Now I have told you all I know, dearest Jack, and I must lay down my pen for the present.

*   *   *   *   *

'All is ready; but I have not had time to add a line to this until now, when it is very late, and I am tired. Madame Vivian came here this afternoon, and had a long talk with Miss Metge. Nothing can exceed the kindness and

consideration of all her arrangements for me.
I fancy she is a very clever woman, though I
am hardly a judge of the indications of talent,
and it may be that she is only unlike any one
whom I have had an opportunity of knowing.
Perhaps all the ladies whom you know—the
people who go to Trescoe Park, for instance—
have that calm, dignified manner, and that
clear, rapid way of judging and deciding ; but
it is quite new to me, and it is delightful. To
all but yourself it would seem an impertinence
for me to pronounce at all upon one so much
my superior as Madame Vivian ; to you I may
say that when I have tried to picture to myself
a woman of genius I have thought of some such
person as she is. My notion of a woman of
genius is one to whom subjects that are distant
from and strange to us common folk are near
and familiar ; to whom difficult things are easy ;
whose thoughts are lofty, and away from self ;
and to whom the petty desires and spites, occupations and interests that fill up the existence

of ordinary beings, are of no more importance than the doings of an ant-colony in an ant-hill.

'I cannot but wish that Madame Vivian were coming to France with me ; it would be so much easier; but I must not complain, everything has gone so well hitherto. She did not say how long she expected to remain in London, but spoke vaguely of business that was detaining her. The young lady must be pretty, if the likeness, which her mother wears in a locket and showed me to-day, be not a flattering one. She has large, solemn, dark eyes, and regular features.

'This letter is all full of myself. That is not because I have been thinking less of you than I am always thinking, but because I know that you will want to learn everything that has occurred. How anxiously I shall await your approval of what I have done !

'Little as we see and hear in this quiet place, we can feel that the attention of the town is fixed on the army and its doings.

Every scrap of news is precious, and sometimes
I can hardly refrain from letting the people
know how much all that concerns the war
means to me. When I lived in London with
my uncle and aunt I never looked at a newspaper. I used to wonder how any one could
take an interest in politics and police cases,
and I thought all newspapers were made up of
those topics. Now I read the papers eagerly,
and even the political side of the war interests
me. I shall not be so ignorant when you
come home as I used to be. When you come
home! I keep my heart and courage up with
those words. They seem to be written on the
air, and my eyes are always fixed on them. I
should stumble and fall if I looked away from
them for a moment.

' The kind of life I am going to is so strange
to me that I cannot even speculate upon it. I
can only make up my mind to do my best, and
I hope there will be a great deal to do. It is
pleasant that Madame Vivian's house is an old

one.   It is not, I dare say, in the least like the
Dame's Parlour-side; but it has had people
living and dying in it for a long, long time,
and I don't think I could ever care for any
house that had not.

'Good night, dearest Jack.   Good-bye for
the present.   I will close this up, take it with
me, and add to it some account of my journey.
I am for ever your own

'MAVIS.'

*   *   *   *   *

Miss Metge was in good spirits.   She liked
Margaret Warne, and it was a satisfaction to her
to be able to serve or gratify Dr. Chad.   Miss
Warne was on her way to the Château de la
Dame Blanche, and Miss Metge felt a pleasant
conviction that the experiment would turn out
well.   She was awaiting the arrival of Madame
Vivian, with whom she was going to the
Adelphi Theatre, where the good old dramas
were still being acted under the auspices of
Mr. Webster and Madame Celeste, by players

whom to remember is a delight. Adorned with a red opera-cloak—the correct thing for theatre dress at that period—Miss Metge sat at the window in the front parlour, where she could keep an eye on the gate, and yet beguile the time with the newspaper.

The 'Times' had just then begun to expose, through its Special Correspondent, the shortcomings of the transport and medical services in the East, and to formulate that famous indictment, to which the poor unnamed fighting-man—the 'food for powder' that does not count—has since owed much mitigation of misery as old as time and war.

As Madame Vivian's carriage was conveying them to the Strand, the friends talked about the Special Correspondent's revelations, and Miss Metge remarked that the state of the postal service at the seat of the war was also a grave calamity, and equally disgraceful to the authorities.

'There is no postmaster at Gallipoli,' Mr.

Russell had recently written, 'nor any person to take care of our letters there. For example, if a letter is put into the post-office in England, directed to "A. B., British Forces, Gallipoli, or Constantinople, viâ Marseilles," it it is put into the Gallipoli bag. The bag is opened by the French postmaster at Gallipoli, and the letters are left lying in a heap till called for. It is obvious that this is a hardship upon the officers and men who have left Gallipoli and gone up to Scutari.'

'Fancy having the misery of uncertainty about one's letters added to all the rest!' said Miss Metge, impatiently.

'Yes,' answered her companion; 'it makes it much worse for people at home, too. I suppose some serious attempt will now be made to remedy so intolerable a hardship.'

This was but a trivial incident of the day, and neither of the speakers remembered it; nevertheless the postal mismanagement at Gallipoli was destined to produce results of grave importance to one of them.

CHAPTER XVII.

THE CHÂTEAU DE RASTACQ.

In more than one record of travel in Brittany, the palm of beauty is assigned to the ancient town of Quimperlé in the province of Finistère. Around the old formerly circumvallated town in the valley through which the rivers Elle and Isole flow, lies a beautiful country; not wanting in the grandeur that abounds in the land of dolmen and menhir, but without the brown-hued desolation that characterises a large portion of Le Morbihan. The air of antiquity still hangs about Quimperlé, although its old monuments are all destroyed, and the successive tragedies of its long history are no longer to be traced in the frowning fortresses and venerable churches that witnessed them.

Only one old tower remains, marking the site of the ancient walls, and giving a touch of antique majesty and meaning to the Rue du Château, whose picturesque lines lie between the two rivers that mingle lower down in the valley.

Thirty years ago Quimperlé still boasted a grand relic of the ancient time, in the Abbaye de la Sainte Croix, which was re-built in 1049 by Alain Caignart, Count of Cornouaille, whose tomb was piously pre-served in the crypt throughout seven peaceful centuries, until the desecrating days of the Revolution. The Count of Cornouaille him-self had come late in the history of the ancient sanctuary, for it was the hermitage of Gunthiern in the sixth century. Those who travel through Brittany now, and linger at Quimperlé, behold only a restoration of the Abbaye in imitation of its ancient form. The church was destroyed in 1862 by the falling of the central tower, when it was undergoing repair, and only the old crypt remains. Where the great Abbaye Blanche once stood, a centre of Dominican learning, the traveller of to-day finds the inn of the Lion d'Or, with a quaint 'Montmorency' of pollarded trees in front of it, and no trace of the old building remaining except one doorway. But for all this there is a restful air of ancient-ness in the place that does not depend upon the presence of ruins; and the sunny, shady peacefulness of the upper town, once the Ville Close, consorts well with the visions of the past that come to the sojourner there. The outlook over the beautiful environs of Quimperlé is a revelation of loveliness, espe-cially when the town has been approached by the rude and sombre route through Le Morbihan.

To the south lies the forest of Carnoët, its grand extent marking the horizon with a dark outline. Over it the sky sharply bends its steely blue; through it the united rivers flow

downward to the Bay of the Forest in one
mingled stream called the Laita, and it is rich
in the wild and beautiful legends of the province. In its most distant recesses lie the grey
and grassgrown ruins of the Abbey of St.
Maurice, a noble structure, whose doorway
bore the proud, vain legend, 'Cette maison
durera jusqu'à ce que la fourmi ait bu la mer,
et que la tortue ait fait le tour du monde.' The
moral of that legend is the moral of Baalbec,
and the moral of the Sphinx. The ant still
drinks, the tortoise still travels; but where are
the great monuments, and where the men who
raised them? In the twelfth century Duke
Conan built this one, now represented by a
cluster of ruins, for the praise of God, and to
the honour of St. Maurice. There are yet
other traces of ancient buildings in the great
forest of Carnoët, and by the side of the Stream
of Gladness (for this, some say, is the meaning
of Laita) fragments of a massive wall reveal
the site of an ancient castle of the dukes of

Brittany, once the abode of the terrible 'Barbe bleue' Comorre.

In comparison with the antiquity of the ruins in its vicinity, the Château de Rastacq, situated near the edge of the forest, was modern. It had, nevertheless, claims to antiquity which in any other province would have been regarded as venerable. The château, with its narrow corps de logis, its leaden roofed, turreted wings, and numerous strait lozenge-paned windows, shining like a beacon on a hill at sundown, stood on a flat plateau, with sloping ground in front of it. The edge of this slope formed the bank of a brawling, foaming little tributary stream that flashed like mingled snow and silver through the landscape. The roughness and untidiness that are features of Brittany as characteristic as its costumes—all unaltered thirty years ago—were much modified in the case of the Château de Rastacq, yet the grounds had a certain bareness of aspect in the front view that was relieved by the

sweep of the forest at the back of the house.
A formal piece of water, with a leaden
fountain in the middle, was divided from a
flat and formal parterre by a railing with a
tall gate in it. The owner of the château
was Madame de Rastacq, a widow, a Parisian,
and the devoted mother of an only son.

In the summer sunshine, the leaden-capped
turrets of the château were turned to silver, the
glass roof of the ' marquise ' glittered, the water
in the pond became a sheet of crystal, the formal flower-beds in the parterre glowed with
glorious colour. The letter-carrier, trudging
wearily up the woodside road, put a little extra
fatigue into his gait on perceiving that a young
lady was on the look-out for him at the 'grille.'
The château was at the far end of his walk,
and a ' chope ' of rough heady cider was his invariable guerdon. The presence of Mademoiselle
indicated, however, a probable gift of a small
coin at the least; perhaps a large one, for
Daniel Grosset had a packet for the young lady

herself. Daniel's expectations were realised; the young lady on the look-out for him at the grille joyfully received the packet which he handed to her, and gave him a pourboire so liberal that the habitual seriousness of his dark face was relieved for a moment by something like a smile. Returning to the 'perron,' the young lady seated herself on one of the broad steps and began to read the welcome letter.

While she was thus engaged, a second figure, emerging from the open door, appeared upon the scene. The new comer was a small, slight, elderly woman. She was richly but appropriately dressed, with a closer observance of the prevailing mode than might have been looked for in a region so remote from the centre of fashion; but she could never have been otherwise than plain in her first youth, or even in her second—a period frequently more favourable than early girlhood to French-women's looks. Madame de Rastacq was not Breton, but Parisian, and as a young woman

she had successfully practised the essentially
Parisian art of charming without beauty. Her
features were insignificant; her small, deep-set
eyes, shrewd of expression and singularly quick
of glance, were of an indefinite colour ; her complexion was evenly dark and sallow ; her thick
black hair had never been lustrous, and only
the perfectly white and even teeth redeemed
her face from positive ugliness. Madame de
Rastacq descended the steps with a light tread,
and laid her still beautiful hand on the shoulder
of ' Mademoiselle.'

'So you have got your letter, Sybille,' she
said, in French as purely Parisian as her gown
and her cap. 'Now you will be tranquil. Eh !
the dear mother writes much ! '

'Does she not ? ' said Sybil Vivian, rising ;
' and it is all so good. Maman makes such
charming plans.'

Madame de Rastacq cast a sharp glance at
the papers in the young lady's hand.

'*She began to read the welcome letter.*'

' Do they include her coming back soon to take you away from me ? '

' No ; she cannot return for some time yet. She has an affair to arrange which is dragging itself, and she must wait to complete it. But I will read her English into our language for you. Did you come to call me to breakfast, dear Madame ? '

' Yes ; and here comes Jean to reproach us with the cooling of the cutlets.'

Madame de Rastacq and her guest entered the house. No one could have detected, under the easy politeness of the elder lady's manner, perfect in its mingling of familiarity and attention, the secret apprehensions with respect to a design on which she was seriously bent, that were besetting her. She was a clever woman in her way and in her degree, but she was narrow in her views, devoid of high-mindedness herself, and incapable of recognising it in others. Not only was she firmly persuaded that Madame

Vivian's chief object in life was to 'marry' her
daughter, but her estimate of the good sense
and maternal virtue of her neighbour would
have been seriously lessened had she been convinced that she was wrong in this belief.   The
whole duty of the mother of a daughter was
comprehended in 'marrying' her.   Not even
the misfortune of Madame Vivian's half-English
blood and breeding could have obscured her
sense of right in that matter.

The mind of Madame de Rastacq was
exercised on two points; one was the unaccountable seclusion in which a lady of such
manifestly easy fortune chose to live, with a
daughter to marry who would be much the
better for seeing and being seen; the other
was the entire silence maintained by her
mother on the subject of Sybil's 'dot.'   The
former was, however, a harmless eccentricity;
and however puzzling it might be to Madame
de Rastacq, it was distinctly fortunate, because
the success of her own design in reference to

her Anglo-French neighbours depended upon their continued residence in the vicinity of Quimperlé. The latter was, however, annoying; not only because it was contrary to custom, but because it gave rise to an uncomfortable sense of insecurity. That detestable liberty in the disposition of their own property which English people were unhappily suffered to enjoy, might exert itself injuriously in the case of Mademoiselle Vivian. It was possible that the fortune was all her mother's, and at her ultimate disposal, and that she might not be inclined to 'doter' Sybil with proportionate liberality; especially as she held the absurd English ideas of love and marriage.

Madame de Rastacq had cherished a design concerning the residents at the Château de la Dame Blanche, from an early period of her acquaintance with them. That acquaintance had been made after due inquiry, and by the advice of M. l'Abbé Foix, curé of a small parish in the environs of Quimperlé, an ecclesiastic whose savoir vivre and savoir faire, might, without any detriment to his piety, have been useful in a more important sphere of action. The mother was half English, but the daughter was virtually French. Sybil had never been in England. She spoke English indeed, but not by preference. Her graceful ways and passive obedience were French. There was about the dark-eyed daughter of Madame Vivian none of the independence of opinion and action which Madame de Rastacq disliked especially because it was so English. There was no personal reason why Madame de Rastacq should not 'marry' her only son René to the young lady of the Château de la Dame Blanche, and there was, presumably, a very sufficient pecuniary motive for making the match if possible. That 'presumably' was the crux, and Madame de Rastacq was bent upon removing it.

When, like the sublime scapegrace of the 'Tale of Two Cities,' Madame de Rastacq 'looked over her hand,' she noted some very good cards in it. The widowhood of Madame Vivian was one of these. A feeling against second marriages was formerly strong amongst French people of condition—its modification is one of the notes of radical change in these latter days—and the possible second marriage of Madame Vivian had never been reckoned by Madame de Rastacq among the chances against her scheme. There had been nothing to suggest such a notion during the five years' residence of the handsome widow at her secluded Breton château. She received visits from the very few families who resided within visiting distance, and her relations with the townspeople, especially the poor, were friendly ; but of the outside world she saw but little. Thirty years ago tourists in Brittany were few. There was no Mrs. Macquoid to tell them what to see and how to see it. Although Madame Vivian's hospitality was occasionally claimed by a savant or an artist, this occurred but rarely.

The next good card was the gentle and pliant disposition of Sybil. Had she been a different kind of girl, had she been more of a ' Meess anglaise,' it would have made no difference in the purpose of Madame de Rastacq, but it might have considerably modified her method, and given her son some trouble. She had, however, nothing of that kind to apprehend. The affair would go quite smoothly, so soon as the two mothers, as high contracting powers, were agreed upon it. René de Rastacq and Sybil Vivian had already met, and the gentleman, who was aware of his mother's plan, had been pleased to declare that she was ' très bien.' There was no evidence that Sybil Vivian had formed any opinion about René de Rastacq; but this too was as it should be.

Not bad cards; but there were others that Madame de Rastacq liked less. These were Madame Vivian's expedition to England, and the indications of serious business by which it had been preceded. She had come to a knowledge of those indications through Sybil's complaints of her mother's preoccupation and absence of mind, and also of her own exile from Madame Vivian's presence for unreasonable spells of Miss Litton's company. Thereupon Madame de Rastacq had played a very good card, by inviting Sybil to her house during the absence of Madame Vivian. She could always make herself agreeable to anybody with little trouble; she liked the girl; here was an opportunity of acquiring influence over Sybil, and strengthening her position with Madame Vivian. Her invitation was gratefully accepted. Miss Litton was properly conveyed back to England; but Madame de Rastacq very soon found that, whatever might be Madame Vivian's business, she had not imparted it to her daughter. Sybil's frank, easy way of talking made the extracting of anything in her power to tell, contemptibly easy to Madame de Rastacq, who would have made a figure in the high-art era of diplomacy.

In the present instance she made the primary mistake of supposing that Madame Vivian must necessarily regard the 'marrying' of Sybil as she herself regarded the 'marrying' of René, and confining her speculations to whether she would conduct the transaction on the French or on the English system. If she meant to adopt the former, the expedition to England became invested with alarming significance; for the whole matter might be arranged without its being thought necessary or expedient to say anything about it. Her mother might return to announce that Sybil was to be married out of hand. If, however, Madame Vivian meant to adopt the latter system, the expedition to England would signify nothing at all, and Madame de Rastacq might prepare Sybil to fall in love with René (according to the odious English fashion and phrase) on his return, covered with glory, from the campaign against Russia.

A more favourable subject for such an

experiment than the girl who faced Madame
de Rastacq at a table, formally placed in the
exact middle à la salle à manger of the dreary
order of French furnishing and arrangement,
it would not have been easy to find. Sybil
Vivian was, in all the ways of the world,

An unlessoned girl, unschooled, unpractised.

Her mind was not uncultivated, but it was
neither expansive nor independent; her disposition was trusting and romantic; her heart
was untouched; her fancy was free. A being
more ignorant of evil, more unsuspicious of
guile, more incapable of comprehending interested motives, more ignorant of 'seems,' did
not exist; nor one who would be more helpless if brought in contact with the hard realities
of life outside a home as effectually sheltered
from them as the Happy Valley of Prince
Rasselas.

The wisest of us is not wise all round.
Madame Vivian, although she had profited by

the lessons of life in her own person, had not escaped from the delusion that so readily besets those whose hearts are garnered up in their children; the fond folly which believes that life may be made something quite different for those children, that their experience may be purged of sorrow, and the Fatal Sisters cheated in their case of the universal toll. Perhaps the fact that she was a weaver of fictions, and lived much in a world of imagination, was chiefly accountable for this flaw in her armour of good sense, and also for the halo of sweet content that in her fancy always surrounded her daughter.

In her hand was the wand of a magician; it conferred or withheld the hearts' desire of those whom the wielder of it summoned up from phantasmal realms. It might be that she had come to wave it outside the sphere of its proper action, and to look for its spiriting in the hard actual world. She could summon up beautiful images of girlhood, set them in her pages, crown them with glory and honour, enrich them with love, fortune, happiness; or she could gently withdraw them from a world that did not appreciate or might fail to satisfy them, by that beneficent expedient of early and poetical death which was not absolutely forbidden to the novelist thirty years ago. Psychology and physiology did not hold their terrors over the story-tellers of those days.

A cordial friendship subsisted between Madame Vivian and Madame de Rastacq, although they were unlike in all but the devotion of each to her only child. The design cherished by Madame de Rastacq could not have been made to appear to her to be traitorous to friendship. She would have declared that the only reason why it had not been avowed from the first was the leaven of English prejudice in the otherwise fine character of Madame Vivian. It was necessary to manage her a little in her own interests, benevolently to scheme for the occasion of bestowing upon

her the privilege and blessing of such an
establishment for her daughter.

It was, therefore, with an untroubled con-
science that Madame de Rastacq played her
game, and she had already won a trick or two.
Her young guest's imagination was impressed
with the idea of the gallant young soldier,
whose mother's love for him was ever manifest
in a thousand nameless ways. The whole
house was full of René, and Sybil's interest was
aroused by the family traditions of the de
Rastacqs. The Château de Rastacq was a
dull and formal dwelling in comparison with
Madame Vivian's handsome country-house.
The latter stood at the head of the grand pass
known as La Roche du Diable, commanding a
magnificent view of the pass, and was adorned
with taste which exceptional circumstances had
enabled her mother to indulge.

The former, however, possessed superior
attractions for Sybil—in that it had a family history ; the armour on the walls of the entrance-

hall; the portraits framed in the panels which lined the corridors; the heavy articles of plate, some displayed upon the black oak buffet in the dining-room, others reposing in old coffers bearing the arms of the family; the collection of old china, not very large nor particularly beautiful, but undeniably authentic, and all linked with the ancestral fortunes of the de Rastacqs—these had a significance different from that of the beautiful things which abounded in her mother's house. Among the latter she might wander at will, making up any stories about them that occurred to her; but she could never associate them with the house, or with the history of any one belonging to herself in the present or the past. The rich and rare arms, the fine old pictures, the objects of gold and silver work, the Oriental porcelain, the gems of ceramic art from all European countries that made her mother's house a wonder, had been brought thither only recently, and were merely purchased things, like the bread the household ate and the clothes that Sybil wore. Among her mother's and her own possessions ancestry had no place. The only kinsman Sybil had ever known was a great-uncle whom she had seen a few times when she was a child, and who had recently died. She had never heard anything about her father's family. Her mother and herself were alone in the world, without a history.

'The world' had no distinct meaning for Sybil. Her experience was almost as limited as that of Hans Christian Andersen's 'ugly duckling,' who, having made its way through the hedge, 'found itself in the wide, wide world.' She was as yet on the safe side of the hedge, and only the eyes of her fancy, fed by the stores of her mother's mind, and aided by Sir Walter Scott's novels, had peered through it.

Sybil was very happy at the Château de Rastacq. Love and indulgence formed her accustomed atmosphere; her sky was not

changed, nor her mind either, when she left
for a while the brighter and more luxurious
Château de la Dame Blanche.

Madame de Rastacq speedily discovered
that the apprehension which Sybil's words had
inspired was unfounded. After their excellent
déjeûner, the young lady put her mother's
letter into French for the benefit of her
hostess.

Madame Vivian's letter was simply the
history of her meeting with Miss Warne, and
of the subsequent arrangements. Sybil was
pleased and excited at the idea of the arrival
of the stranger, and by her own unusual
importance on this occasion. Her mother
wished her to return to the Château de la Dame
Blanche as soon as possible after the arrival of
Miss Warne

At the latter portion of Madame Vivian's
directions to her daughter, the expressive eyebrows of Madame de Rastacq met in a frown.
Here was an instance of her friend's unaccount-

able departure from custom ; of that deplorable originality which was a result of her English breeding. Two young girls to be left to their own devices, without any surveillance! it was altogether unheard of. And the headstrong folly of Madame Vivian's selecting a companion for her daughter at least ten years too young for the position, simply because she happened to sing well! was there ever anything so English? That Madame Vivian should think her daughter required a companion at all was a cause of offence to Madame de Rastacq. This was a result of the engrossing studies to which she so needlessly devoted herself; but for those long hours passed among books and papers, Sybil would need no other society than her mother's.

With such tenacity did Madame de Rastacq cling to her cherished purpose, that she had come to regard Sybil more in the light of her own daughter-in-law than in that of Madame . Vivian's daughter. She was positively impatient

of the solicitude with which Sybil's mother
guarded against her losing the habit of speaking English, and kept her supplied with
English books. The young lady had no great
love of books ; and René de Rastacq's wife need
speak no other language than René's.

'How nice all this is!' said Sybil, unconscious of the elder lady's disapprobation.
'Grégoire is to come for me. I hope Mademoiselle Warne likes to walk out a great
deal, and that she loves dogs and birds and
flowers.'

'It will be the duty of your companion to
like what you like, and to accommodate herself
to you,' said Madame de Rastacq, dryly.

'Mademoiselle Litton did not think so. She
hated walking ; she always believed every dog
she saw was bent upon biting her ; she did not
know a blackbird from a sparrow-hawk, and
flowers made her head ache. She cared for
nothing but eating, and could talk with pleasure
of nothing but lords and ladies. I hope Made-

moiselle Warne does not know any. I am so
tired of them. How soon do you think she
will arrive?'

'Much sooner than I wish, Sybille, since she
is to take you from me,' answered Madame de
Rastacq, in the caressing tone that she reserved
for Sybil only; 'in three or four days at the
latest, I fear. I am glad, however, that you
will not have to leave me until after the next
news from Scutari comes in. You will like to
hear what René has to say?'

'Yes, yes, indeed,' answered Sybil, with
satisfactory alacrity; 'it is so interesting, and
M. le Capitaine writes so well.'

Sybil Vivian had some of the defects of an
only and idolised child. She entertained a
natural conviction that the feelings which en-
grossed and the subjects which interested her
must be engrossing and interesting to those
about her, while she sometimes failed to return
the taken-for-granted sympathy in kind. Her
mother had occasionally put her shortcomings

in this respect before her, and although she was
not generally observant, she did just now perceive that Madame de Rastacq was not particularly interested in her speculations concerning
the new-comer, to whom that lady alluded once
or twice as Madame Vivian's ' oiseau bleu.'
Although Sybil did not detect in this a shade
of ridicule of her mother's supposed impulsive-
ness, it checked her and made her uncomfortable.   Here Madame de Rastacq made a small
mistake in her play. Sybil resolved to keep off
the subject, to be as cheerful as possible, to talk
to Madame de Rastacq about the family stories,
portraits, and legends, and also about M. le
Capitaine ; likewise to wait for the coming of
Grégoire patiently.   But she ardently hoped
that Grégoire's coming would not be long de-
layed, and she read her mother's letter over
and over again, almost as often and attentively
as though it had been one of those love-letters
which deplorable English custom permits young
persons to receive.

Sybil's patience was destined to a more protracted trial than she had foreseen. A whole week elapsed, and Grégoire had not made his appearance, driving Madame Vivian's handsome grey ponies in the London-built open carriage, which was still an object of curiosity in the neighbourhood. Neither did the long-haired letter-carrier, in the loose trousers and the cartwheel hat, bring any more letters for Mademoiselle to the Château de Rastacq.

The expected letter from M. le Capitaine arrived duly, and made an agreeable diversion. Not so agreeable, however, as it might have been had M. le Capitaine written in better spirits; for he admitted that there was a great deal of sickness among the troops in the allied camps, and he recorded one or two losses which affected him deeply. There had not been any fighting as yet; but the ugly realities of war, its sufferings of the baser sort, its wasteful casualties, wringing many hearts, but readily overlooked in the sum of its gigantic misery, had already beset the hosts under the united standards.

A day after the expiry of the week, Madame de Rastacq and Sybil were in the salon, the former working steadily at a large piece of embroidery for church uses, the latter frankly idle, and lost in contemplation of the beauty of a snow-white kitten curled up on her knees. A servant entered the room and, presenting a letter to Madame de Rastacq, said :

'A man on horseback has just brought this.'

Sybil was at the other end of the long room, and did not hear what was said. She took no notice until Madame de Rastacq called to her. Then she looked up and perceived that something had happened. She set the kitten down, and hastily approached Madame de Rastacq.

'What is it? News from home?'

'Yes. Mademoiselle Warne has been at the château for two days—but the maid is ill. Here, you had better read what she says.'

Sybil read the following, written in stiff, but correct French :

' MADAME,—I venture to address you, being in great perplexity.   Mademoiselle Vivian is, I am aware, prepared for my arrival here, and is expecting that the carriage shall be sent for her, according to instructions.   I have taken it upon myself to postpone sending for her in consequence of the unfortunate illness of Eliza Blount, the English maid who has been engaged for Mademoiselle Vivian, and has accompanied me from London.   She was apparently well at the beginning of our journey, but soon showed signs of indisposition, and arrived here so ill that Grégoire sent for Dr. Renouf.   He pronounces the malady to be fever, although he cannot yet say of what kind.   At present the case is not alarming.   I have written to Madame Vivian, and Grégoire has secured the services of a person capable of helping me in the necessary care of the patient.   This woman's name is Jeanne Penhoël; Grégoire tells me she is

well known to Mademoiselle Vivian. I entertain no doubt, Madame, that you will not permit Mademoiselle Vivian to return home under
the present circumstances, and I beg to assure
you, and also Mademoiselle Vivian, that I will
do all in my power for the sick woman. Dr.
Renouf is satisfied of that, and has sanctioned
my writing to you. Grégoire would have taken
this letter himself, only that he fears to leave
the château for any length of time. I regret to
have to make so distressing a communication,
and am yours respectfully,

'MARGARET WARNE.'

'Oh, how dreadful! How unfortunate!
What must I do? She can't be left there
alone!'

'My dear!' said Madame de Rastacq, firmly,
taking the letter out of her hand, 'you must
stay where you are, and keep as quiet as you
can. I will go and speak to the man, and you
may write to this young lady. I must say she

is behaving very well. She has good sense, that is clear.'

Referring to the letter again, Madame de Rastacq turned over the leaf:

'See,'—she said. 'Here is a line from Grégoire':—

'MADEMOISELLE' — he wrote,—'Be not frightened. Keep quiet. Do not come near the fever. The new English lady is an angel. And with a head!—Your devoted servant,

'GRÉGOIRE.'

CHAPTER XVIII.

THE STORY OF MAVIS.

'Château de la Dame Blanche; near Quimperlé,
Finistère: June, 1854.

'DEAREST JACK,—I resume my story a few hours after my arrival at my journey's end. All that I saw was full of interest for me, especially after we left railways behind and took to the diligences—vehicles which I knew from books, but find much calumniated. I did not mind the short sea voyage, though it was my first, and I should have enjoyed the whole journey thoroughly, only for the illness of the English maid. She is a young woman ; her name is Eliza Blount. Madame Vivian was especially induced to engage her by the fact that she speaks no French at all ; so that Miss Vivian, whose attendant she is to be, will

be obliged to speak English with her. I soon
saw that she was not very fit to travel, and she
acknowledged that she had felt ill at starting.
I had much ado to get her through it. For
the last few miles of the journey we had a
carriage of Madame Vivian's sent to fetch us,
and on our arrival Grégoire and I agreed that
the doctor should be summoned in the morning. She is quiet now, and says she would
rather be alone, so that I have time for resting
and writing.

'With every hour, my anxiety to learn
what you think of all that I have told you
grows greater. I may soon have a letter in
reply to my first from Liverpool, although there
were many complaints of delay and irregularity in the post-office business before I left
London. When I have heard from you I dare
say this desolate feeling will pass off, but just
now it is very oppressive. I realise so fully
how young I am, and how lonely—with my
secret history and my assumed name.

' I have as yet seen nothing outside of the château, and have made acquaintance with only a small portion of the inside. The whole house would take some time to study, for it is like a museum—in earnest, I mean, not only in Miss Nestle's sense. The approach from the road is very picturesque, and the house itself is quite unlike the bare and grey, though sometimes imposing structures which we passed on our way hither. It is not old, for Brittany, and Madame Vivian has made several altera- tions " in the English sense," as Grégoire explained. I wonder what you would think of the château ? You are accustomed to great houses, and might not be impressed by it, for I fancy it is not what would be called a great house in England ; but I have only Bassett in my mind to compare with it, and there is no likeness between the two. I am afraid I shall not be able to describe it so as to make you see it, for it belongs to a style of architecture whose name I do not know.

M 2

'The approach from the high road is through a fine avenue of many kinds of trees, the poplar and the pine in particular. I was delighted to see the endless rows of poplar-trees as we travelled along; I knew them from books, and my Uncle Jeffrey had a few pictures of French scenery. The front of the house, of grey and white stone, is almost clothed with greenery. I never saw such a profusion of foliage and flowers of the creeping and climbing kind, and the blossoms are very brilliant in colour. The casements of my own room are actually framed in yellow roses of some early and hardy kind; sprays of them in their first bloom trail down from above and wave gently before the window-panes. There are two wings to the house; these project on either side of the front, but the whole building is on a line at the back. When I was conducted by Grégoire (evidently interested in the effect upon me) through the great open hall, or, "salle de réunion," as he calls it, into a wide corridor furnished as a sitting-room, with pictures on the inner wall, marble statues and vases of flowers at intervals throughout its length, and an outer wall of glass from floor to ceiling, with doors opening upon a verandah whose pillars are all wreathed with foliage and flowers, and Grégoire in a tone of triumph bade me look out, I was as much startled and delighted as he expected me to be.

'The château stands at the head of a wild and rugged pass called La Roche du Diable, and from the gallery and verandah at the back the actual Devil's Rock is visible, with its sheer descent to the bed of the swift dark river on one side, and its grand upreared masses of precipice on the other. From the face of the rock spring pine-trees that seem to cling to it at all sorts of angles, and in the most desperate positions, and sturdy oaks are embedded among the masses of stone. The wildness and grandeur of the scene, far surpassing anything I had ever beheld, made me gasp, and brought tears into my eyes. The house commands a long grand sweep of the pass downwards, with the river appearing here and there along the curving line—in one place it looks as though it were quite shut in by the lofty pinnacled rocks, and lies within their enclosure like a lake—to a great distance below the beautiful niche in which the château is placed.

'The sudden strong contrast between the park-like country in front, with a steep, green-banked, flower-gemmed road leading to it, and the wild and majestic gorge at the back, could not fail to strike even those who have been accustomed to grand scenery. I asked Grégoire, before he hurried me away to eat and drink after my journey, whether there was any possibility of getting down into the gorge and reaching the river's brink. He told me with pride that there are miles of footpaths among the woods, rocks, and boulders; so I shall soon be exploring the valley. It must be terrific enough in winter, but the beauty of it on such a day as this is wonderful; and then the height and the blueness of the sky! It must do one good and bring one peace to live in so beautiful a part of the world.

'The house is simply furnished; all the decoration is white and gold; there are lofty ceilings and tall doors and windows on the ground-floor. There are but two storeys, and the centre roof is flat, with a queer bell turret in the middle of it. There is a parapet with loopholes all along the front. The wings have leaden-roofed cupolas with odd lozenge-shaped windows in them, and the same sort of loopholed parapet on the projecting front and sides. There is no courtyard, so I presume the house ought not properly to be called a château. As yet I have only seen the sitting-rooms on the ground-floor, my own "apartment," and the room prepared for Miss Vivian's English maid. The right wing is occupied by MadameVivian, and the rooms are closed during her absence. The pretty " apartment " allotted to me is in the left wing, and I was not a little delighted to find that my sitting-room commands a perfect view of the pass, and opens on the verandah.

'If I may judge by the arrangements made for the comfort of Miss Vivian's companion, I have fallen into exceptional hands. I have two large, airy, handsome rooms, one opening into the other, prettily furnished in a light polished wood, and some French material which I have never before seen—the colour is blue, with a leaf-and-flower pattern in white. The floors are polished, and a square carpet of the same colours is laid down in each room. This does not sound pretty, but it is so. The open fire-places remind me of the Dame's Parlour-side, but they are smaller, and all shining with blue and white tiles and brass " dogs." Of course there are no fires, but a neat pile of logs in a carved box is placed in readiness for use. On the walls are some water-colour drawings, and above the mantelpiece is a large mirror. This is rather uncomfortable ; I never before occupied a room in which I must be constantly catching sight of myself. I have a writing-table, a work-table, and two easy-chairs ; a pretty timepiece and lovely china ornaments adorn the mantel-shelf. There is a book-case, with a number of books in both French and English. The collection has evidently been made with care. I recognise, though I have only given the shelves a glance, some of the authors whom my Uncle Jeffrey held in esteem.

'I have often pictured to myself what a house might be like in which everything was beautiful and orderly ; where there was plenty of money, and no discord ; where the ruling spirits were wise and kindly, and full of the tastes and interests that must make life so full and so delightful when they exist with wealth. Not that I should ever care to be rich, dearest Jack ; you know that, and how happy I am to think that there will always be a great deal for me to do in the home to which you will one

day take me.   If I say these things it is only
because it is such an unspeakable delight to
talk to you as if you were present, and could
answer me.   I have often thought of such a
house, just as I have often pictured foreign
countries and old historical scenes in my mind's
eye.   Now I think I have come to such a one.
The first impression the house produces is that
of peaceful orderly brightness.   I imagine it to
be among houses something like what Madame
Vivian is among women.

'Darkness has now settled down over the
beautiful scene outside my windows.   I have
been watching the closing of the curtains of
night, and the clear shining of a few stars.
By-and-by the arch of heaven will be studded
with them, and your eyes will be seeking them
too.   This thought always makes a starlit night
precious to me; I feel nearer to you than in
the sunny day, which has no object common
to us both to show me.   I am not tired, although
I am supposed to be greatly fatigued by the

journey, and I have been attended by the
servants in a way that says much for their
mistress. I must write on for a little longer.
There is so much to say, although the sense
always comes over me when I am writing to
you, dearest Jack, that it is so feeble and
insufficient. I have a thousand thoughts and
impressions that I cannot convey to you at all ;
of the one abiding feeling in my heart how
little can I say !

' The steel-blue heaven now stretches its
great arch over a multitude of shining globes ;
they hang in the space between it and us. I
have never seen the stars look like that in
England. The stillness is so deep, that, leaning over the rail of the verandah just now, I
could hear the soft lapse of the river far down
below. In the winter I suppose there is a
rapid rush of water, and the sound would be
quite loud up here. How different from our
own river, flowing so peacefully through the
flat fields and past the old walls. I wonder

whether Mr. Reckitts uses our boat, and whether Reuben has been kept at the farm. I spoke hardly a dozen times to Mr. Reckitts, but once, when I had an opportunity, I told him about Jack and Jill, and he said he would look after them. I said a good word for Isaac too, and poor Sarah and I had the comfort of seeing that the dear " black man," as you used to call him, was at least not afraid of the stranger. Fieldflower Farm, the Dame's Parlour-side, the river, the swans, they are a thousand miles and a hundred years away from me ; only you, and the words we spoke that last day, are always present. Good-night, dearest Jack.'

The following was written a day later :—

' It is again evening, and I am once more with you, but I do not resume my pen with a calm mind. I could hardly resume my letter were it not that it must be posted three days hence, so as to go out by the next mail. This has been a trying day. I arose early, and

found that the scene which had been so
beautiful the night before was even more
beautiful in the morning light, and I had gone
out on the verandah when Grégoire came to
look for me. He told me that Eliza Blount
had passed a bad night, and he, fearing she was
seriously ill, had sent a messenger to the doctor
again to beg that he would come to the
château without delay. Grégoire seemed to
think it was a matter for my choice whether
I would or would not see the sick woman, but
of course I went to her at once, and was with
her when the doctor arrived. He is an elderly
man, with a gruff manner, a clever face, and an
unreasonable temper. He seemed quite angry
because his poor patient could only speak
English, treating the fact as obstinacy or
stupidity on her part; but as she did not
understand a word he said, this did not frighten
or abash her. He flurried me a good deal, but
I interpreted between them as well as I could,
and presently he became mollified, and told me

that Eliza Blount would undoubtedly have a
long illness, its nature being fever, although of
what kind he could not as yet pronounce.   He
asked about Madame Vivian and her daughter ;
I told him they were absent, and explained my
position in the house.   He said I must consider
well what I was doing if I remained there, and
that, as he could not say whether the malady
would prove to be infectious or not, it would be
well to prevent the return of Miss Vivian.   He
then went away, promising to send a person in
whom he has confidence to assist me in the
care of the patient.   This I at once told him I
should undertake.   Then Grégoire and I had
a conference, which ended in my taking it upon
myself to write to Madame de Rastacq, with
whom Mademoiselle Vivian is staying, telling
her the state of the case, and suggesting that
the young lady should not come home.
Grégoire was to have gone to fetch her to-
morrow.   I have also written to Madame
Vivian.   What she will do I cannot tell ; but

from the way in which she spoke of the urgency
of her business in England, I do not think she
will allow this occurrence to change her plans ;
especially as I hope she will trust to my doing
the best I can.

'My last letter to you was written by the
side of a death-bed.   Once more I am tending
a sufferer ; this time, indeed, a stranger, if
I can use that word about a person who is
suffering, and has no one but me to understand
her complainings and interpret her wants.   I
have passed a very anxious day, and I am now
released from my watch for a few hours by the
arrival of the nurse.   As the patient cannot
understand her, or she the patient, I shall not
be able to be much away from the sick-room ;
but the doctor forbade my sitting up to-night,
and as the illness must run its course, it would
be foolish of me to tire myself out in the
beginning of it.   Grégoire would have amused
me to-day, if anything could have done so ; he
was in such a state of mind about Mademoiselle

Sybille ! That she should be alarmed, or dis-
appointed, or vexed in any way would seem to
be in his eyes the greatest of misfortunes, an
impossible, unheard-of thing! Mademoiselle
is so delicate, so nervous, so "sensible," and
Madame is so desirous that nothing should
ever "contrarier" her. How strange it is to
think of the difference in the lives of people.
I can hardly realise any girl's being brought
up in that way, and made of so much account.
I suppose it is the custom among people not of
my station, but of hers and yours. It stands
to reason that to be sheltered and considered,
and, so to speak, worshipped, always to have
beautiful things to look at and to use, must
make young girls very happy, charming, and
elegant ; and I am afraid I envy those unknown
beings, not because they have so much to
enjoy, but because they must be so much
beautified and refined by it. For myself, I
should never think of those things, but I am,
in that one respect, like your favourite Portia.

I should like to be for your sake all that any woman ever was, and " treble twenty times myself," or rather, dearest Jack, what you think me. Grégoire's anxiety set me pondering on this vast difference. I hope I may not find Mademoiselle Vivian a spoilt child whom her mother takes for an angel. There is a lovely portrait of her in the outer salon; if she be selfish and capricious her disposition contradicts her face.

' I have not been out of the house to-day, and I am now going to walk on the verandah.

' It is not surprising that my spirits should be low to-night; the strangeness of the place and the solitariness, which must now continue for some time, would be enough to excuse that ; but there is more than all this. Nothing changes my mind about Sarah ; there is not a moment in which I am not thankful that she is dead ; but I grow more and more troubled about my father. I am obliged to remind myself of the facts, to go over and over them, forcibly

to restrain my fancy from practising any decep-
tion upon me, in order to ward off doubt and
self-reproach concerning what I have done.   I
shall not be really at rest until I know what
you think, and have your sanction for writing
to my father, to explain my conduct and its
motives.

'To-day I have seen Madame Vivian's own
rooms, in the wing opposite mine.   I wanted
something out of the medicine-chest for the sick
woman, and Grégoire took me to Madame
Vivian's apartment to get it.   There are four
rooms—a salon, a library, a bed-room, and an
oratory.   The first is a museum of curiosities ;
the actual furniture is as simple as that of all
those other rooms which I have seen, but the
walls are lined with cases containing objects of
great beauty, and, I should think, value.   I had
only a passing glimpse of these things, as I
would not, of course, intrude during Madame
Vivian's absence.   They include some enamels
and a number of gold-mounted miniatures.   The

library commands a superb view of the pass
and the Devil's Rock. It is a beautiful room,
and the walls are fitted with bookcases from
the ceiling to the floor. Of this room, too, I
had only a passing glimpse; but I observed a
pile of English newspapers on a table, and asked
Grégoire whether they were regularly received
at the château. It appears that a parcel arrives
once a week. Grégoire offered to bring the
next that comes to my room; he answers for
the permission of Madame Vivian. This is a
great relief. Among the things that were
troubling me was my having forgotten to make
any arrangement for having the 'Times' sent to
me, and not knowing how to do it from hence.
There ought to be some news in soon, and with
that a letter from you. How strange and sad
it will be to read, notwithstanding the delight
of it; for unless I am quite out in my calcula-
tion of time, it will have been despatched before
my first letter posted at Liverpool can have
reached you.

' The messenger brought back Madame de Rastacq's reply to my letter, and a pretty note from Mademoiselle Vivian.   Madame de Rastacq thanks me in the name of her absent friend for my prompt action, pays me some undeserved ompliments, and informs me that Mademoiselle Vivian's visit to the Château de Rastacq will terminate only when it is perfectly safe for her to return to her own home.   The young lady sends me a cordial assurance that in all this she chiefly regrets the postponement of her meeting with me.

' 11.30 P.M.—The hours are very slow and heavy to-night; I am " so troubled that I cannot sleep."   There is no danger of my disturbing any one with my singing at this side of the house, so I have sung my evensong from the verandah, to the sky, the rocks, the trees, and the river.   You know that I used to sing it at the window of the Dame's Parlour, when I could just trace by the starlight the course of the iver you had crossed, and the dim line of the fields beyond. I used to think how wonderful it was that I could be the same creature who had sung those old hymns at that window when there was no hope in my heart, no joy in my soul, no love in my life. What a poor creature I was in those past days, dearest Jack. I do not think I knew their full dreariness; I should have been more frightened by the prospect that was the only one I then had to look forward to, if I had realised it. How rich I am now! although you are so far away, and it may be so long before you come for me.

'I must have disturbed a bird with my evensong, for since I came in from the verandah one has been uttering rich plaintive notes; all else around is profoundly still. Oh, for one moment's sight of you, and the hearing of one word from your lips! You told me that in every letter I was to say: " I love you ; I am yours." And I have not failed to do so. " I love you ; I am yours," that is what I am always saying to you in my heart ; but beyond

and above those words there is something that
has no words, that nothing can disturb, and
that is as immortal as our two souls.'

The following lines were added on the next
day :—

'Eliza Blount continues very ill.   The
malady is running its course.   The doctor
gives no decided opinion, but approves of all
I have done.   I had a few lines this afternoon
from Madame Vivian, and they make me all
the more sorry that I have been obliged to
send her distressing news from home.   She
writes : " I am obliged to leave you and my
daughter to do the best you can for each other
more indefinitely than I intended at first.
Some bad news from Scutari, deeply affecting
a friend of mine, just received, but not confirmed, puts it out of my power to name a day
for my arrival at home.   This uncertainty makes
me all the more anxious to hear from you that
all is well."   So there is news from Scutari,
and for some poor people it is bad !   Your
letter ought to have arrived at the same time

with this news. I shall write to Jane Price
to-night, to give her this address. Oh, how
ardently I hope she may have a letter to forward to me. I am glad to know that Madame
Vivian has friends who are interested· in the
war ; she will be more likely to talk of it, and
to tell me all she knows. Although I must
not say anything about you to her until I have
your permission, I feel that there will be a sort
of help in her being anxious and interested
too. But, " bad news from Scutari " ! The
words turned me cold.

'I shall probably be unable to write much
more on account of the patient, and Grégoire
tells me my " courrier " must be ready early in
the day. After the despatch of this packet, I
shall begin to keep a regular journal for you.
It is impossible to describe the sinking of my
heart as I finish this page ; and, having written
the words " Good-bye, my dear dear love,"
press my lips upon them that you may find the
kiss there.'

    *   *   *   *   *

CHAPTER XIX.

ONE DAY—MORNING.

LOOKING down the valley from the verandah
which commanded the view of the pass called
La Roche du Diable, the observer might suppose that the Château de la Dame Blanche,
from its dominant site near the head of the
grand gorge, surveyed no residence of man.
In the sense of any rival or similar abode, this
was so ; but at a considerable distance from
the château, on the opposite side of the pass, a
thin column of blue smoke might be seen to
rise amid the rocks and pines, indicating the
existence of a dwelling at that place. Only
the smoke was visible from the verandah of the
château, for a steep projection from the precipitous side of the pass, on which huge rocks

were piled in Titanic masses, with the river
bed making a sudden sweep into a sort of
little sheltered bay behind it, hid the house
from view.

Mavis, contemplating the scene on the
morning after her arrival, had observed that
thin column of smoke with a pleasant feeling
of relief from the oppressive sense of rugged
ness and loneliness that almost overpowered
the admiration inspired by a spectacle so novel
to her. The deep-down murmur of the river;
the slow flight of a bird of prey poised above
the precipice in the luminous air, then discerning a quarry and darting down upon it out of
her sight, with the surprising swiftness of its
kind; the glinting sunshine that revealed the
mighty masses of rock with sparkles all over
their face in the light, but whose black frown
came with the evening; the trees that had taken
foothold in the scanty earth, like assailants
swarming up the walls of a fortress, while others
had gained and held the place, and which were

motionless now and silent in the summer-time but for a faint rustling, but would make terrible moan in the winter; all these impressed Mavis. Never had she looked on any scene so beautiful, so grand, or so solitary.

'The verandah was supported by a wall, covered with flowering plants; at its foot was a broad smooth walk laid upon the sheer rock, with a strong iron railing at its outer edge. This walk led, at some distance from the house, to the steep shoulder of a rocky hill with a crescent* of pines on its brow, forming an effectual shelter for the château on that side.

'There's another house in the valley, then,' said Mavis to herself, when she perceived the smoke; 'but there's no bridge that I can see; so they must be as lonely there as we are here. I suppose all the life of the place is on the road-side of the château. I am glad there is another house to be guessed at, though not seen from the verandah. It must be because I have lived nearly all my life in a town that this beautiful place almost frightens me. If Jack were with me I should not care though there was not another house within a hundred miles of us.' She turned away, unconscious of the tears that were stealing down her cheeks, and went to receive the morning's report of the patient from Grégoire.

Grégoire's favourable opinion of the new importation from England had undergone no modification. He continued to regard Miss Warne with distinguished consideration on account both of her heart and her head; but he was not quite so well pleased with her looks this morning. Having told her that the patient was no worse, he respectfully advised her to breakfast after the English fashion before she went to the sick-room, and also to go out presently in the fresh air. While Mavis ate her breakfast, Grégoire imparted his views to the nurse whom she was to relieve, and that kindly person, declaring that she was not tired, and

also that the patient was doing well, confirmed
the old man's advice with authority.

Mavis was glad to obey. Her spirits had
flagged very much since the preceding night.
She did not feel ill, and she had no fear of
illness, but she was oppressed. Very soon now
she would have Jack's letter; it would have
reached Bassett yesterday, she calculated; it
would have been forwarded to Liverpool to-day,
and Jane would lose no time in sending it on
its comparatively tedious journey to South
Brittany. Why was it that the time she had
still to live through before Jack's next letter
could arrive, seemed harder to endure than all
the days that had come and gone since his last
had blessed her sight?

Mavis thought she had got the better of her
changeable moods, of those fits of despondency
that had beset her in the dark days at Fieldflower Farm—the very last of them had befallen her just before the 'budding morrow'
had come to its perfect blossom in her 'mid-

night.' Such moods must be for ever inexcusable henceforth. Those were the fitful humours of a girl ; she was a woman now, and Jack loved her. In life and death, for time and eternity, she was his.

' Very well, Jeanne,' she answered, with that sweet smile which had a charm for most observers in whom there was any good thing, ' I will go out for two hours. Indeed, I have been longing to get down into the pass. Grégoire tells me there is an easy way from the end of the terrace walk, and a path up and down through the rocks quite to the end of the valley.'

' So there is, but Mademoiselle will not want to walk all that way,' said Jeanne Penhoël, in the tone of conscious superiority of one who is explaining local matters to a stranger from afar. ' It is a much longer bit of road than it looks from the windows up there. Mademoiselle will go no farther than the Devil's Rock, if she gets to that ; but the way is easy enough and safe.

Mademoiselle will perhaps meet some children collecting rushes for the basket-makers, for nobody else comes into the valley except on fête days. The way through the park into the town is much prettier, however, and more gay, and I am sure, if Mademoiselle wishes it, Grégoire will send some one to accompany her.'

'No, no,' said Mavis, 'I am well used to lonely walks. I prefer to be alone. Grégoire shall show me the way down from the terrace walk, and I will be back in two hours punctually.'

Mavis prepared for her walk with lightened spirits. She passed for a moment into her sitting-room, to set the window open, and lock the drawer of the writing-table. As she paused with her hand on the key, she thought she would take one—only just one—of Jack's letters; it would be so delightful to read it in some sunny, shady nook of that wild, beautiful, strange place below there. So she drew one of her treasures from their neat silken case of her own making, and, after glancing at the thick sealed packet which was to be confided to Grégoire that evening for post, she placed the precious paper in her bosom, and locked the drawer.

' Thank you, Grégoire, that will do ; pray do not come down those steep steps ; I cannot possibly fail to find my winding way. But,' she paused on the second step, ' that smoke,' pointing to it, ' comes from the other side of the pass, does it not ? There's a house there ; who lives in it ? '

Grégoire made answer that Mademoiselle was right ; that in effect there was a house there, at the other side of the pass, just at the back of the Devil's Rock, and that Jeanne Penhoël and her husband lived in it. He added that the house had formerly been a ' sportsman's rest,' but that was long ago. There was not so much wolf and boar hunting in the district of late years, and when by an odd chance

in the hard winter the chase came that way the
'rest' was not used.

'A very lonely place to live in,' said the
listener.

Mademoiselle was again right ; but the pass
was narrow beyond Penhoël's cottage, and the
road to the nearest village, though steep, was
not long.   If Mademoiselle wished, she might
see the village one day ; for there was a means
of crossing the pass.   It would, however, be
better to go in the carriage, taking the road by
the head of the valley—a promenade much
enjoyed by Miss Vivian.

'I was just going to ask whether Jeanne
had to walk all that long, slow way round,'
said Mavis, 'for I remember she arrived here
on foot.'

Grégoire permitted himself a respectful
smile at the young English lady's notion of the
local estimate of distance and time.

'She would think nothing of it,' he
answered, 'although she is not of the country ;

she is French.' (Mavis already knew that the true Breton repudiates with scorn the imputation of being French.) 'But there's a ready way to get across, just above the Devil's Rock. The people from the village come down with eggs and fowls and baskets in the summer. Sometimes in the winter the Giant's Stepping-Stones are covered with the waters—the river runs deep and strong in the winter—Mademoiselle will see that. Then the planks are withdrawn, and there is no crossing from this side.'

Mavis descended the long flight of steps, hardly touching the handrail attached to the sheer side of the cliff. Grégoire gravely waited until she had reached the wide rocky ledge beneath, when she waved her hand to him, and he returned to the house.

'Glorious summer' was truly abroad that day, and the power and delight of it came fully to the girl as she descended by the winding way into the pass that had looked so difficult of approach from the verandah of the château. Some new beauty of the scene became visible at each bend of the narrow rock-bounded path, with its height above, its lower depth beneath, and, beyond the slope, the shining river. On the side of the pass which she was following, the variety was greater than on the other, where the grey precipice rose harsh, grim, and rugged from the river bed, and the red and brown rocks—about which, doubtless, the river whirled and churned in the winter, but now circled quietly enough —seemed to have been flung down from behind the precipitous cliffs. On the opposite side the declivity was more gentle, sloping grandly indeed, but less ruggedly, to the river's bed, and the great boulders were intermixed with trees, plants, grasses, and patches of sand. Close by the river, willows, rushes, and reeds grew in beautiful profusion, and a narrow strip of pebbly strand bordered the water. The wind was deliciously warm ; the stillness was not oppressive, for birds were astir in the trees,

and the hum of insects was in the air. Looking upward and backward, Mavis was almost
startled to find how soon and suddenly she had
lost sight of the château, how completely the
gorge shut out all beyond itself. She climbed
to the top of a large sloping rock, and looked up
and down the valley. The head of the pass
might have been one end of the world, the
vanishing point below might have been the
other.

She walked on very slowly, pausing to gaze
and wonder at the immense masses of stone
lying about that playground of giants in every
fantastic position that a dream of incongruity
could picture. Some were seemingly so in-
secure on their immemorial perches that a
moderate shove might send them tearing down
the declivity, to clash with their separated
brethren in the flood below. It was all so
different from what it had been like, seen from
above, that she soon lost her hold of Grégoire's
instructions, and the sheer height of the preci-

pice on the opposite side hid the guiding smoke
for which she had intended to look, making the
crossing to Jeanne Penhoël's cottage the limit of
her walk. After some time she got down to
the strip of pebbly strand by the river, and
there she rested awhile, sitting under the shade
of a willow tree, reading her lover's letter, and
thinking of their own river, flowing through the
rich flat fields at home, murmuring along under
the old walls down to the weir, with Jack and
Jill sailing stately on its quiet breast. The
scene before her eyes, and the scene supplied
by her fancy, were in their combination too
much for Mavis. With a cry of 'Oh Jack,
Jack!' she fell into such a passion of tears as
she had never known yet.

When the paroxysm was over, Mavis rose,
and reascended the declivity, intending to take
the homeward path at once. She was vexed
with herself; this was unlike all she had resolved upon; she was at her moods again!
That must not be; she had boundless cause for

thankfulness ; Jack's new letter was on its way
to her. She took her hat off and fanned her
tear-stained eyes with it ; the moving of the
sweet air restored her ; she kissed the old
letter and replaced it in her bosom with a
smile ; then looking around she found the scene
changed by the bending of the path she had
taken, and recognised, opposite and lower
down, the redoubtable Devil's Rock.

This huge slab of stone projects from
the grey precipice which at that point thrusts
a vast shoulder into the river, and then,
curving back to form a little bay of irre-
gular shape, something like a horseshoe, juts
out again, much less lofty and grim of aspect,
as its long rugged line descends the valley.
Beyond the Devil's Rock was a fierce whirl of
water ; the river, broken and vexed by the
huge obstruction, rushed and tumbled there
amid masses of stone that were but playthings
in comparison with that imperturbable impedi-
ment. She stood for several minutes gazing at

this grand object, and then, remembering that Grégoire had told her the means of crossing the pass was in the vicinity of the Rock, she looked about for it.

The narrowest part of the river which she had yet seen was just above the Rock—she understood now why it was that from the verandah it looked at that point like a dark lake surrounded by masses of stone—and she could see the heads of four rocks, so massive and even that they might be of man's masonry instead of nature's making, protruding a clear couple of feet above the smoothly-flowing water. On these gigantic stepping-stones broad planks were laid. The crossing was safe and easy, and Mavis, having again descended to the water's edge, promised herself that she would return on the first opportunity, and get a view of the pass from the opposite side. She had not a watch, and she could not tell the time by the sun, but as she lingered there came towards her from the other side of the river the music of the Angelus bell, and she knew that it was noon. She had outstayed her promise; it would take her half an hour to get back to the château.

Mavis began to retrace her steps hurriedly, and, climbing obliquely up the declivity, had almost lost sight of the Devil's Rock, when footsteps coming towards her from the direction in which she was advancing caught her ear. This was not the tread of a child, straying about, collecting rushes for basket-making; it was the rapid heavy step of a man walking with a purpose. In a few moments the man came in sight. He was on a higher level than Mavis, and there were masses of stone and some straggling trees between them. With instinctive fear she crouched behind a rock, and held her breath, as he passed at a distance of a few feet from her, unconscious of her presence, while she saw him distinctly.

He was a young man, strongly built, shabbily dressed, not in the characteristic costume of the country, but in clothes of the kind that idlers about towns wear. He was not ill-looking, but, if the expression of his face was to be trusted, the impulse that made Mavis hide herself was a fortunate one. A cloth cap with a peak, worn to one side, revealed the coal-black hair that covered his head with metal-like ridges of hard curls, coming down on the thick red neck and the low brooding forehead. Ruffianism and cupidity might be read in the lurid black eyes, and the coarse lips which displayed strong white teeth. The man had not the gait or bearing of a sailor, but his skin had the red-brown tint usually due to the salted wind of the sea, and the outlook of his evil eyes had the keenness generally to be noted in the gaze of seafaring folk. Dogged and skulking, brutal and merciless, was the expression of the young man's face, revealed in the freedom of his supposed solitude, and Mavis crouched closer to the rock, in the shrinking aversion with which he inspired her.

The man passed on ahead for a short distance, and she, watching him round a corner of her shelter, thought he was going down the valley on the same side ; but he abruptly descended the slope, and crossed the bridge of planks. Mavis saw him disappear on the other side ; then she sprang up and walked back to the château at her utmost speed ; now reproaching herself for her unreasonable terror—for she had not seen the man when she hid from him —and again recalling his ruffianly appearance with horror.

On reaching the château she at once went to the sick-room, and begged Jeanne Penhoël to take some rest. Jeanne liked the young lady's looks still less than in the morning, and asked her whether she was over-tired by her walk.

'No,' replied Mavis, ' I am not very tired. But I was startled by seeing a wicked-looking man. He did not see me, but I got a foolish fright; for I was not expecting to meet any body. I wonder whether he belongs to this place.'

'A young man, did Mademoiselle say?'

'Yes, a young man.' Mavis described the person whom she had seen in the pass. Jeanne Penhoël, who was standing near the door and in the shadow while Mavis spoke, answered that no such person was known in the immediate neighbourhood, and that the man was probably a sea-faring stranger. She then withdrew, leaving Mavis to take her watch.

Whether she was tired or not Jeanne had no present purpose of repose. She went to the room allotted to Madame Vivian's major-domo, and found him seated before a ponderous bureau, busy with his accounts.

'What's the matter?' exclaimed Grégoire, rising to his feet with his first glance at the intruder. 'Is your patient worse?'

'No, no, Grégoire; it does not concern the patient, it concerns me. I must go home, my good friend, and at once. Jean is here again!

Mademoiselle met him in the valley, and he has gone to the house. She did not know him, of course, but I knew him when she drew his portrait for me. I will come back before night, but I must go home now, and get rid of him somehow. Penhoël is alone. God send he does not do him a mischief.'

She hurried away, and Grégoire resumed his work with a sigh.

'The "mauvais garnement," ' he muttered, ' will at all events be the death of that woman, if he is not the death of somebody else first, and does not get put out of the way himself. It is well Madame is not here, or she would bribe him again, and to the same purpose. Now, what Jeanne has not got she cannot give. The rascal will have to work this time.'

CHAPTER XX.

ONE DAY—EVENING.

In a sheltered nook, with the curving face of the grey precipice for its background, a sloping patch of sandy grass plat dividing it from the pebbly strand of the river, stood the house whose blue smoke Mavis had observed. A steep path, with fir trees in serried ranks on both sides of the cutting, led from the secluded dwelling, through the rugged edge of the pass, to the upland and the village beyond. There was little in its external appearance to distinguish the home of Jeanne Penhoël from any other dwelling of its modest pretensions in the country. It was rather larger, a difference accounted for by its original purpose, and the doorway was wider; but the heavy roof was low, and the walls were of rough grey stone.

On either side of the door was a long narrow casement, and a penthouse projected from the eaves, lessening the light that reached the interior of the house, but helping to form a summer workshop for Jacques Penhoël, who was a basket-maker.

It was in the interior arrangements of her house that the foreign origin of its mistress revealed itself. Jeanne Penhoël, formerly Veuve Lebeau of Paris, had not introduced the startling innovation of boards for the flooring of the cottage, but she had gone to the extent of tiles, in a land of earthen floors. Those tiles were of the reddest and the smoothest ; they were likewise kept in a state of mirror-like brightness. White curtains bordered with red adorned the casements, and in the furniture of the three good-sized rooms there was a considerable departure from the established order of things. Neither pigs nor poultry ever invaded the kitchen. The picturesque green and yellow pottery of the country abounded, producing

' bits of colour,' not much talked about in
Jeanne's time, and the plenishing boasted many
an article of foreign origin and use.   The walls,
though only washed with colour, displayed a
few good prints instead of the flaming monstrosities, then, and now, accounted art treasures
by the peasants of Brittany.   Box-beds, fitted
into recesses in the walls, with perforated slid-
ing doors, such as may still be seen of a ruder
form in Scotland, and chests of carved wood,
household coffers for the goods of dead-and-
gone generations, occupied the invariable places.
But these were only traditions, monumental
remains, kept—as funereal urns may hereafter
be kept upon the mantelpieces or in the cup-
boards of our own posterity, if the cremationists
get their way—as inconvenient, but irremovable
memorials.

The most foreign-looking piece of furniture was a combination of glazed bookcase
and chest of drawers in real Honduras ma-
hogany.   This occupied a place of honour

in the living-room—that is to say, the kitchen. Jeanne Penhoël was frankly proud of her 'bibliothèque,' which, with all the other exotic articles in the house, was the gift of Madame Vivian. As a receptacle for books the ' beau meuble,' as its owner fondly designated it, was in but moderate request. The Penhoël library was a small one, and oddly composed; for of the books rigidly locked up behind the shining glass doors, one half were devotional, and the other half theatrical. Librettos of once popular operas, programmes of concerts whose echoes had long since died out of the air, collections of ' opinions of the press ' upon the performances of artists whose very names were forgotten, records of the triumphs of ' Divas ' and the discovery of tenors whose ' golden-throated ' glory was remembered no more ; such and such like were the unaccountable contents of a portion of Jeanne Penhoël's bookshelves. One entire shelf was assigned to a collection of expensive but mutilated toys, and a second to artificial

wreaths and dried bouquets. The wreaths
hung at the back of the shelf on nails concealed
by bows of ribbon, the bouquets were placed
in vases and glasses in the front of the upper
shelves. These decorative objects were regarded
with much admiration by the neighbours.

One of the rooms was used as a store for
the materials of Penhoël's handicraft.

On this bright summer's day the basket-maker
was busy with his work in the front of the house;
his bench was set in the shade; on a rough
table by its side lay his simple tools, and a
bundle of osiers prepared for use. The house-
door was open. The front casement was
hooked back, and a birdcage hung in the free
air. The scene was a peaceful and happy one,
and Jacques Penhoël presented a pleasant image
of cheerful industry. He was a handsome man
of barely middle age, with a grave dark face,
and a large, well-built, seemingly powerful
frame. Nevertheless, he was a cripple, and a

pair of crutches was placed within his reach in the angle of the doorway.

Jacques Penhoël had formerly been a sailor. The dexterity with his hands that he had acquired in his seafaring life had helped him to a new industry when he was terribly injured by an accident, shortly after his marriage with the comely widow Lebeau.

It was noon; the Angelus rang out from the old church in the village. Jacques Penhoël put down the half-made basket, removed his broad-leaved hat, and reverently repeated the archangelical salutation. He then got upon his feet with difficulty, and by the aid of his crutches entered the house.

'Babette should have been back by this time,' said Penhoël to himself, as he renewed the fire in the stove and made a few preparations for the meal that ought to have been in readiness by noon.

'She is gossiping above there, no doubt.

Nothing ever goes quite right when Jeanne is not here.   Does it, Mistigris ? '

He addressed this question to a handsome grey cat who had followed him into the house, and was keenly alive to Babette's unpunctuality.

'Somebody's coming ; but the other way.' Footsteps had caught Penhoël's quick ear, and he limped back to the open door.   The young man whom Mavis had seen in the pass confronted him at a few yards' distance, and, without any form of greeting, demanded roughly :—

'Where is my mother ? '

'You here, Jean? Where have you come from ? '

'What affair is that of yours ?   I'm here. That ought to satisfy you ; you are so glad to see me, you know.   Where is my mother, I ask you again ? '

'Will you not come in ? '

Penhoël, whose face betrayed the trouble

he felt, moved out of the doorway to let the young man pass.

'Yes, I will come in.'

He entered the house, contriving to convey aggression and insult to the owner of it, by both look and gesture. A glance showed him that the person he sought was not there, and that Penhoël was alone. He flung himself into a chair, and repeated his question.

'Your mother is up at the château,' said Penhoël, mildly. 'There is sickness there. She has been away from home for some days.'

'I must see her. I will go there, when I have had something to eat. Does no one here dine, because my mother has turned servant again?'

'Babette will be in presently, and she will get dinner for you. But—I am forced to remind you that Madame has forbidden you the château.'

The young man answered by an insolent laugh.

' Let my mother come out of it then ; for I will see her, I swear.'

' Here comes Babette,' said Penhoël, as a sturdy young woman, carrying a heavily laden basket with as much ease as if she had been a mountain pony, appeared at the threshold.

' Babette, my girl, make us a good dinner; Jean has arrived.'

With a look of anything but welcome on her broad ugly face, the woman busied herself with her cooking. Penhoël limped out to his former place, where he sat dejectedly, making no attempt to talk to the new-comer.

The latter lounged about the room, kicking the chairs, and swearing at the delay of the meal. His insolence elicited no remark from either of the persons to whom it was addressed, and it was plainly a cover for some uncertainty or uneasiness of his own. The blustering of the bully was overdone. At length a good cabbage-soup was set smoking upon the table, which had been decently laid, and the two men sat down

to eat together, but with the same mutual
avoidance. The new-comer ate greedily and
coarsely, and drank largely of the strong cider
for which he called, though grumbling at its
quality. Penhoël's manner was that of a man
enduring the inevitable, and waiting for a
revelation of evil to come. At the conclusion
of the meal, Penhoël still keeping silence, the
young man rose and repeated his resolution to
go to the château.

'You had better not, Jean. I say it for
yourself, not for us. You will be turned from
the door. The last time you were told that it
would be the last, and you know Madame is
one who keeps her word.'

'I know more than *that* about Madame.'

The young man laughed, and showed his
white teeth in a singularly unpleasant manner.

'I might have a word to say to Mademoiselle that would keep the door open a bit longer
for me. What! The rich woman up there,

and my fool of a mother, thought they had got rid of me, did they?'

'You are absurd,' said Penhoël, with a glance at the young man which had more grief than anger in it. He was thinking of the mother. 'You cannot do any injury to either Madame or Mademoiselle; they do not occupy themselves with you; it is an easy thing for gentlefolk to rid themselves of the importunate. Think of it, my poor Jean; a word to the commissary and where would you be?'

The fury with which the young man had listened to the first words of the speaker abated suddenly as the last were uttered. The colour in his florid face faded, the craven in him succeeded to the bully. 'The commissary.' This was a word to conjure with. The dread of ' an officer' was as strong in this ruffian as in any of Shakespeare's poor rogues.

'What an old owl you are, stepfather!' he said jeeringly. 'You needn't take me so solemnly. Who's going to do them any harm

up there, with their big house and their pots
of money? Do you and they let a poor devil
live, and not turn my mother against me, and
the " état civil " of Madame may regularise
itself for me.'

He was standing in front of the house now,
and this dialogue had passed out of hearing by
Babette.

Penhoël was evidently surprised at the effect
of his own words, and this sudden change of
mood.

'I have nothing to do with it,' he said, ' as
you know well. If I gain my own living, dis-
abled as I am, it is because Madame has given
us the house ; but I do no more—neither
hinder you nor help you, my poor Jean.'

Here the inflection of pity in Penhoël's voice
made the young man grind his teeth with
wrath, so simple and sincere was it.

'It is your mother whom you have despoiled,
it is not me, and she has sworn to take no more
money from Madame to be put to such uses.

You come for money, I suppose, and have lost
what work you had. Well; you know how it
was the last time. There was little then; there
is less now. This will finish ill, Jean, this will
finish ill.'

He spoke without passion or even reproach;
but only with the hopeless weariness of long
striving with a reprobate.

'She will have to go back of her oath, then;
unless you want me at home, to be the spoiled
child of the house. Hein! how would you like
that? I am not going to starve, I promise you,
and I am not going to lead the dog's life of dock
work at Lorient any longer. So, whether it
pleases Madame or does not please her, I am
going to see my mother at the château. She
can come out to me if her generous patroness
forbids the door to her son. "A tantôt," stepfather; I'm coming back to sleep. Hein! here
comes my mother!' he added, as Jeanne
Penhoël, breathless with haste and apprehension, approached the house from the cliff-side.

She hurried up to the front of the house, and exclaimed, with a quick glance at her husband:

' What brings you here, Jean? Is there any new misfortune?'

' There's a tender mother! Am I not to have an embrace and the maternal blessing? No! Very well then, I can do without them. You arrive in time, my very loving mother; I was just about to visit you at the château.'

' Is there any new misfortune?'

' Well—perhaps—a little affair. There was a " rixe " below there, and some of us were rather too ready with our knives. Peste! Where's the use of this?' with a sudden change to ferocity. 'What do you care, or I? I have escaped with my skin, but no more, and here I am. The less delay I make about quitting the country the better; the sooner you give me the means of going the better. Yes, yes; you need not keep looking at your man there, to see whether you are to believe me or not. It

is quite true what I tell you. I'm not so fond
of this hole of a place, and the black looks of
yourself and your cripple, as to trouble it of
my own free choice. It's a question of money;
to take or to leave. Here I stay until you find
me the means of placing myself again, and in
safety; unless my stepfather thrusts me out by
the strength of his manly arm, or my tender
mother denounces me to the police.'

The mother and son stood facing each other,
while Jean Lebeau uttered these words, with
every aggravation of insolent tone and gesture
that could be added to their cynical brutality.

He now lighted a pipe leisurely, and, leaning against the wall with his hands in his
pockets, waited for his mother's reply.

'I believe your story,' she said at length.
'We had nothing else to expect. If the police
want you, it is here they will look for you.
You cannot stay here.'

'Give me money, then, and let me go.'

'Where will you go? What will you do?'

'That is my affair. I have a comrade who
can put me in the way of doing something ; he
has a share in a boat trading with England.
Give me money, I say, and I will be off as soon
as you like.'

'Come into the house with me.'

She led the way, and Jean, with an exultant
grin, followed her. Penhoël resumed his work.
Babette was busy in the 'basse-cour'; the
mother and son were alone. Jeanne approached
the book-case, which was the pride of her
housewifely heart, and drew from her pocket a
bright key. The eyes of her son glistened.
He had never known where she kept her
money ; if he had had any notion it was in so
easily accessible a place, he might have helped
himself on former occasions.

'Jean,' said his mother, 'when you went
away the last time, taking with you money
which my good mistress had given me, to rid
me of you and save me from shame, I told you
that you should never touch money of hers

again. I meant it then, and I mean it now
What I possess I will give you; but you may
be sure, as sure as you are of death, that it is the
last you will ever touch. You will have left
me nothing then, and it is better so. I shall be
more at rest when nothing is possible for me to
do, no matter what comes. I say nothing to
you; it is all in vain. You must go your own
way, and come to your own fate. It takes a
long time to convince a mother of such a thing
as that; but I am convinced. I will give you
all I have'—here she unlocked the book-case
—'only, for your own sake, remember that there
will be no more.'

She, too, spoke without heat or anger; she,
too, seemed hopelessly weary; her glance
hardly rested on him.

'That's enough,' he said impatiently; 'I
don't care for sermons; but I don't run my
head against stone walls either. Give me the
money.'

She put her hand upon the shelf on which the

broken toys were displayed, and took down from behind the medley a ' tirelire,' a little common money-box. Her son was much surprised ; but after all, he thought, it was not such a bad idea to keep money in so obtrusively unsafe a place. He would have looked for it in the rafters of the roof, or under the tiles of the flooring.

Jeanne turned out the contents of the box upon a table, and reckoned them. Twenty golden louis. She pushed them towards her son's outstretched hand. He clutched them eagerly.

'Yes,' she said, as if to herself, ' there is nothing left now. There will be no blame to us whatever may come, and they will give us our grave.'

'No fear,' said her son, with a coarse laugh ; ' you and your cripple will have Christian burial all right, and my father's son will console himself with the shiners. Adieu, tenderest of parents.'

With this he walked out of the house, passed before Penhoël's bench without a word, and took the upper path in the direction of the village.

Jeanne stood where he had left her for a few moments. A slow, cold shudder passed over her.

'Mon Dieu,' she muttered, 'it might have been his father. The same face, the same voice, the same cruel, hard, bad heart. Two such men in the lot of one woman! It is too much!'

The husband and wife had nothing consoling to say to each other. The young man was the curse of their otherwise happy lives— a hopeless, irretrievable, ungrateful scoundrel. The resolution at which Madame Vivian had arrived, to do no more for him, had been formed in the interest of his unfortunate mother. The generous and grateful woman, whose faithful friend and servant Jeanne was, knew the world too well not to be aware that there are cases in which that hard utterance, 'Va-t-en tc faire pendre ailleurs!' is obligatory. This was such a case.

When the sun was going down, Jeanne, wishing to cross the pass before it grew dark, left her husband, with many instructions to Babette for his comfort, and the pleasant assurance that the patient at the château would not require her attendance for very long.

'Poor Jeanne, poor woman!' said Penhoël to himself, after she was gone; 'hers is a sore that has no plaster. She often says I make up for most things that have happened to her in her life, but I cannot make up for that. The miserable "garnement" is on the road to the galleys or the scaffold.'

Jeanne gave Grégoire a brief account of what had happened, and received his report of things at the château. Mademoiselle Warne was unremitting in her attention to the patient. She had hardly taken time for her dinner, and was in the room now. He had sent Mademoiselle the English papers to amuse her a little.

Entering the sick-room with a noiseless tread, Jeanne saw all in order : the patient as she had left her, the screen on the off side of the bed, shading the light which was placed on a table beyond, with an easy-chair for the watcher by its side. In the room, save for the slight murmur of the patient as she turned restlessly on the pillow, all was still. Jeanne passed by the foot of the bed to the other side of the screen, and there lay Miss Warne upon the floor—insensible or dead.

Some newspapers were scattered on the table, and one lay near her on the ground. Presently, when Miss Warne had been carried to her room, these papers were collected and put in their proper place in Madame Vivian's library. It occurred to no one there to connect them with the illness of the young English lady. Her swoon was taken to be the beginning of a fever like that of her compatriot. It was, how ever, a line in one of those newspapers that, like a stone from the sling of fate, had struck down

'There lay Miss Warne upon the floor.'

Mavis—a line which recorded among the names of some officers who had succumbed to the illness rife in the English camp, but at first confined to the men only—John Bassett, of the Rifle Brigade.

CHAPTER XXI.

THE DAME'S PARLOUR-SIDE—SUMMER.

THE 'glorious summer' that was investing
Mavis Wynn's new abode with romantic beauty,
was abroad in her old home also.   Looking at
Fieldflower Farm on the day when this story
returns for a while to Mr. Bassett, it was hard
to realise that anywhere under the golden sunshine, strife, bloodshed, and deliberate destruc-
tion were being systematically carried on with
the sanction of great names and high-sounding
principles.   The spirit of peace seemed to
possess the tranquil English scene ; the genius
of home to be present in it.   The river ran so
low in the hot weather that the boat could no
longer be pushed into the water, or pulled up
on the bank, by a girl's hands; the grass-fields
were browning, the rees were laden with

leaves, the hedgerows were thick set with wild flowers, and the prim flower-beds on the Dame's Parlour-side were bedecked with glowing tints and exquisite forms. The music of the time was in the air; from the song of birds to the busy hum of bees at their quest among the flower-beds. Mr. Bassett, sitting by the open casement of the Dame's Parlour, loved to hear the cawing of the Bassett rooks as they flew to and from his own woods, and to watch the swallows wheeling over the surface of the river. He came to love that quiet little stream very much. It was the same that watered his own grounds; but from the house on the hill it was not visible. Its inner bank soon replaced the terrace walk on which he had been wont to pass many meditative hours. The gentle murmuring lapse of the water, the wide-spreading fields opposite, with their slight upward slope, the dark border of pine trees beyond, each one of them a familiar friend—all had a charm for the Squire. That charm was not strong

enough to make him forget his garden and his
shrubberies, but it rendered contentment, which
he would in any case have cultivated as a moral
duty, easier to him.   Perhaps it is paradoxical
to say of the Squire that he was essentially a
man of habit, and yet that he sat loosely to external things ; but so it was.   The cheerfulness
with which he accepted the changed conditions
of his life was as genuine as its expression in
his letters to his son.

Could Mavis Wynn, thinking of the home
that had been hers for so short a time, but
which was glorified in her remembrance by the
dawn of her love, and the earth and stones of
it consecrated by the presence of her lover,
have had a vision of Fieldflower Farm just
about the time when she arrived at the Château
de la Dame Blanche, great would have been
her amazement.   The installation of the Squire
had been rapidly effected, and he had early
adopted the river-side walk, the swan settle-
ment, the summer-house where the boat lay, and

the turret-bower, as favourite resorts Jack
and Jill received their daily dole of bread
with a monastic regularity. Isaac, with the
sagacity of his tribe, after a leisurely inspection
of the new-comers, had migrated from the
Farm-side to the Dame's Parlour-side, and
speedily ingratiated himself with the Squire.
His method was perhaps only what we call in-
stinct, but it had all the effect of philosophical
research put in action. Mr. Bassett's was a
generous nature, to which spontaneous confidence never appealed in vain. Isaac, who
had understood Farmer Wynn's ways, and
defended himself against them with great
astuteness, took the Squire's measure readily,
and appealed to him with spontaneous confidence.

'The beautiful, black-robed, topaz-eyed
creature walked in and took up a position on
the arm of my chair,' said the Squire, on a later
occasion, 'as if not the slightest doubt of his
being welcome could possibly exist. Yet there

was no impudence about him; it was pure, noble confidence, like that of a child who does not know such a thing as a hard word or a blow is possible.'

The Squire, regarding Isaac with great pride, as the big black beauty lay across his lap with his shining head tucked into the breast of his master's wadded dressing gown, addressed these remarks to a person who happened to know something of the previous history of this child of nature. His auditor had his own reasons for disputing Mr. Bassett's theory.

'Not a bit of it,' was his comment, 'Isaac is much sharper than you take him for. He's had more kicks than kickshaws in his time; but like all cats, he can read the human countenance, and having read yours, he very naturally came home to you. It's more complicated, you see, but it's also cleverer.'

Mavis had timidly endeavoured to propitiate Mr. Reckitts in Isaac's favour; but Reckitts,

although a good sort of man, had not the fine
instincts indispensable to a sympathetic comprehension of animals.   Isaac might be well
fed, comfortably housed, and not unkindly
treated, but he would be 'incompris.'   There
would be nobody to talk to him, to indulge his
ever-active curiosity about the household proceedings, to interpret the movements of his ears
and the wags of his tail, to know that he liked
to drink water out of a certain glass sugar-basin,
or to remember that he delighted in the scent
of flowers, and required his milk warm with a
lump of sugar in it after the 'turn' of the year.
In the shock, grief, and apprehension of her
own uprooting, Mavis had suffered many a pang
on Isaac's account.   If only she could now have
known how well it was with him !   Finding the
intelligence of the Squire equal to his good-will,
the cat had gradually trained the man to his
own harmless, happy ways, and admitted him
to full companionship.

The Squire's one difficulty had been Trotty

Veck. Jack's dog was a sacred animal. How would he be disposed towards Isaac? Would he too be touched by the fearless confidence of the cat? When Trotty Veck returned from a constitutional into the village in company with Miss Nestle, and, coming into the Dame's Parlour, found Isaac there in occupation of a big footstool, the Squire observed his conduct with much interest. It was perfectly friendly; he sniffed at Isaac for a moment; this attention was acknowledged by a yawn and a stretch, expressive of patronage as well as leisurely composure on the part of the cat. Presently Trotty lay down amicably by the side of the footstool, and they had a good long sleep together, equivalent to the ' drink ' which seals the bond of certain human amities.

The Squire was delighted; his darling boy's darling dog had fully justified Jack's good opinion of him. To receive after this fashion a stranger, an ' alien in blood, race, and reli-

gion ' (for Isaac could know nothing of
Trotty's God Almighty—who was Jack), was
really fine. Mr. Bassett told Miss Nestle about
it with a kind of grandfatherly pride; but
neither was aware that in reality Trotty Veck
and Isaac were old friends, merely renewing an
interrupted intercourse. The two were close
allies thenceforward, and no doubt discussed
the changes that had taken place in their re-
spective circles. They had many tastes in common, although Isaac could not make out why
Trotty wanted go on long walks, and Trotty
wondered why Isaac never proposed a bath or
a boating excursion. They were, besides, united
by the strong bonds of a common aversion. It
would be difficult to say whether Trotty or
Isaac detested Miss Nestle's parrot Belshazzar
most cordially. Any slight breach between
the two—moultings of the feather of friendship
did occasionally arise on nice questions of tit-
bits—would be instantly healed by the provoca-
tive voice of that detestable bird calling ' Isaac,

Isaac,' or 'Trotty, Trotty Veck, I say,' with a
peculiar horny, rattly scornfulness in its utterance, that made the dog howl and the cat spit
with rage. They would sit side by side and
gaze distressfully at the Squire while this aggression was being perpetrated by Belshazzar, con-
vincingly conveying a sentiment identical with
that which Mr. Thackeray put into the mouth
of the royal sturgeon, when it was intruded
upon by Mr. Buckland's porpoise :—

> ' From the bottom at once of my heart and my pond,
>   I wish the porpoise was dead.'

Mr. Bassett had no horses at Fieldflower
Farm. It was part of his contract with Reckitts
that the carrying business of the small household should be done by the farmer, and that
the Squire should have the use of the round
car and the services of Reuben when required.
Mr. Lansdell had proposed to purchase the
Squire's horses and carriages ; but this offer had
been declined. The horses had been sold at

Chester, with the brougham and pony-carriage. The Squire retained Jack's dog-cart, and had consented that it should still stand in the big coach-house at Bassett. When his son came home he would find his favourite vehicle, and a good horse in Reckitts's stable for his use. The Squire never wanted to go beyond walking distance, unless it might be to the railway station, and he probably should not do even so much until he went to meet Jack. That moment was always in his thoughts; that event formed the horizon of his hopes; that desire was the burthen of his prayers, ' uttered or unexprest.' The Squire was a man much given to prayer of both kinds.

Mr. Lansdell's parting injunction to Mr. Dexter was general in one sense, but particular in another. It was that in every way Mr. Bassett should be induced to maintain his interest in Bassett. His eccentric tenant had not contented himself, as the Squire soon found, with enjoining this upon Mr. Dexter; he had sent instructions to all the heads of departments whom he had retained. The steward was to consult Mr. Bassett about things in general; the gardener was to observe the methods pursued under the old régime ; supplies of fruit and flowers were to be despatched to the farm with unfailing regularity. No persons to whom the Squire had been in the habit of affording assistance were to suffer, because the house on the hill had passed into the hands of a man of wandering ways and cosmopolitan tastes, who liked to have a country place ' to run down to whenever he felt inclined,' but had no notion when the fancy might take him, and no intention of being bothered about the place until it did. Mr. Dexter was not slow to point out to Mr. Bassett, that although it was a singular instance of good fortune that such an accommodating tenant should have come in his way, the advantages were mutual. Mr. Lansdell could not have a better guarantee for the care of his interests than the continued influence of the

Squire over the persons in the employment of the new and absent master.

As for the pain of the situation, it was only a choice between two kinds : that of getting used to Bassett, no longer his own home; or that of never seeing the place at all. The first of these two kinds of pain would certainly be the sooner surmounted, especially as the Squire would have no strange faces to encounter. Mr. Dexter at the time, and Jack Bassett when he came to know it later, felt a more cruel concern for the Squire's position than there was any need for. He was a man about whom those who cared for him troubled themselves beyond the common, because of the gentleness of his unworldly nature, and again, because his transplantation was a difficult thing to realise. Nevertheless it took place easily, because the ' stuff in his thoughts' was more important. He now knew the worst that could happen to him in money matters. That worst was better than he could have anticipated when

the consequences of the legal decision had
been made plain, by the full measure of his
exceptional tenant at Bassett.   In his new
home—new, but not strange—he would await,
with all the patience that the Divine grace
might grant to him, and so much pursuit of
his accustomed studies as he could school his
mind to, the return of his son ; to be then, as
always, the motive and the meaning of his life,
now a man, a soldier, widely different from the
child, the boy, the youth, but as infinitely
dear.

The Dame's Parlour-side was transformed,
under the orders and the eye of Miss Nestle,
into a residence, which, although she privately
disparaged it as a ' nutshell,' and a ' poor place
for the Squire,' had a certain charm for a man
of his quiet tastes and ways.   The best portions
of the antique furniture were retained, and did
not blend ill with the things that were brought
from Bassett.   The simple furniture of Jack's
own room was transferred in its completeness,

and his quarters were arranged as though the morrow were to see his arrival. The Squire's books found lodging on shelves put up by the village carpenter on every bit of untapestried wall ; his big writing-table was set facing the needlework Nativity, and the deep window seat boxes accommodated his maps and manuscripts conveniently enough.

The old oak cabinet in which Mavis had concealed her treasure was admitted even by Miss Nestle to be good enough for the Squire ; but she turned out the spinning-wheel as ' rubbish.' The winged hour-glass was permitted to hold its place undisturbed in the niche over the door, after its wings had been subjected to the first thorough dusting they had received for half a century. A narrow door, covered with tapestry, led from the Dame's Parlour into the adjoining room, where a high carved buffet of antique form, and an oak table on trestles, remained to indicate that in former days it had served the purpose to which the Squire

now put it   This dining-room was panelled in
oak on two sides, on the third was the long
casement, in the centre of the fourth was the
door opening on the corridor; on either side
of it deep shelved roomy presses reached from
wall to ceiling. Great was the consolation that
the Squire derived from those presses. To the
shrunken dimensions of his own kingdom he
was indifferent, but his heart sank when he
thought of Miss Nestle severed from the
Museum. Here was a not too despicable sub-
stitute. With such powers of packing as she
possessed, a fairly proportionate quantity of
her beloved ' stores ' might be transferred to
Fieldflower Farm.

'Then,' said the Squire to himself, ' with
me, a miniature museum, Belshazzar, a couple
of women to keep up to their work, and sub-
sidies for Jack to look after, the dear old
woman will soon recover her spirits.'

The Squire's anticipations proved correct;
but, indeed, Miss Nestle's conduct had been

from the first admirable. The attitude of reserve that she had adopted towards Mrs. Wynn and Mavis she had rigidly preserved towards everybody, the Squire included, after the communication of the disaster which was made to her by the Squire himself.

'It's the law that has done it, sir,' she said, after she had heard him to the end in silence, but with an occasional nervous start.

'Yes, I have told you the law was against me.'

'Then God forgive the law,' ejaculated Miss Nestle, so plainly in the spirit of Queen Elizabeth's famous words to Lady Nottingham, that the Squire smiled to find his expectation exactly realised. From that day he acquired a fresh claim to the zeal and fidelity of Miss Nestle ; he was a victim of injustice. She asked no questions concerning the 'interloper ' who, favoured by the misdeeds of the law, was to fill the Squire's place ; she merely observed that nothing should ever make her believe that anybody but a Bassett could have any right to live at Bassett. She made no comment upon Mr. Lansdell's accommodating readiness to leave persons and things in their places; she maintained rigid composure under all the trying circumstances of the 'flitting'; she presented a deceitful appearance of cheeriness, combined with added scrupulosity of respect in her demeanour towards the Squire —indeed, she made him uncomfortable by her unusual acquiescence. On one point only had she 'turned rusty,' as Jack would have expressed it. It was in this wise :—

On a lovely day in June, when the Squire, attended by Trotty Veck, was reading a newspaper in the river-side arbour, Miss Nestle was interrupted in the task of cataloguing the contents of the museum in miniature by the arrival of the second gardener from Bassett. The man brought a superb bunch of the Squire's favourite cabbage-roses, and desired to speak with Miss Nestle.

He had been sent to tell her that the house-keeper from London had arrived at Bassett, and that she had Mr. Lansdell's authority for asking Miss Nestle to do her the favour of coming to see her when she could make it convenient. The message was carefully worded and respectfully transmitted, but it overthrew Miss Nestle's composure. Across the broad disk of her face, angry colour flew; she had to hold back her answer for full two minutes, or risk the not keeping herself in her place, by letting Griffith Jones detect her feel-ings. Griffith was a jovial person, with a wholesome scent of horticulture about him ; he did not mind waiting the two minutes, but he noted Miss Nestle's colour, and surmised that ' some one had been catching it.'

' I am obliged to the new person's house-keeper,' said Miss Nestle at length, ' but you can say that I have no time for visiting.'

Griffith Jones was disconcerted.

' She—she gave me the message herself,'

he said, ' at the terrace door. She's a lady, you know.'

' Oh, indeed ! Lady-housekeepers have come up since my time. I hope you may all like the change. Not that it has anything to do with you, of course, or that it is any business of mine. I dare say it is all very well for new persons. So good morning, Griffith Jones.'

' Good morning, ma'am.'

Miss Nestle went back to her lists and her labels. The angry red was slow of fading from her face ; her dexterous fingers trembled. She did not mention this incident to the Squire, or to anybody, but the first time Farmer Reckitts got an opportunity of talking to her, she gave the conversation a turn that elicited certain information for which nothing would have induced her directly to ask.

Farmer Reckitts was ' Church.' A pew in the parish church had been rented in Mr. Lansdell's name, so that the ' new person at

Bassett' was presumably of the same persuasion. In the sacred edifice, Reckitts had a good view of the Bassett housekeeper, and he reported to Miss Nestle that she was a quiet-seeming lady, neither old nor young, not to say handsome or ugly, but sensible-looking, and with a noticing way about her. Miss Nestle remarked to herself that she would want *that* if she was to be anything of a housekeeper. He could tell that she was dressed in black, but whether it was mourning he would not undertake to say. She looked quite the lady. Miss Nestle observed that it was well if ' fallalism ' were not brought in at Bassett by new people who knew nothing of the ways of the place, and observed that they had not yet heard of any arrival. Farmer Reckitts could assure her that none was expected. A lady—he understood she was the housekeeper's sister—had come with her in a fly from Chester to Bassett quite early in the morning, but she had gone back the same evening. He concluded by opining that it would be pretty lonely for the lady-housekeeper; but the remark failed to elicit any response from Miss Nestle.

The combination of loftiness and quietude of mind that was characteristic of Mr. Bassett rendered many things easy, because unimportant to him, which would have been trying to a less happily endowed nature. Miss Nestle was as right as she usually was where the Squire was concerned, when she said (to herself) that having to say 'no,' where he had always said 'yes,' would come hardest to him. No one more correctly estimated the duty, or more fully appreciated the luxury of giving, than did this unostentatious gentleman.

Again, Miss Nestle said in her thoughts, 'It's the law's doing, and the poor have got to suffer by it. God forgive the law!'

On a Sunday morning late in June, Mr. Bassett—being on his way to the little Catholic church, which he would have found inconveniently far off had he not struck into the

path through his own woods, at the spot wher e
Jack and Mavis first saw each other—met a
lady. She advanced towards him under the
leafy arcade, and the Squire perceived that she
was a stranger. She was plainly dressed in
black, and there was nothing remarkable about
her face, except that it was intelligent and pale.
The Squire raised his hat, and the lady acknowledged the courtesy with a bow, as they passed
each other.

'One of the new people,' said the Squire to
himself, and thought no more about this casual
meeting. But the lady walked on with a hurried step, and it was some minutes before the
colour that had faded at sight of him returned.

Mr. Bassett mentioned to Miss Nestle that
he had seen a strange lady in the beechwood
walk, and that he presumed, as she was not
going in the direction of the church, she was
one of the new residents at Bassett. Miss
Nestle received this communication in her dry-
est manner. She did not correct his impres-

sions by her more accurate knowledge, and
privately 'hoped' that the 'lady,' who, thanks
to the law, occupied an usurped position at
Bassett, would at least have the decency to
keep her own place to the extent of not in-
truding on the Squire.

Resolutely as she hid her discomfiture,
things were going hard with Miss Nestle. She
had no private cares or personal interests of
any kind ; the first serious trouble that had
assailed her for many years was composed of
the uneasiness with which Jack's acquaintance
with Mavis Wynn had inspired her, and the
hard necessity of seeing her idol depart to
share the inevitable hardships and dangers of
the war. The first of these grievances had
been disposed of by the departure of the
farmer's family ' for good '; the second she
must just bear with ; but then came the astounding removal from Bassett, and the necessity of contemplating her beloved master in
the light of a despoiled, injured, and un-

'*She advanced towards him under the leafy arcade.*'

resisting victim. She hated the idea of his being shut out from the place that he loved, from the woods, the gardens, the terrace, and the rooms; but she hated even more the notion of his visiting all these by the courtesy of that hateful 'new person at Bassett,' whom she regarded as an accomplice of the law.

Time passed, and although the Squire had visited the Bassett woods and gardens more than once, he had said nothing of any second meeting with the obnoxious lady-housekeeper. He had received some friendly visits, including one from the new curate in charge. Mr. Gale recommended himself to Mr. Bassett by his nice discernment of the antiquarian merits of the Dame's Parlour-side, and his appreciation of the peaceful landscape. The county families were for the most part in town, either for the whole season, or a bit of it, according to custom; but Sir Henry Trescoe, being at his country place for a few days, came over to visit the Squire immediately, and by so doing helped to reconcile Miss Nestle to human nature. In a world—she argued with herself—ruled by anything so monstrous as a law which could put new people in the place of Bassetts at Bassett, anything might be looked for; even persons capable of siding with the law, and holding Mr. Bassett of less importance at Fieldflower Farm than under his ancestral roof.

The Squire was out of doors when Sir Henry Trescoe reached the farm, and was conducted by Reuben to the river-side arbour. There he found his old friend, with Trotty Veck at his feet, Isaac fast asleep on the green table close to his elbow, and Balthazar Gracian's 'Homme Universel' in his hand. He rose to receive the visitor with alacrity, and as Sir Henry preferred to remain in the air, the Squire proposed that they should walk along the river bank. The picturesque old building was new to Sir Henry, and he examined it with interest. The conversation soon turned, of course, on Jack. Sir Henry told Mr. Bassett that he was

ordered by his daughters Jane and Caroline
to bring them full particulars of what Jack
wrote to his father.

Nothing loth, the Squire quoted Jack's
cheery, gay-hearted letters, in which the best
was made of everything, and the blunders which
shortly assumed such gigantic dimensions, and
led to such terrible loss and suffering, were
barely admitted. Everything was 'couleur de
rose' with the ardent young soldier. Jack declared that he was 'learning his trade'—as Mr.
Dexter called the acquisition of military science
—making friends among his brother officers, and
in all respects doing well. The 'points noirs'
were the terrible sickness among the men, and
the irregularity of the postal service. Everybody felt the hardship inflicted by the unpar-
donable neglect and mismanagement in the latter
department. Nothing could be more calculated
to produce disheartenment and discontent.

'Jack is very strong on this point,' said the
Squire; 'and it is indeed a cruel hardship. His

letters have reached me all right, so far as I know, but he has not had all mine. Here is his last.' The Squire took the document from his breast pocket, and turned to the last page. 'Our mails are long overdue; no doubt they are lying at Gallipoli, a place which people at home seem to believe is a short walk from Scutari. I cannot describe my longing for letters. Of course I know you have written, and that it is no fault of yours, but pray write everything all over again. Take it for granted the letters have been lost—if they ever turn up they will be doubly welcome—and tell me every bit of news there is about home, and everybody—man, woman, child, and dog—in the place. We know that several bags have been lost in landing, and we can only guess that many more of our letters have gone astray on our way up here, for they are sent on "anyhow" when sent at all. There is no help for it; nobody is responsible. I dwell on this to make you understand that you must not take it for granted I know anything you have written to me.'

'A very unpleasant state of affairs for him,' said Sir Henry Trescoe, ' and a great nuisance to you too—especially if you don't like letter-writing, which is my case.'

'I don't dislike writing to Jack ; but it's a long story to go over again, all about this.' He indicated his removal to the farm by a comprehensive sweep of his right arm.

' What, did not Jack know you were coming here when he went out ? '

' No, he did not, and my letter of explanation is one of those he has not got—unless it has turned up since he wrote.'

Presently the Squire and Sir Henry went into the house, and Mr. Bassett took his guest through the quaint old rooms.

'Jack gave my girls a charming description of the Dame's Parlour,' said Sir Henry, ' with its long casements, its tapestry, and its old oak.'

'Did he?' remarked the unsuspecting Squire; 'I should have thought he had hardly ever seen them.'

It was already late in the afternoon when the Squire and Sir Henry started from the farm to walk to the village, where Sir Henry's dog-cart was put up at the 'Bassett Arms.' Business was pretty brisk at the general shop. In the postal department, Mr. Williams was sorting the letters just deposited per post-cart; on the other side Mrs. Williams was distributing the contents of the London parcel to customers who called in person for their papers; while the errand-boy waited for his share before starting on his round. There was daylight still; but Mr. Williams had a flaring light in his dark little hutch, and to this a lady who had just bought a newspaper was holding it up, searching eagerly for something in its columns. The two gentlemen observed her as they strolled past the shop on their way to the inn, and Mr. Bassett recognised her as the stranger he had met in the beechwood path. No remark was made; they went on; the lady continued her search. Presently she crushed the newspaper between her hands, left the shop, and walked rapidly up the village street in the direction of Bassett.

The Squire, after a cordial parting with Sir Henry at the inn door, turned his steps homeward. On the edge of the village he came up with the errand-boy from Williams's, and good-naturedly dispensed him from a part of his walk by taking the newspapers for the farm. At this moment a gig passed the Squire at a rattling pace, and just as he came within sight of the farm the same vehicle again passed him, going in the direction of the village. He went in by the Farm-side entrance, to give Reckitts his paper, and passed through to the Dame's Parlour-side, admitting himself by his key. At the top of the stairs he made out the figure of Miss Nestle in the dim light; behind her he could see through the nearly closed door

of the Dame's Parlour that the room was
lighted.

'Is that you, sir?' asked Miss Nestle.

Her voice gave him a start.

'Yes.   Is anything the matter?'

'I hope not—I am sure not'—she laid her
hand on his sleeve, trying to detain him for a
moment; 'but there's a magnetic thing come,
and——'

'Where is it?'

'In there.'

He went in, and found the message on the
table, where a lighted lamp stood.   On the
threshold was Miss Nestle, her eyes upon his
face.   He read the lines to himself, passed his
hand over his forehead, read them again, and
said in a thick, uncertain voice,—

'But what—what is the statement?'

'Oh, sir,' implored Miss Nestle, coming up
to the table, 'what is it?   For God's sake tell
me.'

'In a minute—wait.'

He laid down the flimsy sheet and snatched up the parcel of newspapers. He spread the 'Times' on the table, and ran down the columns with eye and finger. Not a sound, not a stir came from the woman facing him ; she watched him in an agony of fear. In a minute he found it—the line that was destined a little later to strike down the girl whom his son had wooed and won in that very room—the line that recorded, among the common occurrences of the time and place, the death of John Bassett of the Rifle Brigade, at the camp at Scutari.

'My God ! '

In a second Miss Nestle had read the words ; in another she had placed him in his chair, and turned it to the open window. The sweet air flowed in softly ; the evening had come with a young moon and a thousand perfumes.

'Rouse yourself, don't die ! oh, don't die ! '

Nothing else could his faithful servant say.

It was all in a moment, but it was meted

with that wonderful measure that sets what we can suffer apart from time. He looked for a few seconds as though death had indeed come and taken him out of the fell grip of intolerable pain, but presently he started up and cried,—

'The message! the message!'

Miss Nestle put it into his hand.

'Tell me what's in it. The worst is there,' she said, pointing to the 'Times.'

The message was from that powerful friend of Mr. Bassett's who had helped in the matter of Jack's commission, and who now held a high official position. It was in these words :—

'There is good hope that the statement is unfounded. The death of an artillery officer of same name is certain ; confusion considered likely. Depend on immediate inquiry and information.'

CHAPTER XXII.

THE DAME'S PARLOUR-SIDE—WINTER.

JACK BASSETT had entered upon his career full of high hope. His resolution was to deserve so well of his country and 'the Service,' that when the time should have come for him to make the avowal of his love, his father should find cause to regard it as that of a man with a right to have his judgment respected as well as his feelings indulged. He had entirely persuaded himself that the sole motive of his conceal-ment of the engagement between himself and Miss Wynn was consideration for the Squire; no misgiving or self-reproach on that score entered into the trouble with which he was soon assailed. His youth, his perfect health, his high spirits, the happiness of his successful love, combined to form a rich endowment for

s 2

the young soldier. Popularity in his corps and far outside it was soon added. No man in the British army went through the earlier phases of the campaign in the East with a lighter heart, or more entirely in the spirit of a vocation, than did Jack Bassett. He wrote to Mavis long letters which did credit to his intelligence, while they breathed the most . devoted love. These letters were despatched with as much regularity as the deplorable postal mismanagement would permit, up to a date beyond the period at which his apprehensions were aroused by the cessation of letters from Mavis.

While Jack was smarting under the dis-appointment of her silence—for two mails had been carried up to the camp in the haphazard fashion described by Mr. Bassett, but had brought nothing to Jack from Mavis—and at the time when he ought to have received her narrative of Farmer Wynn's resolution and its results, posted at Liverpool, he actually did

learn from his father the astounding facts that
the Wynns had sailed for Melbourne, and that
the Squire had taken up his abode at Fieldflower Farm. The effect of this news upon
Jack would have been bad enough, told as
Mavis told it in her letter—lost with hundreds of others in 'the Slough of Despond'
—but reaching him thus, with hardly a comment upon that portion which was of vital
importance to him, it was bewildering.

The Squire, considering chiefly how he
might best let Jack down to the knowledge
that the sacrifice demanded by his money
troubles was heavier than his son had at first
understood it to be, treated the matter with
intentional levity and brevity. Being unaware
that Jack had any special acquaintance with
Farmer Wynn and his family, he confined
himself to the bare mention of them, and,
indeed, discharged a thunderbolt at Mavis
Wynn's lover in this wise :—

'Wynn had been thinking, for some time

past, of joining a brother of his in Australia, and cleared out with his wife and daughter just in time for me. Reckitts is a very good sort of man, and the arrangement is in every respect a successful one. I don't think you will dislike the farm as a residence; I like it much. I believe you know the old rooms; they have been made very comfortable by Miss Nestle, who has taken the changes of all kinds better than I expected.'

The Squire then dwelt at length upon the good fortune that had befallen him with regard to the letting of Bassett, but he returned no more to the topic of the Wynns.

Mavis had not overrated the effect upon her lover of her enforced departure for Australia. It was greater than she had imagined by the measure of his more accurate knowledge of what such a voyage implied. His compassion for Mrs. Wynn was as profound as Mavis knew it would be.

It was with feelings almost of desperation

that he took in the full meaning of this event, and realised that there was only too surely no communication from Mavis. The distance that divided them, his powerlessness to interfere, the knowledge that this horrible thing was an accomplished fact, the sudden conviction that the concealment of his engagement to Mavis from his father had been a fatal mistake, disturbed and tore Jack's mind between them, driving him nearly wild. He lost sight of what the actual position of affairs had been, in the shock of this new development, bitterly reproached himself for the very thing that had appeared to be the best at the time, and declared angrily to himself that if he had but trusted the Squire's affection, confessed the truth, and commended Mavis to his care and kindness, this catastrophe would have been averted.

What had he done ? He had left her helpless, friendless, bound by his injunction of secrecy, and powerless to oppose her father's

will by convincing him that it would be to his
own interest to leave her in England—an argu-
ment to which he believed that Wynn would
have been amenable. Painful as Jack's state
of mind was while he awaited the long-delayed
communication from Mavis, being unable to
write to her because of his ignorance of the
date of Wynn's departure, or even his exact
destination—for the Squire had vaguely said
'Australia,'—it was much more pitiable as
time wore on, and no word from her reached
him.

How this happened has already been re-
lated. Mavis's letter, posted at Liverpool, had
been lost. The history of her flight, her stay
in London, her journey to Brittany, her first
days at the Château de la Dame Blanche, was
lying, all the time that he was longing for a
word from her, in a drawer of her writing-
table, made up into a parcel that also con-
tained his letters. This parcel was sealed with
Jack's own seal, and on the cover the following

words were written : 'I request that, if I die
in this house, this packet may be burned un-
opened.—M. W.'

A dead blank of hopeless silence, of almost
unbearable suspense, now befell Jack. . He
could not resist the conviction that Mavis had
already left England, and that he was doomed
to suffer that suspense for many months. Some
accident had occasioned the loss of her last
letters written before she left England. In
those days the voyage to Australia was a
lengthsome undertaking. In a kind of de-
spairing frenzy he counted off the months that
must elapse before he could hear from his
betrothed. That she was in any way to blame,
never entered his mind for a moment, nor did
it occur to Jack to inflict upon himself the
sentimental miseries of doubt and jealousy.
Of the love and fidelity of Mavis he was as
seriously certain as of his own love and fidelity
—that is to say, he accepted them just as he
accepted the fact that he existed. Their sepa-

ration had assumed a new and far more painful character; that was all. It was as much as Jack could bear, and the position was not destined to be alleviated by his father's response to his eager inquiry about the Wynns, and his request to be informed of the time of their departure and of their exact destination.

The Squire answered Jack's question about the date of Wynn's departure, and added that he believed the farmer's brother, Lewis Wynn, was settled in Melbourne, and that Wynn would land there. He went on to say that, so far as he knew, no one at Bassett had heard from Wynn from Liverpool, and no particulars of Mrs. Wynn's death, which must have been rather sudden, were known. Of this event the Squire wrote, evidently thinking that he had mentioned it in his former letter. The intelligence was a fresh shock to Jack. To picture Mavis, alone with her father in a strange land, was very grievous, although his notions of Wynn's treatment of his daughter were vague.

It was well for Jack that in the interval before this meagre reply to his inquiries reached him the active business of the campaign had set in, and he was brought face to face with experiences which took boyishness out of him for evermore.

In the later days of June the British army was in Bulgaria, and 'the country round Varna was one vast camp.' The story of July was that of sickness, monotony, expectation, and uncertainty ; bad surroundings amid which to suffer from heavy care. August was somewhat relieved by the decrease of sickness, and the preparations for the departure of the allied forces. The destination of the troops was kept secret. On the 14th of September Mr. Russell wrote, 'We are an army of occupation at last. The English and French armies have laid hold of a material guarantee in the shape of some score square miles of the soil of the Crimea, and they are preparing to extend the area of their rule in their progress towards Sebastopol.'

The war had begun in earnest. On the 19th the allies got their first sight of the enemy. It was on this occasion that, as Marshal St. Arnaud passed the 55th regiment, he exclaimed, ' English ! I hope you will fight well to-day !' and was answered from the ranks by an Irishman, 'Hope! Ah, sure, you know we will !' Of this first brush with the enemy, the writer who has come nearest to doing that which he declares to be impossible, *i.e.* describing war, wrote, 'It was admitted that as a military spectacle, the advance of our troops and the little affair of artillery, as well as the management of the cavalry, formed one of the most picturesque and beautiful that could be imagined. No pencil could do it justice, for the painter's skill fails to impart an idea of motion, and the painter has not yet been born who can describe with vividness and force, so as to bring the details before the reader, the events of even the slightest skirmish.'

This was the prelude to the battle of the

Alma, and the other great events of the first year of the Crimean war followed in quick succession.

The winter of that year, charged with misery to the allied forces at the scene of conflict, but more especially to the English army, was also particularly rigorous to us at home. Dark, dismal, and pitiless were the closing weeks of 1854 ; pitiless, dismal, and dark were the opening weeks of 1855. Even those who were so fortunate as to have none of their dear ones among the victims, read with equal sympathy and indignation of the sufferings of the troops, and the daily accumulating evidence of official incapacity, with its terrible result in the waste of life and treasure.

Those were dark days indeed—notwithstanding the victories of the Alma and of Inkermann—that preceded the Christmastide of 1854.

As a matter of fact we were always at war somewhere. English soldiers were always killing or being killed, suffering hardship and sickness.

withdrawn from the productive and industrial
pursuits of life, and costing a heavily burthened
country large sums of money at one point or
another of the world's surface.   But we did not
think about that.   The fighting was in Hindo-
stan or Afghanistan, in Burmah or in China,
and we could go on very comfortably, forgetting
all about it, and repeating on Sundays, with
quiet minds, the collects ordered to be used in
time of peace.   The struggle with ' the Colossus
of the North ' was, however, presented to the
imagination of the whole community with vividness and vitality, which the young people of
the present day could hardly realise ; while the
gloomy weather seemed to indicate that for once
nature was sympathetic with those unconsidered
trifles called human beings.

Fieldflower Farm did not form a complete
exception to the prevalent mood ; but it afforded
an illustration of that trite saying to which we
are so often forced to turn for consolation, that
few things are so bad but they might be worse

So strongly was this truth impressed upon Squire Bassett, that when the end of January—the terrible ' General January ' that was to fight Czar Nicholas's battles for him—came, he was ready to acknowledge what it brought to him as positively good, regarded by the lurid light of what might have been, and to accept it with thankfulness.

One of the first explorers of the wonderful Yellowstone region has told us how he crawled on hands and knees to the brink of the great cañon, and looked over into its depths; then crawled away—he never knew after how short or long a time—and lay prone, barely alive, dimly conscious of sublime grandeur and awfulness existing outside of his senses, and of something that was himself being too weak to cope with the idea or endure the sight of them. Something like that bodily experience we may suppose to be the mental experience of one who, having looked into the bottomless gulf of an irremediable grief, has been plucked away from

the brink of it, to recover calmness and strength
upon the flat common earth.

If we could attain to a true comprehension
of the feelings of one who has escaped an im-
measurable, irremediable calamity, so barely
that its terror and its agony have been revealed
with the completeness said to attend the vision
of the past that flashes upon a man drowning
or falling from a precipice, we should find that
joy is slow of coming to the rescued. The relief
is exhausting, and, like sleep after fierce physical pain, lethargic.

It was to a glimpse only of the gulf of grief
that the Squire had been condemned. The
supposition of the message proved to be correct,
and his suspense was not of long duration. Mr.
Bassett bore the ordeal with a manly patience
that tried Miss Nestle's nerves almost to break-
ing-down point, and took the relief when it
came with quiet gratitude. But he aged a good
deal in the time. The summer had passed since
then. News from the seat of war was looked

for in England with ever-growing anxiety and heart-sickness.

Jack Bassett had been in the battle of the Alma, among that ' foam of skirmishes ' that shows so brilliantly in Mr. Russell's vivid picture of ' one of the most bloody and determined struggles in the annals of war,' and he had escaped unhurt. He was also in the memorable battle of Inkermann, and on both occasions he behaved with distinguished gallantry, which was recognised by the chiefs. After the second battle Jack found himself promoted by the terrible ' death vacancies ' to the rank of captain. Through the thick of the fight he had come with only a few ' scratches,' as horrid hurts which make mothers and wives shudder at the thought of them are called in the military jargon abhorred of Mr. Dexter. He was not, however, to escape so easily.

Early in this story it was declared to be of the humble kind that does not deal with stricken fields and deeds of high emprise, but only with 'the non-combatants below.' There is, however, one episode of the great battle of Inkermann that has to find a place here, because it was fraught with grave consequences to Jack Bassett. This episode Mr. Russell relates as follows :—

'About ten o'clock a body of French infantry appeared on our right, a joyful sight to our struggling regiments. The Zouaves came on at the *pas de charge.* The French artillery had already begun to play with deadly effect on the right wing of the Russians. Three battalions of the Chasseurs d'Orléans rushed by, the light of battle on their faces. They were accompanied by a battalion of Chasseurs Indigènes—the Arab sepoys of Algiers. Their trumpets sounded above the din of battle, and when we watched their eager advance right on the flank of the enemy, we knew the day was won. Assailed in front by our men, broken in several places by the impetuosity of our charge, renewed again and again, attacked by the

French infantry on the right, and by artillery
all along the line, the Russians began to retire,
and at twelve o'clock they were driven pell-
mell down the hill towards the valley, where
pursuit would have been madness, as the roads
were all covered by their artillery. They left
mounds of dead behind them.'

Among the officers of the Chasseurs d'Orléans
who rushed by with the light of battle on their
faces, was one, light of tread, bright of visage,
bravest of the brave, a gallant young Frenchman, with whom John Bassett had formed a
close friendship. On the morning after the
battle the mounds of dead still lay upon the
battle-field, and the piercing wind swept over
the moaning ghastly heap. When the search-
parties were busy at their terrible task of seeking among the peaceful dead for mutilated
wretches whose wounds were stiffening in the
cold, Jack Bassett learned that René de Rastacq
was among the ' missing.'

The place of the Chasseurs d'Orléans in the battle was easy to find, and Jack went out with the search-party. He was heavy-hearted indeed, for the ambulances had been at work for hours, and the tale of the wounded was supposed to be nearly complete. Over the brow of a hill on the English right the French had rushed and fallen on the flank of the Russian column with which our troops were engaged. On that spot the English, French, and Russian dead lay together in the 'mounds,' and there, crushed by the weight of a dead Russian who had fallen across his legs, and with his face as close to the shattered skull of a Zouave as though both were resting on the same pillow, René de Rastacq was found. It was Jack who found him, pulled away the dead Russian, lifted his friend's bare head, its dark curls all stiffened and crusted with blood (not his own), from its terrible contact with the dead Zouave, and believed that he still lived. Jack moistened his cold cracked lips with brandy, placed him in a litter, and directed the bearers to start with their load.

The bearers had gone on a few steps in advance ; a moan of pain from the wounded man, produced by the inevitable jerking of the litter, had borne its testimony to the fact that there still was life in him. Jack, having lingered behind to glance over the surrounding scene in the hope of discerning a medical uniform, either French or English, was following, when a burst of smoke arose out of the valley from the head of the harbour, and a shell came whizzing overhead, exploding near the trench in which English soldiers were burying the Russian dead.

A splinter from the shell struck Jack in the right arm, and he fell. The bearers set down the litter on which René de Rastacq lay, and ran to him, shouting for aid. Some of the burial party hurried to the spot. The wounded officer's shattered arm was tied up, and a second litter was brought. Side by side the

two maimed men were carried off the fatal field
of Inkermann.

The Frenchman was the first to recover
from his wounds, notwithstanding the terrible
night upon the battle-field. In three weeks he
was on his feet, and not much the worse for
what had befallen him ; but when he made
inquiry for his English friend, he learned that
John Bassett had been less fortunate. He had
all but died of loss of blood, for the fragment
of shell that hit him had fearfully lacerated
the forearm, and the makeshift bandage had
but imperfectly checked the bleeding. The
surgeons looked grave when poor Jack came
under their hands, and they looked grave for
many a day after, while he wasted with fever,
raving and muttering in delirium, and when
that left him, lying weak as a child with the
terrible greyness in his pinched face, and the
terrible anxiety in his sunken eyes, that those
who have watched mortal, or well-nigh mortal,
sickness recognise with dread. A comparatively

slight but very painful wound in the neck added much to his sufferings, and not a little to his danger, for it kept up the fever, and the mail that left the Crimea on the 18th of November took a dubious report of his condition to England. It also carried a letter for Mr. Bassett from one of the generals, an old friend and schoolfellow of the Squire's, in which a warm eulogium was passed upon the young officer. This praise of his beloved son, so kindly meant, hardly affected the Squire at all when he read the simple soldierly phrases in which it was conveyed. He laid it by with a dim consciousness of what its value might be to him in a dark future near at hand, and once more disciplined himself for the endurance of suspense.

Many times during the ensuing weeks death drew very near to Jack, and for almost all that time he was too ill to be much affected by the surroundings that were so dreadful to the friends of the victims of the war, who read of

them at home in decency and comfort.   When
he was questioned afterwards about the miseries
of that experience, Jack never seemed clear
upon the point ; at all events he protested that
the best that was possible had been done for
everybody, and that lots of fellows were much
worse off than he.   When he ceased to be in
danger of death, it became evident that his
convalescence must be slow, and that a long
time must elapse before he would be fit for
service.   The siege was dragging its slow
length along ; the terrible weather, an impartial
enemy to all, was warring victoriously against
Russia and the allies alike ; things were at the
worst and gloomiest, when Jack Bassett was
sent home with a batch of invalids.   After a
voyage in which he suffered so severely that he
escaped with his life almost as narrowly as
after Inkermann, he reached England at the end
of January 1855.

   *   *   *   *

A wood fire was burning cheerfully upon

the open hearth in the Dame's Parlour, and the old room looked bright and comfortable. The prospect outside was dreary enough ; showers of rain and sleet swept across the fields, blurring the view of the leafless woods on the horizon, and swelling the current of the river, which was also indistinct in the drizzle.

In a great chair on one side of the hearth, with a table covered with papers at his side, and Trotty Veck at his feet, sat Jack Bassett. Opposite to him, and quietly observant of him, sat the Squire with a book in his hand. Three days had passed since Jack's arrival at Field-flower Farm, and his father was comparatively used to the change in his looks that had so shocked him. There was a greater change in Jack than that wrought by his grim experience, by the sight of terrible things, by physical hardship and suffering, or even by the immediate menace of death, not only on the battle-field, but during the slow weeks of pain and illness that had ensued upon his wounds. All

these things were written in the wasted frame,
the still useless arm, the darkened complexion
which yet showed pallor so plainly, the thinned
hair that had lost its crisp curliness, the lank
brown hands, the unsmiling gravity of the eyes,
formerly so merry, bright, and blue. Something more than all this ailed the Squire's
son, whom he no longer thought of as ' the
boy.'

The Squire had the strangest feelings about
Jack ; feelings which had their origin in his
own imaginative and reflective nature, and in
the seclusion and tranquility of his own life.
A curious shyness and silence came over him
when he looked at the young fellow to whom
a few months had brought actual experience
of the things which he himself had only read
and thought about ; an experience that had
altered him almost out of recognition. The
man of books felt himself weak, ignorant, nowhere, in comparison with the man of action ;
and although his sympathies were, in the ab-

stract, as far removed from Jack's profession as
ever, he was full of pride in his gallant son.

To this sentiment Miss Nestle had administered an early corrective, in her characteristic
way. Nothing could exceed her satisfaction
on learning that Jack was coming home, except
the consternation with which his altered looks
struck her when he arrived.

'Not fit for service for a long time,' she
repeated, after the Squire informed her of the
medical verdict upon Jack; 'that's a good
hearing, sir, indeed. And I hope the war will
be over, and that all the poor creatures who are
to be killed, what for nobody knows, will be
out of their misery long before Mr. Jack is able
to go back and help to kill them. He's a deal
better at home: and now he has seen what it's
like for himself, I'm sure he'll be sensible. It's
just like his watch. When he was little—don't
you remember, sir?—he was never done poking
and scraping at the works, to see how it was
put together, until at last the inside came right

out of it. Then he was satisfied, and you had
it mended for him. You couldn't have kept
him at home, sir; but he's had his fling, and
enough of it too, bless his heart! with his
poor thin face, and his clothes just hanging
on him.'

From this attitude Miss Nestle was not to
be moved. She applied herself to the care of
the invalid with skill and assiduity all her own;
but there was no hero-worship about her.
She regarded Jack as having been engaged in
the inevitable process of sowing his wild oats,
and paying for it pretty dearly; that was all.

The weather had been comparatively fine in
the morning, and Jack had walked down to the
village and back. This was quite enough to
fatigue him, and it might have been only the
exertion that made him look so worn and
anxious as he turned over his papers; but his
father felt vaguely apprehensive that there was
some trouble untold. He recalled the circumstances that had occurred a year before, and he

wondered whether Jack, in spite of his warning, had kept back any debt that he ought to have avowed then, and was worried about it now. It was a proof of the curious change in Jack, and of his father's acute perception of it, that the Squire felt as shy of approaching the probable difficulty as if Jack had been a man of his own age.

The matter in Jack's thoughts was far different. The time had come when there was to be no longer a secret between himself and his father. He had only put off speaking to the Squire until to-day, because there had remained one inquiry for him to make before he could place the whole story with every detail before the Squire. That inquiry he had made at the post-office at Bassett.

Mr. Williams would hardly have made a difficulty about answering a question put by the Squire's son, but Jack removed all scruples from the postmaster's mind by stating when he asked whether certain letters addressed to Miss

Wynn, post-office, Bassett, and posted in London, were still in his charge, that he, the questioner, was the writer of those letters. Mr. Williams betrayed no surprise, but perfect readiness to give the required information. In pursuance of Miss Wynn's instructions, all letters for her had been forwarded to 108 Cecil Street, Liverpool. Mr. Williams produced the book in which he had recorded this address, and added that the last letter which had arrived for Miss Wynn had been forwarded several months previously, but, he believed, after Farmer Wynn had sailed for Australia.

As he left the general shop, and turned homewards, leaning heavily on his stick, and walking with a slow and heavy tread, which Mavis would not have recognised for his, a lady passed him on the narrow footway, and looked at him with undisguised interest. Jack was too much absorbed in his own thoughts to notice her His resolution was taken; he knew what he had to do.

'Father,' said Jack, after a considerable interval of silence, and pushing away his papers, 'I have something to tell you. Can you give me your attention now?'

There was a sudden brightening all over the Squire's face, as, laying down his book and rolling his chair nearer to his son's, he answered with eagerness, 'I thought you had something to tell me, Jack. What is it?'

END OF THE SECOND VOLUME.

LONDON : PRINTED BY
SPOTTISWOODE AND CO.. NEW-STREET SQUARE
AND PARLIAMENT STREET

CHATTO & WINDUS'S
LIST OF BOOKS.

* * * * * * * * * * * * *

About.—The Fellah: An Egyp-
tian Novel. By EDMOND ABOUT.
Translated by Sir RANDAL ROBERTS.
Post 8vo, illustrated boards, 2s.; cloth
limp, 2s. 6d.

Adams (W. Davenport), Works
by:

A Dictionary of the Drama. Being
a comprehensive Guide to the Plays,
Playwrights, Players, and Playhouses of the United Kingdom and
America, from the Earliest to the
Present Times. Crown 8vo, half-
bound, 12s. 6d.   [*Preparing.*

Latter-Day Lyrics. Edited by W.
DAVENPORT ADAMS. Post 8vo, cloth
limp, 2s. 6d.

Quips and Quiddities. Selected by
W. DAVENPORT ADAMS. Post 8vo,
cloth limp, 2s. 6d.

Advertising, A History of, from
the Earliest Times. Illustrated by
Anecdotes, Curious Specimens, and
Notices of Successful Advertisers. By
HENRY SAMPSON. Crown 8vo, with
Coloured Frontispiece and Illustra-
tions, cloth gilt, 7s. 6d.

gony Column (The) of "The
Times," from 1800 to 1870. Edited,
with an Introduction, by ALICE CLAY.
Post 8vo, cloth limp, 2s. 6d.

Aide (Hamilton), Works by:

Carr of Carrlyon. Post 8vo, illustrated boards, 2s.

Confidences. Post 8vo, illustrated
boards, 2s.

Alexander (Mrs.).—Maid, Wife,
or Widow? A Romance. By Mrs.
ALEXANDER. Post 8vo, illustrated
boards, 2s.; cr. 8vo, cloth extra, 3s. 6d.

Allen (Grant), Works by:
Crown 8vo, cloth extra, 6s. each,

The Evolutionist at Large. Second
Edition, revised.

Vignettes from Nature.

Colin Clout's Calendar.

Nightmares: A Collection of Stories.

Architectural Styles, A Hand-
book of. Translated from the German
of A. ROSENGARTEN, by W. COLLETT-
SANDARS. Crown 8vo, cloth extra, with
639 Illustrations, 7s. 6d.

Art (The) of Amusing: A Col-
lection of Graceful Arts, Games, Tricks,
Puzzles, and Charades. By FRANK
BELLEW. With 300 Illustrations. Cr.
8vo, cloth extra, 4s. 6d.

Artemus Ward:

Artemus Ward's Works: The Works
of CHARLES FARRER BROWNE, better
known as ARTEMUS WARD. With
Portrait and Facsimile. Crown 8vo,
cloth extra, 7s. 6d.

Artemus Ward's Lecture on the
Mormons. With 32 Illustrations.
Edited, with Preface, by EDWARD P.
HINGSTON. Crown 8vo, 6d.

The Genial Showman: Life and Adventures of Artemus Ward. By
EDWARD P. HINGSTON. With a
Frontispiece. Crown 8vo, cloth extra,
3s. 6d.

Ashton (John), Works by:
A History of the Chap-Books of the
Eighteenth Century. With nearly
400 Illusts., engraved in facsimile of
the originals. Cr. 8vo, cl. ex., 7s. 6d.
Social Life in the Reign of Queen
Anne. From Original Sources. With
nearly 100 Illusts. Cr.8vo,cl.ex.,7s.6d.
Humour, Wit, and Satire of the
Seventeenth Century. With nearly
100 Illusts. Cr. 8vo, cl. extra, 7s. 6d.
English Caricature and Satire on
Napoleon the First. 120 Illusts. from
Originals. Two Vols., demy 8vo, 28s.

Bacteria.—A Synopsis of the
Bacteria and Yeast Fungi and Allied
Species. By W. B. GROVE, B.A. With
87 Illusts. Crown 8vo, cl. extra, 3s. 6d.

Balzac's " Comedie Humaine "
and its Author. With Translations by
H. H. WALKER. Post 8vo, cl. limp.2s. 6d.

Bankers, A Handbook of London; together with Lists of Bankers
from 1677. By F. G. HILTON PRICE.
Crown 8vo, cloth extra, 7s. 6d.

Bardsley (Rev. C.W.),Works by:
English Surnames: Their Sources and
Significations. Third Ed., revised,
Cr. 8vo, cl. extra, 7s. 6d. [Preparing,
Curiosities of Puritan Nomencla-
ture. Crown 8vo, cloth extra, 7s. 6d.

Bartholomew Fair, Memoirs
of. By HENRY MORLEY. With 100
Illusts. Crown 8vo. cloth extra, 7s. 6d.

Basil, Novels by:
A Drawn Game. Three Vols., cr. 8vo.
The Wearing of the Green. Three
Vols., crown 8vo.   [Shortly.

Beaconsfield, Lord: A Biography. By T. P. O'CONNOR, M.P. Sixth
Edit., New Preface. Cr.8vo,cl.ex.7s.6d.

Beauchamp. — Grantley
Grange: A Novel. By SHELSLEY
BEAUCHAMP. Post 8vo, illust. bds., 2s.

Beautiful Pictures by British
Artists: A Gathering of Favourites
from our Picture Galleries. In Two
Series. All engraved on Steel in the
highest style of Art. Edited, with
Notices of the Artists, by SYDNEY
ARMYTAGE, M.A. Imperial 4to, cloth
extra, gilt and gilt edges, 21s. per Vol.

Bechstein. — As Pretty as
Seven, and other German Stories.
Collected by LUDWIG BECHSTEIN.
With Additional Tales by the Brothers
GRIMM, and 100 Illusts. by RICHTER.
Small 4to, green and gold, 6s. 6d. ;
gilt edges, 7s. 6d.

Beerbohm. — Wanderings in
Patagonia; or, Life among the Ostrich
Hunters. By JULIUS BEERBOHM. With
Illusts. Crown 8vo, cloth extra, 3s. 6d.

Belgravia for 1885.   One
Shilling Monthly. A Strange Voyage,
by W. CLARK RUSSELL, will be begun
in the JANUARY Number and continued
throughout the year. This Number
will contain also the Opening Chapters
of a New Story by CECIL POWER, Author of " Philistia," entitled Babylon,
and Illustrated by P. MACNAB.
. Now ready, the Volume for JULY to
OCTOBER 1884, cloth extra, gilt edges,
7s. 6d.; Cases for binding Vols., 2s. each.

Belgravia Annual. With Stories
by F. W. ROBINSON, J. ARBUTHNOT
WILSON, JUSTIN H. McCARTHY, B.
MONTGOMERIE RANKING, and others.
Demy 8vo, with Illusts., 1s. [Preparing.

Bennett (W.C.,LL.D.),Works by:
A Ballad History of England. Post
8vo, cloth limp, 2s.
Songs for Sailors. Post 8vo, cloth
limp, 2s.

Besant (Walter) and James
Rice, Novels by. Post 8vo, illust.
boards, 2s. each; cloth limp, 2s. 6d.
each; or crown 8vo, cloth extra,
3s. 6d. each.
Ready-Money Mortiboy.
With Harp and Crown.
This Son of Vulcan.
My L'ttle Girl.
The Case of Mr. Lucraft.
The Golden Butterfly.
By Celia's Arbour.
The Monks of Thelema.
'Twas in Trafalgar's Bay.
The Seamy Side.
The Ten Years' Tenant.
The Chaplain of the Fleet.

Besant (Walter), Novels by:
All Sorts and Conditions of Men:
An Impossible Story. With Illustra-
tions by FRED. BARNARD. Crown
8vo, cloth extra, 3s. 6d ; post 8vo,
illust. boards, 2s ; cloth limp, 2s. 6d.
The Capta'ns' Room, &c. With
Frontispiece by E. J. WHEELER.
Crown 8vo, cloth extra, 3s. 6d ; post
8vo, illust. bds., 2s ; cl. limp, 2s. 6d.
All in a Garden Fair. With 6 Illusts.
by H. FURNISS New and Cheaper
Edition. Cr. 8vo. cl. extra, 3s. 6d.
_ Dorothy Forster. New and Cheaper
Edition. With Illustrations by CH.
GREEN. Crown 8vo, cloth extra,
3s. 6d.   [Preparing.

The Art of Fiction. Demy 8vo, 1s.

Betham-Edwards (M.), Novels by. Crown 8vo, cloth extra, 3s. 6d. each.; post 8vo, illust. bds., 2s. each.
Felicia. | Kitty.

Bewick (Thos.) and his Pupils. By AUSTIN DOBSON. With 95 Illustrations. Square 8vo, cloth extra, 10s. 6d.

Birthday Books:—
The Starry Heavens: A Poetical Birthday Book. Square 8vo, handsomely bound in cloth, 2s. 6d.

Birthday Flowers: Their Language and Legends. By W. J. GORDON. Beautifully Illustrated in Colours by VIOLA BOUGHTON. In illuminated cover, crown 4to, 6s.

The Lowell Birthday Book. With Illusts., small 8vo, cloth extra, 4s. 6d.

Blackburn's (Henry) Art Handbooks. Demy 8vo, Illustrated, uniform in size for binding.

Academy Notes, separate years, from 1875 to 1883, each 1s.

Academy Notes, 1884. With 152 Illustrations. 1s.

Academy Notes, 1875-79. Complete in One Vol.,with nearly 600 Illusts. in Facsimile. Demy 8vo, cloth limp, 6s.

Academy Notes, 1880-84. Complete in One Volume, with about 700 Facsimile Illustrations. Cloth limp, 6s.

Grosvenor Notes, 1877. 6d.

Grosvenor Notes, separate years, from 1878 to 1883, each 1s.

Grosvenor Notes, 1884. With 78 Illustrations 1s.

Grosvenor Notes, 1877-82. With upwards of 300 Illustrations. Demy 8vo, cloth limp, 6s.

Pictures at South Kensington. With 70 Illustrations. 1s.

The English Pictures at the National Gallery. 114 Illustrations. 1s.

The Old Masters at the National Gallery. 128 Illustrations. 1s. 6d.

A Complete Illustrated Catalogue to the National Gallery. With Notes by H. BLACKBURN, and 242 Illusts. Demy 8vo, cloth limp, 3s.

Illustrated Catalogue of the Luxembourg Gallery. Containing about 250 Reproductions after the Original Drawings of the Artists. Edited by F. G. DUMAS. Demy 8vo, 3s. 6d.

The Paris Salon, 1884. With over 300 Illusts. Edited by F. G. DUMAS. Demy 8vo, 3s.

ART HANDBOOKS, *continued*—
The Art Annual, 1883-4. Edited by F. G. DUMAS. With 300 full-page Illustrations. Demy 8vo, 5s.

Boccaccio's Decameron; or, Ten Days' Entertainment. Translated into English, with an Introduction by THOMAS WRIGHT, F.S.A. With Portrait, and STOTHARD's beautiful Copperplates. Cr. 8vo, cloth extra, gilt, 7s. 6d.

Blake (William): Etchings from his Works. By W. B. SCOTT. With descriptive Text. Folio, half-bound boards, India Proofs, 21s.

Bowers'(G.) Hunting Sketches:
Canters in Crampshire. Oblong 4to, half-bound boards, 21s.

Leaves from a Hunting Journal. Coloured in facsimile of the originals. Oblong 4to, half-bound, 21s.

Boyle (Frederick), Works by:
Camp Notes: Stories of Sport and Adventure in Asia, Africa, and America. Crown 8vo, cloth extra, 3s. 6d.; post 8vo, illustrated bds., 2s.

Savage Life Crown 8vo, cloth extra, 3s. 6d.; post 8vo, illustrated bds., 2s.

Brand's Observations on Popular Antiquities, chiefly Illustrating the Origin of our Vulgar Customs, Ceremonies, and Superstitions. With the Additions of Sir HENRY ELLIS. Crown 8vo, cloth extra, gilt, with numerous Illustrations, 7s. 6d.

Bret Harte, Works by:
Bret Harte's Collected Works. Arranged and Revised by the Author. Complete in Five Vols., crown 8vo, cloth extra, 6s. each.
Vol. I. COMPLETE POETICAL AND DRAMATIC WORKS. With Steel Portrait, and Introduction by Author.
Vol. II. EARLIER PAPERS — LUCK OF ROARING CAMP, and other Sketches —BOHEMIAN PAPERS — SPANISH AND AMERICAN LEGENDS.
Vol. III. TALES OF THE ARGONAUTS —EASTERN SKETCHES.
Vol. IV. GABRIEL CONROY.
Vol. V. STORIES — CONDENSED NOVELS, &c.

The Select Works of Bret Harte, in Prose and Poetry. With Introductory Essay by J. M. BELLEW, Portrait of the Author, and 50 Illustrations. Crown 8vo, cloth extra, 7s. 6d.

Gabriel Conroy: A Novel. Post 8vo, illustrated boards, 2s.

BRET HARTE'S WORKS, *continued—*

An Heiress of Red Dog, and other Stories. Post 8vo, illustrated boards, 2s.; cloth limp, 2s. 6d.

The Twins of Table Mountain. Fcap. 8vo, picture cover, 1s.; crown 8vo, cloth extra, 3s. 6d.

Luck of Roaring Camp, and other Sketches. Post 8vo, illust. bds., 2s.

Jeff Briggs's Love Story. Fcap. 8vo, picture cover, 1s.; cloth extra, 2s. 6d.

Flip. Post 8vo, illustrated boards, 2s.; cloth limp, 2s. 6d.

Californian Stories (including THE TWINS OF TABLE MOUNTAIN, JEFF BRIGGS'S LOVE STORY, &c.) Post 8vo, illustrated boards, 2s.

Brewer (Rev. Dr.), Works by :

The Reader's Handbook of Allusions, References, Plots, and Stories. Fourth Edition, revised throughout, with a New Appendix, containing a COMPLETE ENGLISH BIBLIOGRAPHY. Cr. 8vo, 1,400 pp., cloth extra, 7s. 6d.

Authors and their Works, with the Dates: Being the Appendices to "The Reader's Handbook," separately printed. Cr. 8vo, cloth limp, 2s.

A Dictionary of Miracles: Imitative, Realistic, and Dogmatic. Crown 8vo, cloth extra, 7s. 6d.; half-bound, 9s.

Brewster (Sir David), Works by:

More Worlds than One: The Creed of the Philosopher and the Hope of the Christian. With Plates. Post 8vo, cloth extra, 4s. 6d.

The Martyrs of Science: Lives of GALILEO, TYCHO BRAHE, and KEPLER. With Portraits. Post 8vo, cloth extra, 4s. 6d.

Letters on Natural Magic. A New Edition, with numerous Illustrations, and Chapters on the Being and Faculties of Man, and Additional Phenomena of Natural Magic, by J. A. SMITH. Post 8vo, cloth extra, 4s. 6d.

Brillat-Savarin.—Gastronomy
as a Fine Art. By BRILLAT-SAVARIN. Translated by R. E. ANDERSON, M.A. Post 8vo, cloth limp, 2s. 6d.

Burnett (Mrs.), Novels by :

Surly Tim, and other Stories. Post 8vo, illustrated boards, 2s.

Kathleen Mavourneen. Fcap. 8vo, picture cover, 1s.

Lindsay's Luck. Fcap. 8vo, picture cover, 1s.

Pretty Polly Pemberton. Fcap. 8vo, picture cover, 1s.

Buchanan's (Robert) Works :

Ballads of Life, Love, and Humour. With a Frontispiece by ARTHUR HUGHES. Crown 8vo, cloth extra, 6s.

Selected Poems of Robert Buchanan. With Frontispiece by T. DALZIEL. Crown 8vo, cloth extra, 6s.

Undertones. Cr. 8vo, cloth extra, 6s.

London Poems. Cr. 8vo, cl. extra, 6s.

The Book of Orm. Crown 8vo, cloth extra, 6s.

White Rose and Red: A Love Story. Crown 8vo, cloth extra, 6s.

Idylls and Legends of Inverburn. Crown 8vo, cloth extra, 6s.

St. Abe and his Seven Wives: A Tale of Salt Lake City. With a Frontispiece by A. B. HOUGHTON. Crown 8vo, cloth extra, 5s.

Robert Buchanan's Complete Poetical Works. With Steel-plate Portrait. Crown 8vo, cloth extra, 7s. 6d.   [*In the press.*

The Hebrid Isles: Wanderings in the Land of Lorne and the Outer Hebrides. With Frontispiece by W. SMALL. Crown 8vo, cloth extra, 6s.

A Poet's Sketch-Book: Selections from the Prose Writings of ROBERT BUCHANAN. Crown 8vo, cl. extra, 6s.

The Shadow of the Sword: A Romance. Crown 8vo, cloth extra, 3s. 6d.; post 8vo, illust. boards, 2s.

A Child of Nature: A Romance. With a Frontispiece. Crown 8vo, cloth extra, 3s. 6d.; post 8vo, illust. bds., 2s.

God and the Man: A Romance. With Illustrations by FRED. BARNARD. Crown 8vo, cloth extra, 3s. 6d.; post 8vo, illustrated boards, 2s.

The Martyrdom of Madeline: A Romance. With Frontispiece by A.W. COOPER. Cr. 8vo, cloth extra, 3s. 6d.; post 8vo, illustrated boards, 2s.

Love Me for Ever. With a Frontispiece by P. MACNAB. Crown 8vo, cloth extra, 3s. 6d.; post 8vo, illustrated boards, 2s.

Annan Water: A Romance. Crown 8vo, cloth extra, 3s. 6d.

The New Abelard: A Romance. Crown 8vo, cloth extra, 3s. 6d.

Foxglove Manor: A Novel. Three Vols., crown 8vo.

Burton (Robert) :

The Anatomy of Melancholy. A New Edition, complete, corrected and enriched by Translations of the Classical Extracts. Demy 8vo, cloth extra, 7s. 6d.

Melancholy Anatomised: Being an Abridgment, for popular use, of BURTON'S ANATOMY OF MELANCHOLY. Post 8vo, cloth limp, 2s. 6d.

Burton (Captain), Works by:

To the Gold Coast for Gold: A Personal Narrative. By RICHARD F. BURTON and VERNEY LOVETT CAMERON. With Maps and Frontispiece. Two Vols., crown 8vo, cloth extra, 21s.

The Book of the Sword: Being a History of the Sword and its Use in all Countries, from the Earliest Times. By RICHARD F. BURTON. With over 400 Illustrations. Square 8vo, cloth extra, 32s.

Bunyan's Pilgrim's Progress.

Edited by Rev. T. SCOTT. With 17 Steel Plates by STOTHARD, engraved by GOODALL, and numerous Woodcuts. Crown 8vo, cloth extra, gilt, 7s. 6d.

Byron (Lord):

Byron's Letters and Journals. With Notices of his Life. By THOMAS MOORE. A Reprint of the Original Edition, newly revised, with Twelve full-page Plates. Crown 8vo, cloth extra, gilt, 7s. 6d.

Byron's Don Juan. Complete in One Vol., post 8vo, cloth limp, 2s.

Cameron (Commander) and

Captain Burton.—To the Gold Coast for Gold: A Personal Narrative. By RICHARD F. BURTON and VERNEY LOVETT CAMERON. With Frontispiece and Maps. Two Vols., crown 8vo, cloth extra, 21s.

Cameron (Mrs. H. Lovett),

Novels by:

Crown 8vo, cloth extra, 3s. 6d. each; post 8vo, illustrated boards, 2s. each.

Juliet's Guardian.

Deceivers Ever.

Campbell.—White and Black:

Travels in the United States. By Sir GEORGE CAMPBELL, M.P. Demy 8vo, cloth extra, 14s.

Carlyle (Thomas):

Thomas Carlyle: Letters and Recollections. By MONCURE D. CONWAY, M.A. Crown 8vo, cloth extra, with Illustrations, 6s.

On the Choice of Books. By THOMAS CARLYLE. With a Life of the Author by R. H. SHEPHERD. New and Revised Edition, post 8vo, cloth extra, Illustrated, 1s. 6d.

The Correspondence of Thomas Carlyle and Ralph Waldo Emerson, 1834 to 1872. Edited by CHARLES ELIOT NORTON. With Portraits. Two Vols., crown 8vo, cloth extra, 24s.

Chapman's (George) Works:

Vol. I. contains the Plays complete, including the doubtful ones. Vol. II., the Poems and Minor Translations, with an Introductory Essay by ALGERNON CHARLES SWINBURNE. Vol. III., the Translations of the Iliad and Odyssey. Three Vols., crown 8vo, cloth extra, 18s.; or separately, 6s. each.

Chatto & Jackson.—A Treatise

on Wood Engraving, Historical and Practical. By WM. ANDREW CHATTO and JOHN JACKSON. With an Additional Chapter by HENRY G. BOHN; and 450 fine Illustrations. A Reprint of the last Revised Edition. Large 4to, half-bound, 28s.

Chaucer:

Chaucer for Children: A Golden Key. By Mrs. H. R. HAWEIS. With Eight Coloured Pictures and numerous Woodcuts by the Author. New Ed., small 4to, cloth extra, 6s.

Chaucer for Schools. By Mrs. H. R. HAWEIS. Demy 8vo, cloth limp, 2s 6d.

City (The) of Dream: A Poem.

Fcap. 8vo, cloth extra, 6s. [In the press.

Cobban.—The Cure of Souls:

A Story. By J. MACLAREN COBBAN. Post 8vo, illustrated boards, 2s.

Collins (C. Allston).—The Bar

Sinister: A Story. By C. ALLSTON COLLINS. Post 8vo, illustrated bds.,2s.

Collins (Mortimer & Frances),

Novels by:

Sweet and Twenty. Post 8vo, illustrated boards, 2s.

Frances. Post 8vo, illust. bds., 2s.

Blacksmith and Scholar. Post 8vo, illustrated boards, 2s.; crown 8vo, cloth extra, 3s. 6d.

The Village Comedy. Post 8vo, illust. boards, 2s.; cr. 8vo, cloth extra, 3s. 6d.

You Play Me False. Post 8vo, illust. boards, 2s.; cr. 8vo, cloth extra, 3s. 6d.

Collins (Mortimer), Novels by:

Sweet Anne Page. Post 8vo, illustrated boards, 2s.; crown 8vo, cloth extra, 3s. 6d.

Transmigration. Post 8vo, illustrated boards, 2s.; crown 8vo, cloth extra, 3s. 6d.

From Midnight to Midnight. Post 8vo, illustrated boards, 2s.; crown 8vo, cloth extra, 3s. 6d.

A Fight with Fortune. Post 8vo illustrated boards 2s.

Collins (Wilkie), Novels by.

Each post 8vo, illustrated boards, 2s; cloth limp, 2s. 6d.; or crown 8vo, cloth extra, Illustrated, 3s. 6d.

Antonina. Illust. by A. CONCANEN.

Basil. Illustrated by Sir JOHN GILBERT and J. MAHONEY.

Hide and Seek. Illustrated by Sir JOHN GILBERT and J. MAHONEY.

The Dead Secret. Illustrated by Sir JOHN GILBERT and A. CONCANEN.

Queen of Hearts Illustrated by Sir JOHN GILBERT and A. CONCANEN.

My Miscellanies. With Illustrations by A. CONCANEN, and a Steel-plate Portrait of WILKIE COLLINS.

The Woman In White. With Illustrations by Sir JOHN GILBERT and F. A. FRASER.

The Moonstone. With Illustrations by G. DU MAURIER and F. A. FRASER.

Man and Wife. Illust. by W. SMALL.

Poor Miss Finch. Illustrated by G. DU MAURIER and EDWARD HUGHES.

Miss or Mrs.? With Illustrations by S. L. FILDES and HENRY WOODS.

The New Magdalen. Illustrated by G. DU MAURIER and C. S. RANDS.

The Frozen Deep. Illustrated by G. DU MAURIER and J. MAHONEY.

The Law and the Lady. Illustrated by S. L. FILDES and SYDNEY HALL.

The Two Destinies.

The Haunted Hotel. Illustrated by ARTHUR HOPKINS.

The Fallen Leaves.

Jezebel's Daughter.

The Black Robe.

Heart and Science: A Story of the Present Time. Crown 8vo, cloth extra, 3s. 6d.

"I Say No." Three Vols., crown 8vo. 31s 6d. [Shortly.

Colman's Humorous Works:

"Broad Grins," "My Nightgown and Slippers," and other Humorous Works, Prose and Poetical, of GEORGE COLMAN. With Life by G. B BUCKSTONE, and Frontispiece by HOGARTH. Crown 8vo, cloth extra, gilt, 7s. 6d.

Convalescent Cookery: A

Family Handbook. By CATHERINE RYAN. Post 8vo, 1s.; cl. limp, 1s. 6d.

Conway (Moncure D.), Works by:

Demonology and Devil-Lore. Two Vols., royal 8vo, with 65 Illusts., 28s.

CONWAY'S (M. D.) WORKS, continued—

A Necklace of Stories. Illustrated by W. J. HENNESSY. Square 8vo, cloth extra, 6s.

The Wandering Jew. Crown 8vo, cloth extra, 6s.

Thomas Carlyle: Letters and Recollections. With Illustrations. Crown 8vo, cloth extra, 6s.

Cook (Dutton), Works by:

Hours with the Players. With a Steel Plate Frontispiece. New and Cheaper Edit., cr. 8vo, cloth extra,6s.

Nights at the Play: A View of the English Stage. New and Cheaper Edition. Crown 8vo, cloth extra, 6s.

Leo: A Novel. Post 8vo, illustrated boards, 2s.

Paul Foster's Daughter. Post 8vo, illustrated boards, 2s.; crown 8vo, cloth extra, 3s. 6d.

Cooper.—Heart Salvage, by

Sea and Land. Stories by Mrs. COOPER (KATHARINE SAUNDERS). Three Vols., crown 8vo.

Copyright. — A Handbook of

English and Foreign Copyright in Literary and Dramatic Works. By SIDNEY JERROLD, of the Middle Temple, Esq., Barrister-at-Law. Post 8vo, cloth limp, 2s. 6d.

Cornwall.—Popular Romances

of the West of England; or, The Drolls, Traditions, and Superstitions of Old Cornwall. Collected and Edited by ROBERT HUNT, F.R.S. New and Revised Edition, with Additions, and Two Steel-plate Illustrations by GEORGE CRUIKSHANK. Crown 8vo, cloth extra, 7s. 6d.

Creasy.—Memoirs of Eminent

Etonians: with Notices of the Early History of Eton College. By Sir EDWARD CREASY, Author of "The Fifteen Decisive Battles of the World." Crown 8vo, cloth extra, gilt, with 13 Portraits, 7s. 6d.

Cruikshank (George):

The Comic Almanack. Complete in Two SERIES: The FIRST from 1835 to 1843; the SECOND from 1844 to 1853. A Gathering of the BEST HUMOUR of THACKERAY, HOOD, MAYHEW, ALBERT SMITH, A'BECKETT, ROBERT BROUGH, &c. With 2,000 Woodcuts and Steel Engravings by CRUIKSHANK, HINE, LANDELLS, &c. Crown 8vo, cloth gilt, two very thick volumes, 7s. 6d. each.

CRUIKSHANK (G.), *continued—*
The Life of George Cruikshank. By BLANCHARD JERROLD, Author of "The Life of Napoleon III.," &c. With 84 Illustrations. New and Cheaper Edition, enlarged, with Additional Plates, and a very carefully compiled Bibliography. Crown 8vo, cloth extra, 7s. 6d.

Robinson Crusoe. A beautiful reproduction of Major's Edition, with 37 Woodcuts and Two Steel Plates by GEORGE CRUIKSHANK, choicely printed. Crown 8vo, cloth extra, 7s. 6d. A few Large-Paper copies, printed on hand-made paper, with India proofs of the Illustrations, 36s.

Cussans.—Handbook of Heraldry; with Instructions for Tracing Pedigrees and Deciphering Ancient MSS., &c. By JOHN E. CUSSANS. Entirely New and Revised Edition, illustrated with over 400 Woodcuts and Coloured Plates. Crown 8vo, cloth extra, 7s. 6d.

Cyples.—Hearts of Gold: A Novel. By WILLIAM CYPLES. Crown 8vo, cloth extra, 3s. 6d.

Daniel. — Merrie England In the Olden Time. By GEORGE DANIEL. With Illustrations by ROBT. CRUIKSHANK. Crown 8vo, cloth extra, 3s. 6d.

Daudet.—Port Salvation; or, The Evangelist. By ALPHONSE DAUDET. Translated by C. HARRY MELTZER. With Portrait of the Author. Crown 8vo, cloth extra, 3s. 6d.

Davenant. — What shall my Son be? Hints for Parents on the Choice of a Profession or Trade for their Sons. By FRANCIS DAVENANT, M.A. Post 8vo, cloth limp, 2s. 6d.

Davies (Dr. N. E.), Works by:
One Thousand Medical Maxims. Crown 8vo, 1s.; cloth, 1s. 6d.
Nursery Hints: A Mother's Guide. Crown 8vo, 1s.; cloth, 1s. 6d.
Aids to Long Life. Crown 8vo, 2s.; cloth limp, 2s. 6d. [*Shortly.*

Davies' (Sir John) Complete Poetical Works, including Psalms I. to L. in Verse, and other hitherto Unpublished MSS., for the first time Collected and Edited, with Memorial-Introduction and Notes, by the Rev. A. B. GROSART, D.D. Two Vols., crown 8vo, cloth boards, 12s.

De Maistre.—A Journey Round My Room. By XAVIER DE MAISTRE. Translated by HENRY ATTWELL. Post 8vo, cloth limp, 2s. 6d.

De Mille.—A Castle in Spain. A Novel. By JAMES DE MILLE. With a Frontispiece. Crown 8vo, cloth extra, 3s. 6d.

Derwent (Leith), Novels by:
Our Lady of Tears. Cr. 8vo, cloth extra, 3s. 6d.; post 8vo, illust. bds., 2s.
Circe's Lovers. Crown 8vo, cloth extra, 3s. 6d.

Dickens (Charles), Novels by:
Post 8vo, illustrated boards, 2s. each.
Sketches by Boz. | Nicholas Nickleby
Pickwick Papers. | Oliver Twist.

The Speeches of Charles Dickens. (*Mayfair Library.*) Post 8vo, cloth imp, 2s. 6d.

The Speeches of Charles Dickens, 1841-1870. With a New Bibliography, revised and enlarged. Edited and Prefaced by RICHARD HERNE SHEPHERD. Crown 8vo, cloth extra, 6s.

About England with Dickens. By ALFRED RIMMER. With 57 Illustrations by C. A. VANDERHOOF, ALFRED RIMMER, and others. Sq. 8vo, cloth extra, 10s. 6d.

Dictionaries:
A Dictionary of Miracles: Imitative, Realistic, and Dogmatic. By the Rev. E. C. BREWER, LL.D. Crown 8vo, cloth extra, 7s. 6d.; bf.-bound, 9s.

The Reader's Handbook of Allusions, References, Plots, and Stories. By the Rev. E. C. BREWER, LL.D. Fourth Edition, revised throughout, with a New Appendix, containing a Complete English Bibliography. Crown 8vo, 1,400 pages, cloth extra, 7s. 6d.

Authors and their Works, with the Dates. Being the Appendices to "The Reader's Handbook," separately printed. By the Rev. E. C. BREWER, LL.D. Crown 8vo, cloth limp, 2s.

Familiar Allusions: A Handbook of Miscellaneous Information; including the Names of Celebrated Statues, Paintings, Palaces, Country Seats, Ruins, Churches, Ships, Streets, Clubs, Natural Curiosities and the like. By WM. A. WHEELER and CHARLES G. WHEELER. Demy 8vo cloth extra, 7s. 6d.

DICTIONARIES, *continued—*
Short Sayings of Great Men. With Historical and Explanatory Notes. By SAMUEL A. BENT, M.A. Demy 8vo, cloth extra. 7s. 6d.

A Dictionary of the Drama: Being a comprehensive Guide to the Plays, Playwrights, Players, and Playhouses of the United Kingdom and America, from the Earliest to the Present Times. By W. DAVENPORT ADAMS. A thick volume, crown 8vo, half-bound, 12s. 6d.   [*In preparation.*

The Slang Dictionary: Etymological, Historical, and Anecdotal. Crown 8vo, cloth extra, 6s. 6d.

Women of the Day: A Biographical Dictionary. By FRANCES HAYS. Cr. 8vo, cloth extra, 6s.

Words, Facts, and Phrases: A Dictionary of Curious, Quaint, and Out-of-the-Way Matters. By ELIEZER EDWARDS. New and Cheaper Issue. Cr. 8vo, cl. ex., 7s. 6d.; hf.-bd., 9s.

Diderot.—The Paradox of Acting. Translated, with Annotations, from Diderot's "Le Paradoxe sur le Comédien," by WALTER HERRIES POLLOCK. With a Preface by HENRY IRVING. Cr. 8vo, in parchment, 4s. 6d.

Dobson (W. T.), Works by:
Literary Frivolities, Fancies, Follies, and Frolics. Post 8vo, cl. lp., 2s. 6d.
Poetical Ingenuities and Eccentricities. Post 8vo, cloth limp, 2s. 6d.

Doran. — Memories of our Great Towns; with Anecdotic Gleanings concerning their Worthies and their Oddities. By Dr. JOHN DORAN, F.S.A. With 38 Illustrations. New and Cheaper Ed., cr. 8vo, cl. ex., 7s. 6d.

Drama, A Dictionary of the. Being a comprehensive Guide to the Plays, Playwrights, Players, and Playhouses of the United Kingdom and America, from the Earliest to the Present Times. By W. DAVENPORT ADAMS. (Uniform with BREWER'S "Reader's Handbook.") Crown 8vo, half-bound, 12s. 6d.   [*In preparation.*

Dramatists, The Old. Cr. 8vo, cl. ex., Vignette Portraits, 6s. per Vol.
Ben Jonson's Works. With Notes Critical and Explanatory, and a Biographical Memoir by WM. GIFFORD. Edit. by Col. CUNNINGHAM. 3 Vols.
Chapman's Works. Complete in Three Vols. Vol. I. contains the Plays complete, including doubtful ones; Vol. II., Poems and Minor Translations, with Introductory Essay by A. C. SWINBURNE; Vol. III., Translations of the Iliad and Odyssey.

DRAMATISTS, THE OLD, *continued—*
Marlowe's Works. Including his Translations. Edited, with Notes and Introduction, by Col. CUNNINGHAM. One Vol.
Massinger's Plays. From the Text of WILLIAM GIFFORD. Edited by Col. CUNNINGHAM. One Vol.

Dyer. — The Folk - Lore of Plants. By T. F. THISELTON DYER, M.A., &c. Crown 8vo, cloth extra, 7s. 6d.   [*In preparation.*

Early English Poets. Edited, with Introductions and Annotations, by Rev. A. B. GROSART, D.D. Crown 8vo, cloth boards, 6s. per Volume.
Fletcher's (Giles, B.D.) Complete Poems. One Vol.
Davies' (Sir John) Complete Poetical Works. Two Vols.
Herrick's (Robert) Complete Collected Poems. Three Vols.
Sidney's (Sir Philip) Complete Poetical Works. Three Vols.

Herbert (Lord) of Cherbury's Poems. Edited, with Introduction, by J. CHURTON COLLINS. Crown 8vo, parchment, 8s.

Edwardes (Mrs. A.), Novels by:
A Point of Honour. Post 8vo, illustrated boards, 2s.
Archie Lovell. Post 8vo, illust. bds., 2s.; crown 8vo, cloth extra, 3s. 6d.

Eggleston.—Roxy: A Novel. By EDWARD EGGLESTON. Post 8vo, illust. boards, 2s.; cr. 8vo, cloth extra, 3s. 6d.

Emanuel.—On Diamonds and Precious Stones: their History, Value, and Properties; with Simple Tests for ascertaining their Reality. By HARRY EMANUEL, F.R.G.S. With numerous Illustrations, tinted and plain. Crown 8vo, cloth extra, gilt, 6s.

Englishman's House, The: A Practical Guide to all interested in Selecting or Building a House, with full Estimates of Cost, Quantities, &c. By C. J. RICHARDSON. Third Edition. Nearly 600 Illusts. Cr. 8vo, cl. ex., 7s. 6d.

Ewald (Alex. Charles, F.S.A.), Works by:
Stories from the State Papers. With an Autotype Facsimile. Crown 8vo, cloth extra, 6s.
The Life and Times of Prince Charles Stuart, Count of Albany, commonly called the Young Pretender. From the State Papers and other Sources. New and Cheaper Edition, with a Portrait, crown 8vo, cloth extra, 7s. 6d.

Eyes, The.—How to Use our Eyes, and How to Preserve Them. By JOHN BROWNING, F.R.A.S., &c. With 37 Illustrations. Crown 8vo, 1s.; cloth, 1s. 6d.

Fairholt.—Tobacco: Its History and Associations; with an Account of the Plant and its Manufacture, and its Modes of Use in all Ages and Countries. By F. W. FAIRHOLT, F.S.A. With Coloured Frontispiece and upwards of 100 Illustrations by the Author. Crown 8vo, cloth extra, 6s.

Familiar Allusions: A Handbook of Miscellaneous Information; including the Names of Celebrated Statues, Paintings, Palaces, Country Seats, Ruins, Churches, Ships, Streets, Clubs, Natural Curiosities, and the like. By WILLIAM A. WHEELER, Author of " Noted Names of Fiction ; " and CHARLES G. WHEELER. Demy 8vo, cloth extra, 7s. 6d.

Faraday (Michael), Works by:
The Chemical History of a Candle: Lectures delivered before a Juvenile Audience at the Royal Institution. Edited by WILLIAM CROOKES, F.C.S. Post 8vo, cloth extra, with numerous Illustrations, 4s. 6d.

On the Various Forces of Nature, and their Relations to each other: Lectures delivered before a Juvenile Audience at the Royal Institution. Edited by WILLIAM CROOKES, F.C.S. Post 8vo, cloth extra, with numerous Illustrations, 4s. 6d.

Fin-Bec. — The Cupboard Papers: Observations on the Art of Living and Dining. By FIN-BEC. Post 8vo, cloth limp, 2s. 6d.

Fitzgerald (Percy), Works by:
The Recreations of a Literary Man ; or, Does Writing Pay? With Recollections of some Literary Men, and a View of a Literary Man's Working Life. Cr. 8vo, cloth extra, 6s.
The World Behind the Scenes. Crown 8vo, cloth extra, 3s. 6d.
Little Essays: Passages from the Letters of CHARLES LAMB. Post 8vo, cloth limp, 2s. 6d.

Post 8vo, illustrated boards, 2s. each.
Bella Donna. | Never Forgotten.
The Second Mrs. Tillotson.
Polly.
Seventy-five Brooke Street.
The Lady of Brantome.

Fletcher's (Giles, B.D.) Complete Poems: Christ's Victorie in Heaven, Christ's Victorie on Earth, Christ's Triumph over Death, and Minor Poems. With Memorial-Introduction and Notes by the Rev. A. B. GROSART, D.D. Cr. 8vo, cloth bds., 6s.

Fonblanque.—Filthy Lucre: A Novel. By ALBANY DE FONBLANQUE. Post 8vo, illustrated boards, 2s.

Francillon (R. E.), Novels by:
Crown 8vo, cloth extra, 3s. 6d. each ; post 8vo, illust. boards, 2s. each.
Olympia. | Queen Cophetua.
One by One.
Esther's Glove. Fcap. 8vo, picture cover, 1s.
A Real Queen. Cr. 8vo, cl. extra, 3s. 6d.

French Literature, History of. By HENRY VAN LAUN. Complete in 3 Vols., demy 8vo, cl. bds., 7s. 6d. each.

Frere.—Pandurang Hari ; or, Memoirs of a Hindoo. With a Preface by Sir H. BARTLE FRERE, G.C.S.I., &c. Crown 8vo, cloth extra, 3s. 6d.; post 8vo, illustrated boards, 2s.

Friswell.—One of Two: A Novel. By HAIN FRISWELL. Post 8vo, illustrated boards, 2s.

Frost (Thomas), Works by:
Crown 8vo, cloth extra, 3s. 6d. each.
Circus Life and Circus Celebrities.
The Lives of the Conjurers.
The Old Showmen and the Old London Fairs.

Fry.—Royal Guide to the London Charities, 1884-5. By HERBERT FRY Showing their Name, Date of Foundation, Objects, Income, Officials, &c. Published Annually. Crown 8vo, cloth, 1s. 6d.

Gardening Books:
A Year's Work in Garden and Greenhouse: Practical Advice to Amateur Gardeners as to the Management of the Flower, Fruit, and Frame Garden. By GEORGE GLENNY. Post 8vo, cloth limp, 2s. 6d.
Our Kitchen Garden: The Plants we Grow, and How we Cook Them. By TOM JERROLD. Post 8vo, cloth limp, 2s. 6d.
Household Horticulture: A Gossip about Flowers. By TOM and JANE JERROLD. Illust. Post 8vo, cl. lp., 2s. 6d.
The Garden that Paid the Rent. By TOM JERROLD. Fcap. 8vo, illustrated cover, 1s.; cloth limp, 1s. 6d.
My Garden Wild, and What I Grew there. By F. G. HEATH. Crown 8vo, cloth extra, 5s.; gilt edges, 6s.

Garrett.—The Capel Girls: A Novel. By EDWARD GARRETT. Post 8vo,illust.bds., 2s.; cr.8vo, cl.ex., 3s 6d.

Gentleman's Magazine (The) for 1884. One Shilling Monthly. A New Serial Story, entitled "Philistia," by CECIL POWER, is now appearing. "Science Notes," by W. MATTIEU WILLIAMS, F.R.A.S., and "Table Talk," by SYLVANUS URBAN, are also continued monthly.
₊ *Now ready, the Volume for* JANUARY *to* JUNE, 1884, *cloth extra, price* 8s. 6d.; *Cases for binding,* 2s. *each.*

German Popular Stories. Collected by the Brothers GRIMM, and Translated by EDGAR TAYLOR. Edited, with an Introduction, by JOHN RUSKIN. With 22 Illustrations on Steel by GEORGE CRUIKSHANK. Square 8vo, cloth extra, 6s. 6d.; gilt edges, 7s. 6d.

Gibbon (Charles), Novels by: Crown 8vo, cloth extra, 3s 6d. each; post 8vo, illustrated boards, 2s. each.

Robin Gray.	Queen of the
For Lack of Gold.	Meadow.
What will the	In Pastures Green
World Say?	Braes of Yarrow.
In Honour Bound.	The Flower of the
In Love and War.	Forest. [lem.
For the King.	A Heart's Prob-

Post 8vo, illustrated boards, 2s. The Dead Heart.

Crown 8vo, cloth extra, 3s. 6d. each. The Golden Shaft. Of High Degree. Fancy Free. Loving a Dream.

By Mead and Stream. Three Vols., crown 8vo. Found Out. Three Vols., crown 8vo. [Shortly.

Gilbert (William), Novels by: Post 8vo, illustrated boards, 2s. each. Dr. Austin's Guests. The Wizard of the Mountain. James Duke, Costermonger.

Gilbert (W. S.), Original Plays by: In Two Series, each complete in itself, price 2s. 6d. each.
The FIRST SERIES contains— The Wicked World—Pygmalion and Galatea — Charity — The Princess — The Palace of Truth—Trial by Jury.
The SECOND SERIES contains—Broken Hearts—Engaged—Sweethearts—Gretchen— Dan'l Druce—Tom Cobb—H.M.S. Pinafore—The Sorcerer—The Pirates of Penzance.

Glenny.—A Year's Work in Garden and Greenhouse: Practical Advice to Amateur Gardeners as to the Management of the Flower, Fruit, and Frame Garden. By GEORGE GLENNY. Post 8vo, cloth limp, 2s. 6d.

Godwin.—Lives of the Necro- mancers. By WILLIAM GODWIN. Post 8vo, cloth limp, 2s.

Golden Library, The: Square 16mo (Tauchnitz size), cloth limp, 2s. per volume.
Bayard Taylor's Diversions of the Echo Club.
Bennett's (Dr. W. C.) Ballad History of England.
Bennett's (Dr.) Songs for Sailors.
Byron's Don Juan.
Godwin's (William) Lives of the Necromancers.
Holmes's Autocrat of the Breakfast Table. With an Introduction by G. A. SALA.
Holmes's Professor at the Breakfast Table.
Hood's Whims and Oddities. Complete. All the original Illustrations.
Irving's (Washington) Tales of a Traveller.
Irving's (Washington) Tales of the Alhambra.
Jesse's (Edward) Scenes and Occupations of a Country Life.
Lamb's Essays of Elia. Both Series Complete in One Vol.
Leigh Hunt's Essays: A Tale for a Chimney Corner, and other Pieces. With Portrait, and Introduction by EDMUND OLLIER.
Mallory's (Sir Thomas) Mort d'Arthur: The Stories of King Arthur and of the Knights of the Round Table. Edited by B. MONTGOMERIE RANKING.
Pascal's Provincial Letters. A New Translation, with Historical Introduction and Notes,byT.M'CRIE,D.D.
Pope's Poetical Works. Complete.
Rochefoucauld's Maxims and Moral Reflections. With Notes, and Introductory Essay by SAINTE-BEUVE.
St. Pierre's Paul and Virginia, and The Indian Cottage. Edited, with Life, by the Rev. E. CLARKE.
Shelley's Early Poems, and Queen Mab. With Essay by LEIGH HUNT.
Shelley's Later Poems. Laon and Cythna, &c.
Shelley's Posthumous Poems, the Shelley Papers, &c

GOLDEN LIBRARY, THE, *continued—*
Shelley's Prose Works, including A Refutation of Deism, Zastrozzi, St. Irvyne, &c.
White's Natural History of Selborne. Edited, with Additions, by THOMAS BROWN, F.L.S.

Golden Treasury of Thought, The: An ENCYCLOPÆDIA OF QUOTATIONS from Writers of all Times and Countries. Selected and Edited by THEODORE TAYLOR. Crown 8vo, cloth gilt and gilt edges, 7s. 6d.

Gordon Cumming (C. F.), Works by:
In the Hebrides. With Autotype Facsimile and numerous full-page Illustrations. Demy 8vo, cloth extra, 8s. 6d.
In the Himalayas and on the Indian Plains. With numerous Illustrations. Demy 8vo, cloth extra, 8s. 6d. *[Shortly.*

Graham. — The Professor's Wife: A Story. By LEONARD GRAHAM. Fcap. 8vo, picture cover, 1s.; cloth extra, 2s. 6d.

Greeks and Romans, The Life of the, Described from Antique Monuments. By ERNST GUHL and W. KONER. Translated from the Third German Edit.on, and Edited by Dr. F. HUEFFER. With 545 Illustrations. New and Cheaper Edition, demy 8vo, cloth extra, 7s. 6d.

Greenwood (James), Works by:
The Wilds of London. Crown 8vo, cloth extra, 3s 6d.
Low-Life Deeps: An Account of the Strange Fish to be Found There. Crown 8vo, cloth extra, 3s. 6d.
Dick Temple: A Novel. Post 8vo, illustrated boards, 2s.

Guyot.—The Earth and Man; or, Physical Geography in its relation to the History of Mankind. By ARNOLD GUYOT. With Additions by Professors AGASSIZ, PIERCE, and GRAY; 12 Maps and Engravings on Steel, some Coloured, and copious Index. Crown 8vo, cloth extra, gilt, 4s. 6d.

Hair (The): Its Treatment in Health, Weakness, and Disease. Translated from the German of Dr. J. PINCUS. Crown 8vo, 1s.

Hake (Dr. Thomas Gordon), Poems by:
Maiden Ecstasy. Small 4to, cloth extra, 8s.

HAKE'S (Dr. T. G.) POEMS, *continued—*
New Symbols. Crown 8vo, cloth extra, 6s.
Legends of the Morrow. Crown 8vo cloth extra, 6s.
The Serpent Play. Crown 8vo, cloth extra, 6s.

Hall.—Sketches of Irish Character. By Mrs. S. C. HALL. With numerous Illustrations on Steel and Wood by MACLISE, GILBERT, HARVEY, and G. CRUIKSHANK. Medium 8vo, cloth extra, gilt, 7s. 6d.

Halliday.—Every-day Papers. By ANDREW HALLIDAY. Post 8vo, illustrated boards, 2s.

Handwriting, The Philosophy of. With over 100 Facsimiles and Explanatory Text. By DON FELIX DE SALAMANCA. Post 8vo, cloth limp, 2s. 6d.

Hanky-Panky: A Collection of Very Easy Tricks, Very Difficult Tricks, White Magic, Sleight of Hand, &c. Edited by W. H. CREMER. With 200 Illusts. Crown 8vo, cloth extra, 4s. 6d.

Hardy (Lady Duffus). — Paul Wynter's Sacrifice: A Story. By Lady DUFFUS HARDY. Post 8vo, illust. boards, 2s.

Hardy (Thomas).—Under the Greenwood Tree. By THOMAS HARDY, Author of "Far from the Madding Crowd." Crown 8vo, cloth extra, 3s. 6d.; post 8vo, illustrated bds., 2s.

Haweis (Mrs. H. R.), Works by:
The Art of Dress. With numerous Illustrations. Small 8vo, illustrated cover, 1s.; cloth limp, 1s. 6d.
The Art of Beauty. New and Cheaper Edition. Crown 8vo, cloth extra, with Coloured Frontispiece and Illustrations, 6s.
The Art of Decoration. Square 8vo, handsomely bound and profusely Illustrated, 10s. 6d.
Chaucer for Children: A Golden Key. With Eight Coloured Pictures and numerous Woodcuts. New Edition, small 4to, cloth extra, 6s.
Chaucer for Schools. Demy 8vo, cloth limp, 2s. 6d.

Haweis (Rev. H. R.).—American Humorists. Includ ng WASHINGTON IRVING, OLIVER WENDELL HOLMES, JAMES RUSSELL LOWELL, ARTEMUS WARD, MARK TWAIN, and BRET HARTE. By the Rev. H. R. HAWEIS, M.A. Crown 8vo, cloth extra, 6s.

Hawthorne (Julian), Novels by.
Crown 8vo, cloth extra, 3s. 6d. each ;
post 8vo, illustrated boards, 2s. each.

Garth. | Sebastian Strome.
Ellice Quentin. | Dust.
       Prince Saroni's Wife.

Mrs. Gainsborough's Diamonds.
Fcap. 8vo, illustrated cover, 1s. ;
cloth extra, 2s. 6d.

Crown 8vo, cloth extra, 3s. 6d. each.
Fortune's Fool.
Beatrix Randolph. With Illustrations
by A. FREDERICKS.

Mercy Holland, and other Stories.
Three Vols., crown 8vo.   [Shortly.

IMPORTANT NEW BIOGRAPHY.
Hawthorne (Nathaniel) and
his Wife. By JULIAN HAWTHORNE.
With 6 Steel-plate Portraits.   Two
Vols., crown 8vo, cloth extra, 24s.
    [Twenty-five copies of an Edition de
Luxe, printed on the best hand-made
paper, large 8vo size, and with India
proofs of the Illustrations, are reserved
for sale in England, price 42s. per set.
Immediate application should be made
by anyone desiring a copy of this
special and very limited Edition.]

Heath (F. G.). — My Garden
Wild, and What I Grew There. By
FRANCIS GEORGE HEATH, Author of
"The Fern World," &c. Crown 8vo,
cl. ex , 5s. ; cl. gilt, gilt edges, 6s.

Helps (Sir Arthur), Works by :
Animals and their Masters.   Post
8vo, cloth limp, 2s. 6d.
Social Pressure. Post 8vo, cloth limp,
2s. 6d.
Ivan de Biron: A Novel. Crown 8vo,
cloth extra, 3s. 6d.; post 8vo, illustrated boards, 2s.

Heptalogia (The); or, The
Seven against Sense.   A Cap with
Seven Bells. Cr. 8vo, cloth extra, 6s.

Herbert. — The Poems of Lord
Herbert of Cherbury. Edited, with
Introduction, by J. CHURTON COLLINS.
Crown 8vo, bound in parchment, 6s.

Herrick's (Robert) Hesperides,
Noble Numbers, and Complete Collected Poems. With Memorial-Introduction and Notes by the Rev. A. B,
GROSART, D.D., Steel Portrait, Index
of First Lines, and Glossarial Index,
&c, Three Vols., crown 8vo, cloth, 18s.

Hesse - Wartegg   (Chevalier
Ernst von), Works by
Tunis: The Land and the People.
With 22 Illustrations. Crown 8vo,
cloth extra, 3s. 6d.
The New South-West: Travelling
Sketches from Kansas, New Mexico,
Arizona, and Northern Mexico.
With 100 fine Illustrations and Three
Maps.   Demy 8vo, cloth extra,
14s.   [In preparation.

Hindley (Charles), Works by :
Crown 8vo, cloth extra, 3s. 6d. each.
Tavern Anecdotes and Sayings: In-
cluding the Origin of Signs, and
Reminiscences connected with
Taverns, Coffee Houses, Clubs, &c.
With Illustrations.
The Life and Adventures of a Cheap
Jack. By One of the Fraternity.
Edited by CHARLES HINDLEY.

Hoey. — The Lover's Creed.
By Mrs. CASHEL HOEY. With 12 Illustrations by P. MACNAB. Three Vols.,
crown 8vo.   [Shortly.

Holmes (O. Wendell), Works by :
The Autocrat of the Breakfast-
Table. Illustrated by J. GORDON
THOMSON. Post 8vo, cloth limp,
2s. 6d.; another Edition in smaller
type, with an Introduction by G. A.
SALA. Post 8vo, cloth limp, 2s.
The Professor at the Breakfast-
Table; with the Story of Iris. Post
8vo, cloth limp, 2s.

Holmes. — The Science of
Voice Production and Voice Preser
vation: A Popular Manual for the
Use of Speakers and Singers. By
GORDON HOLMES, M.D. With Illus-
trations. Cr. 8vo, 1s.; cl. limp, 1s. 6d.

Hood (Thomas):
Hood's Choice Works, in Prose and
Verse. Including the Cream of the
Comic Annuals. With Life of the
Author, Portrait, and 200 Illustra-
tions. Crown 8vo, cloth extra, 7s. 6d.
Hood's Whims and Oddities. Com-
plete. With all the original Illus-
trations. Post 8vo, cloth limp, 2s.

Hood (Tom), Works by :
From Nowhere to the North Pole,
A Noah's Arkæological Narrative.
With 25 Illustrations by W. BRUN-
TON and E. C. BARNES. Square
crown 8vo, cloth extra, gilt edges, 6s.
A Golden Heart: A Novel. Post 8vo,
illustrated boards, 2s.

Hook's (Theodore) Choice Humorous Works, including his Ludicrous Adventures, Bons Mots, Puns and Hoaxes. With a New Life of the Author, Portraits, Facsimiles, and Illusts. Cr. 8vo, cl. extra, gilt, 7s. 6d.

Hooper.—The House of Raby: A Novel. By Mrs. GEORGE HOOPER. Post 8vo, illustrated boards, 2s.

Horne.—Orion: An Epic Poem, in Three Books. By RICHARD HENGIST HORNE. With Photographic Portrait from a Medallion by SUMMERS. Tenth Edition, crown 8vo, cloth extra, 7s.

Howell.—Conflicts of Capital and Labour, Historically and Economically considered: Being a History and Review of the Trade Unions of Great Britain, showing their Origin, Progress, Constitution, and Objects, in their Political, Social, Economical, and Industrial Aspects. By GEORGE HOWELL. Cr. 8vo, cloth extra, 7s. 6d.

Hugo. — The Hunchback of Notre Dame. By VICTOR HUGO. Post 8vo, illustrated boards, 2s.

Hunt.—Essays by Leigh Hunt. A Tale for a Chimney Corner, and other Pieces. With Portrait and Introduction by EDMUND OLLIER. Post 8vo, cloth limp, 2s.

Hunt (Mrs. Alfred), Novels by: Crown 8vo, cloth extra, 3s. 6d. each; post 8vo, illustrated boards, 2s. each.
Thornicroft's Model.
The Leaden Casket.
Self-Condemned.

Ingelow.—Fated to be Free: A Novel. By JEAN INGELOW. Crown 8vo, cloth extra, 3s. 6d.; post 8vo, illustrated boards, 2s.

Irish Wit and Humour, Songs of. Collected and Edited by A. PERCEVAL GRAVES. Post 8vo, cl. limp, 2s. 6d.

Irving (Washington),Works by: Post 8vo, cloth limp, 2s. each.
Tales of a Traveller.
Tales of the Alhambra.

Janvier.—Practical Keramics for Students. By CATHERINE A. JANVIER. Crown 8vo, cloth extra, 6s.

Jay (Harriett), Novels by. Each crown 8vo, cloth extra, 3s. 6d.; or post 8vo, illustrated boards, 2s.
The Dark Colleen.
The Queen of Connaught.

Jefferies (Richard), Works by: Nature near London. Crown 8vo, cloth extra, 6s.
The Life of the Fields. Crown 8vo, cloth extra, 6s.

Jennings (H. J.), Works by: Curiosities of Criticism. Post 8vo, cloth limp, 2s. 6d.
Lord Tennyson: A Biographical Sketch. Crown 8vo, cloth extra, 6s. [*In the press.*

Jennings (Hargrave). — The Rosicrucians: Their Rites and Mysteries. With Chapters on the Ancient Fire and Serpent Worshippers. By HARGRAVE JENNINGS. With Five full-page Plates and upwards of 300 Illustrations. A New Edition, crown 8vo, cloth extra, 7s. 6d.

Jerrold (Tom), Works by: The Garden that Paid the Rent. By TOM JERROLD. Fcap. 8vo, illustrated cover, 1s.; cloth limp, 1s. 6d.
Household Horticulture: A Gossip about Flowers. By TOM and JANE JERROLD. Illust. Post 8vo.cl.1p.,2s.6d.
Our Kitchen Garden: The Plants we Grow, and How we Cook Them. By TOM JERROLD. Post 8vo, cloth limp, 2s. 6d.

Jesse.—Scenes and Occupations of a Country Life. By EDWARD JESSE. Post 8vo, cloth limp, 2s.

Jones (Wm., F.S.A.), Works by: Finger-Ring Lore: Historical, Legendary, and Anecdotal. With over 200 Illusts. Cr. 8vo, cl. extra, 7s. 6d.
Credulities, Past and Present; including the Sea and Seamen, Miners, Talismans, Word and Letter Divination, Exorcising and Blessing of Animals, Birds, Eggs, Luck, &c. With an Etched Frontispiece. Crown 8vo, cloth extra, 7s. 6d.
Crowns and Coronations: A History of Regalia in all Times and Countries. With One Hundred Illustrations. Cr. 8vo, cloth extra, 7s. 6d.

Jonson's (Ben) Works. With Notes Critical and Explanatory, and a Biographical Memoir by WILLIAM GIFFORD. Edited by Colonel CUNNINGHAM. Three Vols., crown 8vo, cloth extra, 18s.; or separately, 6s. each.

Josephus,The CompleteWorks of. Translated by WHISTON. Containing both "The Antiquities of the Jews" and "The Wars of the Jews." Two Vols., 8vo, with 52 Illustrations and Maps, cloth extra, gilt, 14s

Kavanagh.— The Pearl Fountain, and other Fairy Stories. By BRIDGET and JULIA KAVANAGH. With Thirty Illustrations by J. MOYR SMITH. Small 8vo, cloth gilt, 6s.

Kempt.— Pencil and Palette : Chapters on Art and Artists. By ROBERT KEMPT. Post 8vo, cloth limp, 2s. 6d.

Kingsley (Henry), Novels by :
Each crown 8vo, cloth extra, 3s. 6d.; or post 8vo, illustrated boards, 2s.

Oakshott Castle. | Number Seventeen

Knight.— The Patient's Vade Mecum : How to get most Benefit from Medical Advice. By WILLIAM KNIGHT, M.R.C.S., and EDWARD KNIGHT, L.R.C.P. Crown 8vo, 1s. ; cloth, 1s. 6d.

Lamb (Charles):
Mary and Charles Lamb: Their Poems, Letters, and Remains. With Reminiscences and Notes by W. CAREW HAZLITT. With HANCOCK'S Portrait of the Essayist, Facsimiles of the Title-pages of the rare First Editions of Lamb's and Coleridge's Works, and numerous Illustrations. Crown 8vo, cloth extra, 10s. 6d.

Lamb's Complete Works, in Prose and Verse, reprinted from the Original Editions, with many Pieces hitherto unpublished. Edited, with Notes and Introduction, by R. H. SHEPHERD. With Two Portraits and Facsimile of Page of the "Essay on Roast Pig." Cr. 8vo, cloth extra, 7s. 6d.

The Essays of Elia. Complete Edition. Post 8vo, cloth extra, 2s.

Poetry for Children, and Prince Dorus. By CHARLES LAMB. Carefully reprinted from unique copies. Small 8vo, cloth extra, 5s.

Little Essays : Sketches and Characters. By CHARLES LAMB. Selected from his Letters by PERCY FITZGERALD Post 8vo, cloth limp, 2s. 6d.

Lane's Arabian Nights, &c. :
The Thousand and One Nights : commonly called, in England, "THE ARABIAN NIGHTS' ENTERTAINMENTS." A New Translation from the Arabic, with copious Notes, by EDWARD WILLIAM LANE. Illustrated by many hundred · Engravings on Wood, from Original Designs by WM. HARVEY. A New Edition, from a Copy annotated by the Translator, edited by his Nephew, EDWARD STANLEY POOLE. With a Preface by STANLEY LANE-POOLE. Three Vols., demy 8vo, cloth extra, 7s. 6d. each.

LANE'S ARABIAN NIGHTS, *continued—*
Arabian Society in the Middle Ages: Studies from "The Thousand and One Nights." By EDWARD WILLIAM LANE, Author of "The Modern Egyptians," &c. Edited by STANLEY LANE-POOLE. Cr. 8vo, cloth extra, 6s.

Lares and Penates ; or, The Background of Life. By FLORENCE CADDY. Crown 8vo, cloth extra, 6s.

Larwood (Jacob), Works by :
The Story of the London Parks. With Illustrations. Crown 8vo, cloth extra, 3s. 6d.

Clerical Anecdotes. Post 8vo, cloth limp. 2s. 6d.

Forensic Anecdotes Post 8vo, cloth limp, 2s 6d.

Theatrical Anecdotes. Post 8vo, cloth limp, 2s. 6d.

Leigh (Henry S.), Works by :
Carols of Cockayne. With numerous Illustrations. Post 8vo, cloth limp, 2s 6d.

Jeux d'Esprit. Collected and Edited by HENRY S. LEIGH. Post 8vo, cloth limp, 2s. 6d.

Life in London ; or, The History of Jerry Hawthorn and Corinthian Tom. With the whole of CRUIKSHANK'S Illustrations, in Colours, after the Originals. Crown 8vo, cloth extra, 7s. 6d.

Linton (E. Lynn), Works by :
Post 8vo, cloth limp, 2s. 6d. each.
Witch Stories.
The True Story of Joshua Davidson.
Ourselves : Essays on Women.

Crown 8vo, cloth extra, 3s 6d each ; post 8vo, illustrated boards, 2s. each.
Patricia Kemball.
The Atonement of Leam Dundas.
The World Well Lost.
Under which Lord ?
With a Silken Thread.
The Rebel of the Family.
" My Love ! " .
Ione.

Locks and Keys.— On the De-velopment and Distribution of Primitive Locks and Keys. By Lieut.-Gen. PITT-RIVERS, F.R.S. With numerous Illustrations. Demy 4to, half Roxburghe, 16s.

Longfellow:

Longfellow's Complete Prose Works. Including " Outre Mer," " Hyperion," " Kavanagh," " The Poets and Poetry of Europe," and " Driftwood." With Portrait and Illustrations by VALENTINE BROMLEY. Crown 8vo, cloth extra, 7s. 6d.

Longfellow's Poetical Works. Carefully Reprinted from the Original Editions. With numerous fine Illustrations on Steel and Wood. Crown 8vo, cloth extra, 7s. 6d.

Long Life, Aids to: A Medical, Dietetic, and General Guide in Health and Disease. By N. E. DAVIES, L.R.C.P. Crown 8vo, 2s; cloth limp, 2s. 6d. _____ [Shortly.

Lucy.—Gideon Fleyce: A Novel. By HENRY W. LUCY. Crown 8vo, cl. extra, 3s. 6d ; post 8vo, illust. bds.,2s.

Luslad (The) of Camoens. Translated into English Spenserian Verse by ROBERT FRENCH DUFF. Demy 8vo, with Fourteen full-page Plates, cloth boards, 18s. _____

McCarthy (Justin, M.P.),Works by :

A History of Our Own Times, from the Accession of Queen Victoria to the General Election of 1880. Four Vols. demy 8vo, cloth extra, 12s. each.—Also a POPULAR EDITION, in Four Vols. cr. 8vo, cl. extra, 6s each.

A Short History of Our Own Times. One Vol., crown 8vo, cloth extra, 6s.

History of the Four Georges. Four Vols. demy 8vo, cloth extra, 12s. each. _____ [Vol. I. in the press.

Crown 8vo, cloth extra, 3s. 6d. each ; post 8vo, illustrated boards, 2s. each.

Dear Lady Disdain.
The Waterdale Neighbours.
My Enemy's Daughter.
A Fair Saxon.
Linley Rochford
Miss Misanthrope.
Donna Quixote.
The Comet of a Season.

Maid of Athens. With 12 Illustrations by F. BARNARD. Crown 8vo, cloth extra, 3s. 6d. _____

McCarthy (Justin H., M.P.), Works by:

Serapon, and other Poems. Crown 8vo, cloth extra, 6s.

An Outline of the History of Ireland, from the Earliest Times to the Present Day. Cr. 8vo, 1s. ; cloth, 1s 6d.

England under Gladstone. Crown 8vo, cloth extra, 6s.

MacDonald (George, LL.D.), Works by :

The Princess and Curdle. With 11 Illustrations by JAMES ALLEN. Small crown 8vo, cloth extra, 5s.

Gutta-Percha Willie, the Working Genius. With 9 Illustrations by ARTHUR HUGHES. Square 8vo, cloth extra, 3s. 6d.

Paul Faber, Surgeon. With a Frontispiece by J. E. MILLAIS. Crown 8vo, cloth extra, 3s 6d.; post 8vo, illustrated boards, 2s.

Thomas Wingfold, Curate. With a Frontispiece by C. J. STANILAND. Crown 8vo, cloth extra, 3s. 6d.; post 8vo, illustrated boards, 2s.

Macdonell.—Quaker Cousins: A Novel. By AGNES MACDONELL. Crown 8vo, cloth extra, 3s. 6d.; post 8vo, illustrated boards, 2s.

Macgregor. — Pastimes and Players. Notes on Popular Games. By ROBERT MACGREGOR. Post 8vo, cloth limp, 2s. 6d.

Maclise Portrait-Gallery (The) of Illustrious Literary Characters; with Memoirs—Biographical, Critical, Bibliographical, and Anecdotal—illustrative of the Literature of the former half of the Present Century. By WILLIAM BATES, B.A. With 85 Portraits printed on an India Tint. Crown 8vo, cloth extra, 7s. 6d.

Macquoid (Mrs.), Works by :

In the Ardennes. With 50 fine Illustrations by THOMAS R. MACQUOID. Square 8vo, cloth extra, 10s. 6d.

Pictures and Legends from Normandy and Brittany. With numerous Illustrations by THOMAS R. MACQUOID. Square 8vo, cloth gilt, 10s. 6d.

Through Normandy. With 90 Illustrations by T. R. MACQUOID. Square 8vo, cloth extra, 7s. 6d.

Through Brittany. With numerous Illustrations by T. R. MACQUOID. Square 8vo, cloth extra, 7s. 6d.

About Yorkshire With 67 Illustrations by T. R. MACQUOID, Engraved by SWAIN. Square 8vo, cloth extra, 10s. 6d.

The Evil Eye, and other Stories. Crown 8vo, cloth extra, 3s. 6d.; post 8vo, illustrated boards, 2s.

Lost Rose, and other Stories. Crown 8vo, cloth extra. 3s. 6d.; post 8vo, illustrated boards, 2s.

Mackay.—Interludes and Undertones: or, Music at Twilight. By CHARLES MACKAY, LL.D. Crown 8vo, cloth extra, 6s.

Magician's Own Book (The): Performances with Cups and Balls, Eggs, Hats, Handkerchiefs, &c. All from actual Experience. Edited by W. H. CREMER. With 200 Illustrations. Crown 8vo, cloth extra, 4s. 6d.

Magic No Mystery: Tricks with Cards, Dice, Balls, &c., with fully descriptive Directions; the Art of Secret Writing; Training of Performing Animals, &c. With Coloured Frontispiece and many Illustrations. Crown 8vo, cloth extra, 4s. 6d.

Magna Charta. An exact Fac-simile of the Original in the British Museum, printed on fine plate paper, 3 feet by 2 feet, with Arms and Seals emblazoned in Gold and Colours. Price 5s.

Mallock (W. H.), Works by:

The New Republic; or, Culture, Faith and Philosophy in an English Country House. Post 8vo, cloth limp, 2s. 6d.; Cheap Edition, illustrated boards, 2s.

The New Paul and Virginia; or, Positivism on an Island. Post 8vo, cloth limp, 2s. 6d.

Poems. Small 4to, bound in parchment, 8s.

Is Life worth Living? Crown 8vo, cloth extra, 6s.

Mallory's (Sir Thomas) Mort d'Arthur: The Stories of King Arthur and of the Knights of the Round Table. Edited by B. MONTGOMERIE RANKING. Post 8vo, cloth limp, 2s.

Marlowe's Works. Including his Translations. Edited, with Notes and Introduction, by Col. CUNNINGHAM. Crown 8vo, cloth extra, 6s.

Marryat (Florence), Novels by: Crown 8vo, cloth extra, 3s. 6d. each; or, post 8vo, illustrated boards, 2s.

Open! Sesame!
Written in Fire.

Post 8vo, illustrated boards, 2s. each.

A Harvest of Wild Oats.
A Little Stepson.
Fighting the Air.

Masterman.—Half a Dozen Daughters: A Novel. By J. MASTERMAN. Post 8vo, illustrated boards, 2s.

Mark Twain, Works by:

The Choice Works of Mark Twain. Revised and Corrected throughout by the Author. With Life, Portrait, and numerous Illustrations. Crown 8vo, cloth extra, 7s. 6d.

The Adventures of Tom Sawyer. Post 8vo, illustrated boards, 2s.

An Idle Excursion, and other Sketches. Post 8vo, illustrated boards, 2s.

The Prince and the Pauper. With nearly 200 Illustrations. Crown 8vo, cloth extra, 7s. 6d.

The Innocents Abroad; or, The New Pilgrim's Progress: Being some Account of the Steamship "Quaker City's" Pleasure Excursion to Europe and the Holy Land. With 234 Illustrations. Crown 8vo, cloth extra, 7s. 6d. CHEAP EDITION (under the title of "MARK TWAIN'S PLEASURE TRIP"), post 8vo, illust. boards, 2s.

A Tramp Abroad. With 314 Illustrations. Crown 8vo, cloth extra, 7s. 6d.; Post 8vo, illustrated boards, 2s.

The Stolen White Elephant, &c. Crown 8vo, cloth extra, 6s.; post 8vo, illustrated boards, 2s.

Life on the Mississippi. With about 300 Original Illustrations. Crown 8vo, cloth extra, 7s. 6d.

The Adventures of Huckleberry Finn. With numerous Illusts. Cr. 8vo, cloth extra, 7s. 6d. [*Preparing.*

Massinger's Plays. From the Text of WILLIAM GIFFORD. Edited by Col. CUNNINGHAM. Crown 8vo, cloth extra, 6s.

Mayhew.—London Characters and the Humorous Side of London Life. By HENRY MAYHEW. With numerous Illustrations. Crown 8vo, cloth extra, 3s. 6d.

Mayfair Library, The:
Post 8vo, cloth limp, 2s. 6d. per Volume.

A Journey Round My Room. By XAVIER DE MAISTRE. Translated by HENRY ATTWELL.

Latter-Day Lyrics. Edited by W. DAVENPORT ADAMS.

Quips and Quiddities. Selected by W. DAVENPORT ADAMS.

The Agony Column of "The Times," from 1800 to 1870. Edited, with an Introduction, by ALICE CLAY.

Balzac's "Comedie Humaine" and its Author. With Translations by H. H. WALKER.

Melancholy Anatomised: A Popular Abridgment of "Burton's Anatomy of Melancholy."

MAYFAIR LIBRARY, *continued*—

Gastronomy as a Fine Art. By BRILLAT-SAVARIN.

The Speeches of Charles Dickens.

Literary Frivolities, Fancies, Follies, and Frolics. By W. T. DOBSON.

Poetical Ingenuities and Eccentricities. Selected and Edited by W. T. DOBSON.

The Cupboard Papers. By FIN-BEC.

Original Plays by W. S. GILBERT. FIRST SERIES. Containing: The Wicked World — Pygmalion and Galatea— Charity — The Princess— The Palace of Truth—Trial by Jury.

Original Plays by W. S. GILBERT. SECOND SERIES. Containing: Broken Hearts — Engaged — Sweethearts— Gretchen—Dan'l Druce—Tom Cobb —H.M.S. Pinafore — The Sorcerer —The Pirates of Penzance.

Songs of Irish Wit and Humour. Collected and Edited by A. PERCEVAL GRAVES.

Animals and their Masters. By Sir ARTHUR HELPS.

Social Pressure. By Sir A. HELPS.

Curiosities of Criticism. By HENRY J. JENNINGS.

The Autocrat of the Breakfast-Table. By OLIVER WENDELL HOLMES. Illustrated by J. GORDON THOMSON.

Pencil and Palette. By ROBERT KEMPT.

Little Essays: Sketches and Characters. By CHAS. LAMB. Selected from his Letters by PERCY FITZGERALD.

Clerical Anecdotes. By JACOB LARWOOD.

Forensic Anecdotes; or, Humour and Curiosities of the Law and Men of Law. By JACOB LARWOOD.

Theatrical Anecdotes. By JACOB LARWOOD.

Carols of Cockayne. By HENRY S. LEIGH.

Jeux d'Esprit. Edited by HENRY S. LEIGH.

True History of Joshua Davidson. By E. LYNN LINTON.

Witch Stories. By E. LYNN LINTON.

Ourselves: Essays on Women. By E. LYNN LINTON.

Pastimes and Players. By ROBERT MACGREGOR.

The New Paul and Virginia. By W. H. MALLOCK.

The New Republic. By W. H. MALLOCK.

Puck on Pegasus. By H. CHOLMONDELEY-PENNELL.

MAYFAIR LIBRARY, *continued*—

Pegasus Re-Saddled. By H. CHOLMONDELEY-PENNELL. Illustrated by GEORGE DU MAURIER.

Muses of Mayfair. Edited by H. CHOLMONDELEY-PENNELL.

Thoreau: His Life and Aims. By H. A. PAGE.

Puniana. By the Hon. HUGH ROWLEY.

More Puniana. By the Hon. HUGH ROWLEY.

The Philosophy of Handwriting. By DON FELIX DE SALAMANCA.

By Stream and Sea. By WILLIAM SENIOR.

Old Stories Re-told. By WALTER THORNBURY.

Leaves from a Naturalist's Note-Book. By Dr. ANDREW WILSON.

Medicine, Family.—One Thousand Medical Maxims and Surgical Hints, for Infancy, Adult Life, Middle Age, and Old Age. By N. E. DAVIES, L.R.C.P. Lond. Cr. 8vo, 1s.; cl., 1s. 6d.

Merry Circle (The): A Book of New Intellectual Games and Amusements. By CLARA BELLEW. With numerous Illustrations. Crown 8vo, cloth extra, 4s. 6d.

Mexican Mustang (On a). Through Texas, from the Gulf to the Rio Grande. A New Book of American Humour. By ALEX. E. SWEET and J. ARMOY KNOX, Editors of "Texas Siftings." 400 Illusts. Cr. 8vo, cloth extra, 7s. 6d.

Middlemass (Jean), Novels by: Touch and Go. Crown 8vo, cloth extra, 3s.6d.; post 8vo, illust. bds., 2s. Mr. Dorillion. Post 8vo, illust. bds., 2s.

Miller.—Physiology for the Young; or, The House of Life: Human Physiology, with its application to the Preservation of Health. For use in Classes and Popular Reading. With numerous Illustrations. By Mrs. F. FENWICK MILLER. Small 8vo, cloth limp, 2s. 6d.

Milton (J. L.), Works by: The Hygiene of the Skin. A Concise Set of Rules for the Management of the Skin; with Directions for Diet, Wines, Soaps, Baths, &c. Small 8vo, 1s.; cloth extra, 1s. 6d. The Bath In Diseases of the Skin. Small 8vo, 1s.; cloth extra, 1s. 6d. The Laws of Life, and their Relation to Diseases of the Skin. Small 8vo, 1s.; cloth extra, 1s. 6d.

Moncrieff —. The Abdication; or, Time Ties All. An Historical Drama. By W. D. SCOTT-MONCRIEFF. With Seven Etchings by JOHN PETTIE, R.A., W. Q. ORCHARDSON, R.A., J. MACWHIRTER, A.R.A., COLIN HUNTER, R. MACBETH, and TOM GRAHAM. Large 4to, bound in buckram, 21s.

Murray (D. Christie), Novels by. Crown 8vo,cloth extra, 3s. 6d. each; post 8vo, illustrated boards, 2s. each.
A Life's Atonement.
A Model Father.
Joseph's Coat.
Coals of Fire.
By the Gate of the Sea.

Crown 8vo, cloth extra, 3s. 6d. each.
Val Strange: A Story of the Primrose Way.
Hearts.
The Way of the World.

North Italian Folk. By Mrs. COMYNS CARR. Illust. by RANDOLPH CALDECOTT. Square 8vo, cloth extra, 7s. 6d.

Number Nip (Stories about), the Spirit of the Giant Mountains. Retold for Children by WALTER GRAHAME. With Illustrations by J. MOYR SMITH. Post 8vo, cloth extra, 5s.

Nursery Hints: A Mother's Guide in Health and Disease. By N. E. DAVIES, L.R.C.P. Crown 8vo, 1s.; cloth, 1s. 6d.

Oliphant. — Whiteladies: A Novel. With Illustrations by ARTHUR HOPKINS and HENRY WOODS. Crown 8vo, cloth extra, 3s. 6d.; post 8vo, illustrated boards, 2s.

O'Connor.—Lord Beaconsfield A Biography. By T. P. O'CONNOR, M.P. Sixth Edition, with a New Preface, bringing the book down to the Death of Lord Beaconsfield. Crown 8vo, cloth extra, 7s. 6d.

O'Reilly.—Phœbe's Fortunes: A Novel. With Illustrations by HENRY TUCK. Post 8vo, illustrated boards, 2s.

O'Shaughnessy (Arth.), Works by:
Songs of a Worker. Fcap. 8vo, cloth extra, 7s. 6d.
Music and Moonlight. Fcap. 8vo, cloth extra, 7s. 6d.
Lays of France. Crown 8vo, cloth extra, 10s. 6d.

Ouida, Novels by. Crown 8vo, cloth extra, 5s. each; post 8vo, illustrated boards, 2s. each.
Held in Bondage.   A Dog of Flanders.
Strathmore.   Pascarel.
Chandos.   Signa.
Under Two Flags.   In a Winter City.
Cecil Castle-   Ariadne.
maine's Gage.   Friendship.
Idalia.   Moths.
Tricotrin.   Pipistrello.
Puck.   A Village Com-
Folle Farine.   mune.
TwoLittleWooden   Bimbi.
Shoes.   In Maremma.

Wanda: A Novel. Crown 8vo, cloth extra, 5s.

Frescoes: Dramatic Sketches. Crown 8vo, cloth extra, 5s.   [Shortly.

Bimbi: PRESENTATION EDITION. Sq. 8vo, cloth gilt, cinnamon edges, 7s. 6d.

Princess Napraxine. Three Vols., crown 8vo, 31s. 6d.

Wisdom, Wit, and Pathos. Selected from the Works of OUIDA by F. SYDNEY MORRIS. Small crown 8vo, cloth extra, 5s.

Page (H. A.), Works by:
Thoreau: His Life and Aims: A Study. With a Portrait. Post 8vo, cloth limp, 2s. 6d.
Lights on the Way: Some Tales with-in a Tale. By the late J. H. ALEXANDER, B.A. Edited by H. A. PAGE. Crown 8vo, cloth extra, 6s.

Pascal's Provincial Letters. A New Translation, with Historical Introduction and Notes, by T. M'CRIE, D.D. Post 8vo, cloth limp, 2s.

Patient's (The) Vade Mecum: How to get most Benefit from Medical Advice. By WILLIAM KNIGHT, M.R.C.S., and EDWARD KNIGHT, L.R.C.P. Crown 8vo, 1s.; cloth, 1s.6d.

Paul Ferroll:
Post 8vo, illustrated boards, 2s. each.
Paul Ferroll: A Novel.
Why Paul Ferroll Killed his Wife.

Paul.—Gentle and Simple. By MARGARET AGNES PAUL. With a Frontispiece by HELEN PATERSON. Cr. 8vo, cloth extra, 3s. 6d.; post 8vo, illustrated boards, 2s.

Payn (James), Novels by.
Crown 8vo, cloth extra, 3s. 6d. each;
post 8vo, illustrated boards, 2s. each.
Lost Sir Massingberd.
The Best of Husbands.
Walter's Word.
Halves. | Fallen Fortunes.
What He Cost Her.
Less Black than we're Painted.
By Proxy. | High Spirits.
Under One Roof. | Carlyon's Year.
A Confidential Agent.
Some Private Views.
A Grape from a Thorn.
For Cash Only. | From Exile.
Post 8vo, illustrated boards, 2s. each.
A Perfect Treasure.
Bentinck's Tutor.
Murphy's Master.
A County Family. | At Her Mercy.
A Woman's Vengeance.
Cecil's Tryst.
The Clyffards of Clyffe.
The Family Scapegrace
The Foster Brothers.
Found Dead.
Gwendoline's Harvest.
Humorous Stories.
Like Father, Like Son.
A Marine Residence.
Married Beneath Him.
Mirk Abbey.
Not Wooed, but Won.
Two Hundred Pounds Reward.

Kit: A Memory. Crown 8vo, cloth
extra, 3s. 6d.
The Canon's Ward. With Portrait
of Author. Cr.8vo, cloth extra, 3s. 6d.
In Peril and Privation: A Book for
Boys. With numerous Illustra-
tions. Crown 8vo, cloth extra, 6s.
[In preparation.

Pennell (H. Cholmondeley),
Works by: Post 8vo, cloth limp,
2s. 6d. each.
Puck on Pegasus. With Illustrations.
The Muses of Mayfair. Vers de
Société, Selected and Edited by H.
C. PENNELL.
Pegasus Re-Saddled. With Ten full-
page Illusts. by G. DU MAURIER.

Phelps.—Beyond the Gates.
By ELIZABETH STUART PHELPS,
Author of "The Gates Ajar." Crown
8vo, cloth extra, 2s. 6d.

Pirkis.—Trooping with Crows:
A Story. By CATHERINE PIRKIS. Fcap.
8vo, p cture cover, 1s.

Planche (J. R.), Works by:
The Cyclopædia of Costume; or,
A Dictionary of Dress—Regal, Ec-
clesiastical, Civil, and Military—from
the Earliest Period in England to the
Reign of George the Third. Including Notices of Contemporaneous
Fashions on the Continent, and a
General History of the Costumes of
the Principal Countries of Europe.
Two Vols., demy 4to, half morocco
profusely Illustrated with Coloured
and Plain Plates and Woodcuts,
£7 7s. The Vols. may also be had
separately (each complete in itself)
at £3 13s. 6d. each: Vol. I. THE
DICTIONARY. Vol. II. A GENERAL
HISTORY OF COSTUME IN EUROPE.
The Pursuivant of Arms; or, Her-
aldry Founded upon Facts. With
Coloured Frontispiece and 200 Illus-
trations. Cr. 8vo, cloth extra, 7s. 6d.
Songs and Poems, from 1819 to 1879.
Edited, with an Introduction, by his
Daughter, Mrs. MACKARNESS. Crown
8vo, cloth extra, 6s.

Play-time: Sayings and Doings
of Baby-land. By EDWARD STANFORD.
Large 4to, handsomely printed in
Colours, 5s.

Plutarch's Lives of Illustrious
Men. Translated from the Greek,
with Notes Critical and Historical, and
a Life of Plutarch, by JOHN and
WILLIAM LANGHORNE. Two Vols.,
8vo, cloth extra, with Portraits, 10s. 6d.

Poe (Edgar Allan):—
The Choice Works, in Prose and
Poetry, of EDGAR ALLAN POE With
an Introductory Essay by CHARLES
BAUDELAIRE, Portrait and Fac-
similes. Crown 8vo, cl. extra, 7s. 6d.
The Mystery of Marie Roget, and
other Stories. Post 8vo, illust.bds.,2s.

Pope's Poetical Works. Complete in One Vol. Post 8vo, cl. limp, 2s.

Power.—Philistia: A Novel. By
CECIL POWER. Three Vols., crown
8vo. *[Shortly.*

Price (E. C.), Novels by:
Valentina: A Sketch. With a Frontispiece by HAL LUDLOW. Cr. 8vo,
cl. ex., 3s. 6d.; post 8vo,illust. bds., 2s.
The Foreigners. Cr. 8vo, cl. ex., 3s.6d.
Mrs. Lancaster's Rival. Crown 8vo,
cloth extra, 3s. 6d.

Proctor (Richd. A.), Works by ;
Flowers of the Sky. With 55 Illusts. Small crown 8vo, cloth extra, 4s. 6d.
Easy Star Lessons. With Star Maps for Every Night in the Year, Drawings of the Constellations, &c. Crown 8vo, cloth extra, 6s.
Familiar Science Studies. Crown 8vo, cloth extra, 7s. 6d.
Rough Ways made Smooth: A Series of Familiar Essays on Scientific Subjects. Cr. 8vo, cloth extra, 6s.
Our Place among Infinities: A Series of Essays contrasting our Little Abode in Space and Time with the Infinities Around us. Crown 8vo, cloth extra, 6s.
The Expanse of Heaven: A Series of Essays on the Wonders of the Firmament. Cr. 8vo, cloth extra, 6s.
Saturn and Its System. New and Revised Edition, with 13 Steel Plates. Demy 8vo, cloth extra, 10s. 6d.
The Great Pyramid: Observatory, Tomb, and Temple. With Illustrations. Crown 8vo, cloth extra, 6s.
Mysteries of Time and Space. With Illusts. Cr. 8vo, cloth extra, 7s. 6d.
The Universe of Suns, and other Science Gleanings. With Illusts. Cr. 8vo, cloth extra, 7s. 6d. [Shortly.
Wages and Wants of Science Workers. Crown 8vo, 1s. 6d.

Pyrotechnist's Treasury (The); or, Complete Art of Making Fireworks. By THOMAS KENTISH. With numerous Illustrations. Cr. 8vo, cl. extra, 4s. 6d.

Rabelais' Works. Faithfully Translated from the French, with variorum Notes, and numerous characteristic Illustrations by GUSTAVE DORÉ. Crown 8vo, cloth extra, 7s. 6d.

Rambosson.—Popular Astro- nomy. By J. RAMBOSSON, Laureate of the Institute of France. Translated by C. B. PITMAN. Crown 8vo, cloth gilt, with numerous Illustrations, and a beautifully executed Chart of Spectra, 7s. 6d.

Reader's Handbook (The) of Allusions, References, Plots, and Stories. By the Rev. Dr. BREWER. Fourth Edition, revised throughout, with a New Appendix, containing a COMPLETE ENGLISH BIBLIOGRAPHY. Cr. 8vo, 1,400 pages, cloth extra, 7s. 6d.

Richardson. — A Ministry of Health, and other Papers. By BENJAMIN WARD RICHARDSON, M.D., &c. Crown 8vo, cloth extra, 6s.

Reade (Charles, D.C.L.), Novels by. Post 8vo, illust., bds., 2s. each; or cr. 8vo, cl. ex., illust..3s. 6d. each.
Peg Woffington. Illustrated by S. L. FILDES, A.R.A.
Christie Johnstone. Illustrated by WILLIAM SMALL.
It is Never Too Late to Mend. Illustrated by G. J. PINWELL.
The Course of True Love Never did run Smooth. Illustrated by HELEN PATERSON.
The Autobiography of a Thief; Jack of all Trades; and James Lambert. Illustrated by MATT STRETCH.
Love me Little, Love me Long. Illustrated by M. ELLEN EDWARDS.
The Double Marriage. Illust. by Sir JOHN GILBERT, R.A., and C. KEENE.
The Cloister and the Hearth. Illustrated by CHARLES KEENE.
Hard Cash. Illust. by F. W. LAWSON.
Griffith Gaunt. Illustrated by S. L. FILDES, A.R.A., and WM. SMALL.
Foul Play. Illust. by DU MAURIER.
Put Yourself in His Place. Illustrated by ROBERT BARNES.
A Terrible Temptation. Illustrated by EDW. HUGHES and A. W. COOPER.
The Wandering Heir. Illustrated by H. PATERSON, S. L. FILDES, A.R.A., C. GREEN, and H. WOODS, A.R.A.
A Simpleton. Illustrated by KATE CRAUFORD.
A Woman-Hater. Illustrated by THOS. COULDERY.
Readiana. With a Steel-plate Portrait of CHARLES READE.
Singleheart and Doubleface: A Matter-of-fact Romance. Illustrated by P. MACNAB.
Good Stories of Men and other Animals. Illustrated by E. A. ABBEY, PERCY MACQUOID, and JOSEPH NASH.
The Jilt, and other Stories. Illustrated by JOSEPH NASH.

Riddell (Mrs. J. H.), Novels by :
Crown 8vo, cloth extra, 3s. 6d. each ; post 8vo, illustrated boards, 2s. each.
Her Mother's Darling.
The Prince of Wales's Garden Party.

Weird Stories. Crown 8vo, cloth extra, 3s. 6d.

Rimmer (Alfred), Works by :
Our Old Country Towns. With over 50 Illusts. Sq. 8vo, cloth gilt, 10s. 6d.
Rambles Round Eton and Harrow. 50 Illusts. Sq. 8vo, cloth gilt, 10s. 6d.
About England with Dickens. With 58 Illusts. by ALFRED RIMMER and C. A. VANDERHOOF. Sq. 8vo, cl. gilt, 10s. 6d.

Robinson (F. W.), Novels by:
Women are Strange Cr. 8vo, cloth
extra, 3s. 6d.; post 8vo, illust. bds., 2s.
The Hands of Justice. Crown 8vo,
cloth extra, 3s. 6d.

Robinson (Phil), Works by:
The Poets' Birds. Crown 8vo. cloth
extra, 7s. 6d
The Poets' Beasts. Crown 8vo, cloth
extra, 7s. 6d. [*In preparation.*]

Robinson Crusoe: A beautiful
reproduction of Major's Edition, with
37 Woodcuts and Two Steel Plates by
GEORGE CRUIKSHANK, choicely printed.
Crown 8vo, cloth extra, 7s. 6d. A few
Large-Paper copies, printed on hand-
made paper, with India proofs of the
Illustrations, price 36s.

Rochefoucauld's Maxims and
Moral Reflections. With Notes, and
an Introductory Essay by SAINTE-
BEUVE. Post 8vo, cloth limp, 2s.

Roll of Battle Abbey, The; or,
A List of the Principal Warriors who
came over from Normandy with William the Conqueror, and Settled in
this Country, A.D. 1066-7. With the
principal Arms emblazoned in Gold
and Colours. Handsomely printed, 5s.

Rowley (Hon. Hugh), Works by:
Post 8vo, cloth limp, 2s. 6d. each.
Punlana: Riddles and Jokes. With
numerous Illustrations.
More Punlana. Profusely Illustrated.

Russell (W. Clark, Author of
"The Wreck of the *Grosvenor*"),
Works by:
Crown 8vo, cloth extra, 6s. each.
Round the Galley-Fire.
On the Fok's'le Head: A Collection
of Yarns and Sea Descriptions.
[*In the press.*]

Sala.—Gaslight and Daylight.
By GEORGE AUGUSTUS SALA. Post
8vo, illustrated boards, 2s.

Sanson.—Seven Generations
of Executioners: Memoirs of the
Sanson Family (1658 to 1847). Edited
by HENRY SANSON. Cr. 8vo, cl. ex. 3s. 6d.

Saunders (John), Novels by:
Crown 8vo, cloth extra, 3s. 6d. each;
post 8vo, illustrated boards, 2s. each.
Bound to the Wheel.
One Against the World.
Guy Waterman.
The Lion in the Path.
The Two Dreamers.

Saunders (Katharine), Novels
by:
Crown 8vo, cloth extra, 3s. 6d. each.
Joan Merryweather.
Margaret and Elizabeth.
Gideon's Rock.
The High Mills.

Heart Salvage, by Sea and Land.
Three Vols., crown 8vo.

Science Gossip: An Illustrated
Medium of Interchange for Students
and Lovers of Nature. Edited by J. E.
TAYLOR, F.L.S., &c. Devoted to Geo-
logy, Botany, Physiology, Chemistry,
Zoology, Microscopy, Telescopy, Phy-
siography, &c. Price 4d. Monthly; or
5s. per year, post free. Each Number
contains a Coloured Plate and numerous Woodcuts. Vols. I. to XIV. may
be had at 7s. 6d. each; and Vols. XV.
to XIX. (1883), at 5s. each. Cases for
Binding, 1s. 6d. each.

Scott's (Sir Walter) Marmion.
An entirely New Edition of this famous
and popular Poem, with over 100 new
Illustrations by leading Artists. Ele-
gantly and appropriately bound, small
4to, cloth extra, 16s.

[The immediate success of "The
Lady of the Lake," published in 1882,
has encouraged Messrs. CHATTO and
WINDUS to bring out a Companion
Edition of this not less popular and
famous poem. Produced in the same
style, and with the same careful and
elaborate style of illustration, regard-
less of cost, Mr. Anthony's skilful
supervision is sufficient guarantee that
the work is elegant and tasteful as well
as correct.]

"Secret Out" Series, The:
Crown 8vo, cloth extra, profusely Illus-
trated, 4s. 6d. each.
The Secret Out: One Thousand
Tricks with Cards, and other Re-
creations; with Entertaining Experi-
ments in Drawing-room or "White
Magic." By W. H. CREMER. 300
Engravings.
The Pyrotechnist's Treasury; or,
Complete Art of Making Fireworks.
By THOMAS KENTISH. With numer-
ous Illustrations.
The Art of Amusing: A Collection of
Graceful Arts, Games, Tricks, Puzzles,
and Charades. By FRANK BELLEW.
With 300 Illustrations.
Hanky-Panky: Very Easy Tricks,
Very Difficult Tricks, White Magic,
Sleight of Hand. Edited by W. H.
CREMER. With 200 Illustrations.

"SECRET OUT" SERIES, *continued*—

The Merry Circle: A Book of New Intellectual Games and Amusements. By CLARA BELLEW. With many Illustrations.

Magician's Own Book: Performances with Cups and Balls, Eggs, Hats, Handkerchiefs, &c. All from actual Experience. Edited by W. H. CREMER. 200 Illustrations.

Magic No Mystery: Tricks with Cards, Dice, Balls, &c., with fully descriptive Directions; the Art of Secret Writing; Training of Performing Animals, &c. With Coloured Frontispiece and many Illustrations.

Senior (William), Works by :

Travel and Trout in the Antipodes. Crown 8vo, cloth extra, 6s.

By Stream and Sea. Post 8vo, cloth limp, 2s. 6d.

Seven Sagas (The) of Prehistoric Man. By JAMES H. STODDART, Author of "The Village Life." Crown 8vo, cloth extra, 6s.

Shakespeare :

The First Folio Shakespeare.—MR. WILLIAM SHAKESPEARE'S Comedies, Histories, and Tragedies. Published according to the true Originall Copies. London, Printed by ISAAC IAGGARD and ED. BLOUNT. 1623.—A Reproduction of the extremely rare original, in reduced facsimile, by a photographic process—ensuring the strictest accuracy in every detail. Small 8vo, half-Roxburghe, 7s. 6d.

The Lansdowne Shakespeare. Beautifully printed in red and black, in small but very clear type. With engraved facsimile of DROESHOUT'S Portrait. Post 8vo, cloth extra, 7s. 6d.

Shakespeare for Children: Tales from Shakespeare. By CHARLES and MARY LAMB. With numerous Illustrations, coloured and plain, by J. MOYR SMITH. Crown 4to, cloth gilt, 6s.

The Handbook of Shakespeare Music. Being an Account of 350 Pieces of Music, set to Words taken from the Plays and Poems of Shakespeare, the compositions ranging from the Elizabethan Age to the Present Time. By ALFRED ROFFE. 4to, half-Roxburghe, 7s.

A Study of Shakespeare. By ALGERNON CHARLES SWINBURNE. Crown 8vo, cloth extra, 8s.

Shelley's Complete Works, in Four Vols., post 8vo, cloth limp, 8s.; or separately, 2s. each. Vol I. contains his Early Poems, Queen Mab, &c., with an Introduction by LEIGH HUNT; Vol. II., his Later Poems, Laon and Cythna, &c.; Vol. III., Posthumous Poems,the Shelley Papers, &c.; Vol. IV., his Prose Works, including A Refutation of Deism, Zastrozzi, St. Irvyne, &c.

Sheridan :—

Sheridan's Complete Works, with Life and Anecdotes. Including his Dramatic Writings, printed from the Original Editions, his Works in Prose and Poetry, Translations, Speeches, Jokes, Puns, &c. With a Collection of Sheridaniana. Crown 8vo, cloth extra, gilt, with 10 full-page Tinted Illustrations. 7s. 6d.

Sheridan's Comedies: The Rivals, and The School for Scandal. Edited, with an Introduction and Notes to each Play, and a Biographical Sketch of Sheridan, by BRANDER MATTHEWS. With Decorative Vignettes and 10 full-page Illustrations. Demy 8vo, cl. bds., 12s. 6d.

Short Sayings of Great Men. With Historical and Explanatory Notes by SAMUEL A. BENT, M.A. Demy 8vo, cloth extra, 7s. 6d.

Sidney's (Sir Philip) Complete Poetical Works, including all those in "Arcadia." With Portrait, Memorial-Introduction, Essay on the Poetry of Sidney, and Notes, by the Rev. A. B. GROSART, D.D. Three Vols., crown 8vo, cloth boards, 18s.

Signboards : Their History. With Anecdotes of Famous Taverns and Remarkable Characters. By JACOB LARWOOD and JOHN CAMDEN HOTTEN. Crown 8vo, cloth extra, with 100 Illustrations, 7s. 6d.

Sims (G. R.)—How the Poor Live. With 60 Illustrations by FRED. BARNARD. Large 4to, 1s.

Sketchley.—A Match in the Dark. By ARTHUR SKETCHLEY. Post 8vo, illustrated boards, 2s.

Slang Dictionary, The : Etymological, Historical, and Anecdotal. Crown 8vo, cloth extra, gilt, 6s. 6d.

Smith (J. Moyr), Works by :

The Prince of Argolis: A Story of the Old Greek Fairy Time. By J. MOYR SMITH. Small 8vo, cloth extra, with 130 Illustrations, 3s. 6d.

SMITH's (J. MOYR) WORKS, continued—
Tales of Old Thule. Collected and Illustrated by J. MOYR SMITH. Cr. 8vo, cloth gilt, profusely Illust., 6s.
The Wooing of the Water Witch: A Northern Oddity. By EVAN DALDORNE. Illustrated by J. MOYR SMITH. Small 8vo, cloth extra, 6s.

Spalding.–Elizabethan Demonology: An Essay in Illustration of the Belief in the Existence of Devils, and the Powers possessed by Them. By T. ALFRED SPALDING, LL.B. Crown 8vo, cloth extra, 5s.

Speight. — The Mysteries of Heron Dyke. By T. W. SPEIGHT. With a Frontispiece by M. ELLEN EDWARDS. Crown 8vo, cloth extra, 3s. 6d. ; post 8vo, illustrated boards, 2s.

Spenser for Children. By M. H. TOWRY. With Illustrations by WALTER J MORGAN. Crown 4to, with Coloured Illustrations, cloth gilt, 6s.

Staunton.—Laws and Practice of Chess; Together with an Analysis of the Openings, and a Treatise on End Games. By HOWARD STAUNTON. Edited by ROBERT B. WORMALD. New Edition, small cr. 8vo, cloth extra, 5s.

Sterndale.—The Afghan Knife. A Novel. By ROBERT ARMITAGE STERNDALE. Cr. 8vo, cloth extra, 3s. 6d.; post 8vo, illustrated boards, 2s.

Stevenson (R. Louis), Works by:
Travels with a Donkey in the Cevennes. Frontispiece by WALTER CRANE. Post 8vo, cloth limp, 2s. 6d.
An Inland Voyage. With Front. by W. CRANE. Post 8vo, cl. lp., 2s. 6d.
Virginibus Puerisque, and other Papers. Crown 8vo, cloth extra, 6s.
Familiar Studies of Men and Books. Crown 8vo, cloth extra, 6s.
New Arabian Nights. Crown 8vo, cl. extra, 6s., post 8vo, illust. bds., 2s.
The Silverado Squatters. With Frontispiece. Cr. 8vo, cloth extra, 6s.
Prince Otto: A Romance. Crown 8vo, cloth extra, 6s. [In preparation.

St. John.—A Levantine Family. By BAYLE ST. JOHN. Post 8vo, illustrated boards, 2s.

Stoddard.—Summer Cruising In the South Seas. By CHARLES WARREN STODDARD. Illust. by WALLIS MACKAY. Crown 8vo, cl. extra, 3s. 6d.

St. Pierre.—Paul and Virginia, and The Indian Cottage. By BERNARDIN ST PIERRE. Edited, with Life, by Rev. E. CLARKE. Post 8vo, cl. lp., 2s.

Stories from Foreign Novelists. With Notices of their Lives and Writings. By HELEN and ALICE ZIMMERN; and a Frontispiece. Crown 8vo cloth extra, 3s. 6d.

Strutt's Sports and Pastimes of the People of England; including the Rural and Domestic Recreations, May Games, Mummeries, Shows, Processions, Pageants, and Pompous Spectacles, from the Earliest Period to the Present Time. With 140 Illustrations. Edited by WILLIAM HONE. Crown 8vo, cloth extra, 7s. 6d.

Suburban Homes (The) of London: A Residential Guide to Favourite London Localities, their Society. Celebrities, and Associations. With Notes on their Rental, Rates, and House Accommodation. With Map of Suburban London. Cr.8vo.cl.ex.,7s.6d.

Swift's Choice Works, in Prose and Verse. With Memoir, Portrait, and Facsimiles of the Maps in the Original Edition of "Gulliver's Travels." Cr. 8vo, cloth extra, 7s. 6d.

Swinburne (Algernon C.), Works by:
The Queen Mother and Rosamond. Fcap. 8vo, 5s.
Atalanta In Calydon. Crown 8vo, 6s.
Chastelard. A Tragedy. Cr. 8vo, 7s.
Poems and Ballads. FIRST SERIES. Fcap. 8vo, 9s. Also in crown 8vo, at same price.
Poems and Ballads. SECOND SERIES. Fcap. 8vo, 9s. Cr. 8vo, same price.
Notes on Poems and Reviews. 8vo 1s.
William Blake: A Critical Essay. With Facsimile Paintings. Demy 8vo, 16s.
Songs before Sunrise. Cr.8vo, 10s.6d.
Bothwell: A Tragedy. Cr.8vo,12s.6d.
George Chapman: An Essay. Crown 8vo, 7s.
Songs of Two Nations. Cr. 8vo, 6s.
Essays and Studies. Crown 8vo, 12s.
Erechtheus: A Tragedy. Cr. 8vo, 6s.
Note of an English Republican on the Muscovite Crusade. 8vo, 1s.
A Note on Charlotte Bronte. Crown 8vo, 6s.
A Study of Shakespeare. Cr. 8vo, 8s.
Songs of the Springtides. Crown 8vo, 6s.
Studies In Song. Crown 8vo, 7s.
Mary Stuart: A Tragedy. Cr. 8vo, 8s.
Tristram of Lyonesse, and other Poems. Crown 8vo, 9s.
A Century of Roundels. Small 4to, cloth extra, 8s.
A Midsummer Holiday, and other Poems. Crown 8vo, 7s.

BOOKS PUBLISHED BY

Symonds.—Wine, Women and Song: Mediæval Latin Students' Songs. Now first translated into English Verse, with an Essay by J. Addington Symonds. Small 8vo, parchment, 6s.

Syntax's (Dr.) Three Tours: In Search of the Picturesque, in Search of Consolation, and in Search of a Wife. With the whole of Rowlandson's droll page Illustrations in Colours and a Life of the Author by J. C. Hotten. Medium 8vo, cloth extra, 7s. 6d.

Taine's History of English Literature. Translated by Henry Van Laun. Four Vols., small 8vo, cloth boards, 30s.—Popular Edition, Two Vols., crown 8vo, cloth extra, 15s.

Taylor (Dr. J. E., F.L.S.), Works by:
The Sagacity and Morality of Plants: A Sketch of the Life and Conduct of the Vegetable Kingdom. With Coloured Frontispiece and 100 Illusts. Crown 8vo, cl. extra, 7s. 6d.
Our Common British Fossils: A Complete Handbook. With numerous Illustrations. Crown 8vo, cloth extra, 7s. 6d. [Preparing.

Taylor's (Bayard) Diversions of the Echo Club: Burlesques of Modern Writers. Post 8vo, cloth limp, 2s.

Taylor's (Tom) Historical Dramas: "Clancarty," "Jeanne Darc," "'Twixt Axe and Crown," "The Fool's Revenge," "Arkwright's Wife," "Anne Boleyn," "Plot and Passion." One Vol., crown 8vo, cloth extra, 7s. 6d.
*** The Plays may also be had separately, at 1s. each.

Tennyson (Lord): A Biographical Sketch. By H. J. Jennings. Crown 8vo, cloth extra, 6s.

Thackerayana: Notes and Anecdotes. Illustrated by Hundreds of Sketches by William Makepeace Thackeray, depicting Humorous Incidents in his School-life, and Favourite Characters in the books of his every-day reading. With Coloured Frontispiece. Cr. 8vo, cl. extra, 7s. 6d.

Thomas (Bertha), Novels by. Crown 8vo, cloth extra, 3s. 6d. each; post 8vo, illustrated boards, 2s. each.
Cressida.
Proud Maisie.
The Violin-Player.

Thomas (M.).—A Fight for Life A Novel. By W. Moy Thomas. Post 8vo, illustrated boards, 2s.

Thomson's Seasons and Castle of Indolence. With a Biographical and Critical Introduction by Allan Cunningham, and over 50 fine Illustrations on Steel and Wood. Crown 8vo, cloth extra, gilt edges, 7s. 6d.

Thornbury (Walter), Works by
Haunted London. Edited by Edward Walford, M.A. With Illustrations by F. W. Fairholt, F.S.A. Crown 8vo, cloth extra, 7s. 6d.
The Life and Correspondence of J. M. W. Turner. Founded upon Letters and Papers furnished by his Friends and fellow Academicians. With numerous Illusts. in Colours, facsimiled from Turner's Original Drawings. Cr. 8vo, cl. extra, 7s. 6d.
Old Stories Re-told. Post 8vo, cloth limp, 2s. 6d.
Tales for the Marines. Post 8vo, illustrated boards, 2s.

Timbs (John), Works by:
The History of Clubs and Club Life in London. With Anecdotes of its Famous Coffee-houses, Hostelries, and Taverns. With numerous Illustrations. Cr. 8vo, cloth extra, 7s. 6d.
English Eccentrics and Eccentricities: Stories of Wealth and Fashion, Delusions, Impostures, and Fanatic Missions, Strange Sights and Sporting Scenes, Eccentric Artists, Theatrical Folks, Men of Letters, &c. With nearly 50 Illusts. Crown 8vo, cloth extra, 7s. 6d.

Torrens. — The Marquess Wellesley, Architect of Empire. An Historic Portrait. By W. M. Torrens, M.P. Demy 8vo, cloth extra, 14s.

Trollope (Anthony), Novels by:
Crown 8vo, cloth extra, 3s. 6d. each; post 8vo, illustrated boards, 2s. each.
The Way We Live Now.
The American Senator.
Kept in the Dark.
Frau Frohmann.
Marion Fay.

Crown 8vo, cloth extra, 3s. 6d. each.
Mr. Scarborough's Family.
The Land-Leaguers.

Trollope (Frances E.), Novels by
Like Ships upon the Sea. Crown 8vo, cloth extra, 3s. 6d.; post 8vo, illustrated boards, 2s.
Mabel's Progress. Crown 8vo, cloth extra, 3s. 6d.
Anne Furness. Cr. 8vo, cl. ex., 3s. 6d.

Trollope(T. A.).—Diamond Cut Diamond, and other Stories. By THOMAS ADOLPHUS TROLLOPE. Crown 8vo, cloth extra, 3s. 6d.; post 8vo, illustrated boards, 2s.

Tytler (Sarah), Novels by:
Crown 8vo, cloth extra, 3s. 6d. each ; post 8vo, illustrated boards, 2s. each.
What She Came Through.
The Bride's Pass.

Saint Mungo's City. Crown 8vo, cloth extra, 3s. 6d. [*Preparing*.

Beauty and the Beast. Three Vols., crown 8vo, 31s. 6d. [*Shortly*.

Tytler (C. C. Fraser-). — Mistress Judith: A Novel. By C. C. FRASER-TYTLER. Crown 8vo, cloth extra, 3s. 6d.

Van Laun.—History of French Literature. By HENRY VAN LAUN. Complete in Three Vols., demy 8vo, cloth boards, 7s. 6d. each.

Villari.—A Double Bond: A Story. By LINDA VILLARI. Fcap. 8vo, picture cover, 1s.

Walcott.— Church Work and Life in English Minsters; and the English Student's Monasticon. By the Rev. MACKENZIE E. C. WALCOTT, B.D. Two Vols., crown 8vo, cloth extra, with Map and Ground-Plans, 14s.

Walford (Edw.,M.A.),Works by:
The County Families of the United Kingdom. Containing Notices of the Descent, Birth, Marriage, Education, &c., of more than 12,000 distinguished Heads of Families, their Heirs Apparent or Presumptive, the Offices they hold or have held, their Town and Country Addresses, Clubs, &c. Twenty-fourth Annual Edition, for 1884, cloth, full gilt, 50s.

The Shilling Peerage (1884). Containing an Alphabetical List of the House of Lords, Dates of Creation, Lists of Scotch and Irish Peers, Addresses, &c. 32mo, cloth, 1s. Published annually.

The Shilling Baronetage (1884). Containing an Alphabetical List of the Baronets of the United Kingdom, short Biographical Notices, Dates of Creation, Addresses, &c. 32mo, cloth, 1s. Published annually.

The Shilling Knightage (1884). Containing an Alphabetical List of the Knights of the United Kingdom, short Biographical Notices, Dates of Creation, Addresses, &c. 32mo, cloth, 1s. Published annually.

WALFORD'S (EDW., M.A.) WORKS, *con.*—
The Shilling House of Commons (1884). Containing a List of all the Members of the British Parliament, their Town and Country Addresses, &c. 32mo, cloth, 1s. Published annually.

The Complete Peerage, Baronetage, Knightage, and House of Commons (1884). In One Volume, royal 32mo, cloth extra, gilt edges, 5s. Published annually.

Haunted London. By WALTER THORNBURY. Edited by EDWARD WALFORD, M.A. With Illustrations by F. W. FAIRHOLT, F.S.A. Crown 8vo, cloth extra, 7s. 6d.

Walton and Cotton's Complete Angler; or, The Contemplative Man's Recreation; being a Discourse of Rivers, Fishponds, Fish and Fishing, written by IZAAK WALTON; and Instructions how to Angle for a Trout or Grayling in a clear Stream, by CHARLES COTTON. With Original Memoirs and Notes by Sir HARRIS NICOLAS, and 61 Copperplate Illustrations. Large crown 8vo, cloth antique, 7s. 6d.

Wanderer's Library, The:
Crown 8vo, cloth extra, 3s. 6d. each.
Wanderings in Patagonia; or, Life among the Ostrich Hunters. By JULIUS BEERBOHM. Illustrated.
Camp Notes: Stories of Sport and Adventure in Asia, Africa, and America. By FREDERICK BOYLE.
Savage Life. By FREDERICK BOYLE.
Merrie England in the Olden Time. By GEORGE DANIEL. With Illustrations by ROBT. CRUIKSHANK.
Circus Life and Circus Celebrities. By THOMAS FROST.
The Lives of the Conjurers. By THOMAS FROST.
The Old Showmen and the Old London Fairs. By THOMAS FROST.
Low-Life Deeps. An Account of the Strange Fish to be found there. By JAMES GREENWOOD.
The Wilds of London. By JAMES GREENWOOD.
Tunis: The Land and the People. By the Chevalier de HESSE-WARTEGG. With 22 Illustrations.
The Life and Adventures of a Cheap Jack. By One of the Fraternity. Edited by CHARLES HINDLEY.
The World Behind the Scenes. By PERCY FITZGERALD.
Tavern Anecdotes and Sayings: Including the Origin of Signs, and Reminiscences connected with Taverns. Coffee Houses, Clubs, &c. By CHARLES HINDLEY. With Illusts.

WANDERER'S LIBRARY, THE, *continued—*
The Genial Showman: Life and Adventures of Artemus Ward. By E. P. HINGSTON. With a Frontispiece.

Tho Story of the London Parks. By JACOB LARWOOD. With Illusts.

London Characters. By HENRY MAY-HEW. Illustrated.

Seven Generations of Executioners: Memoirs of the Sanson Family (1688 to 1847). Edited by HENRY SANSON.

Summer Cruising in the South Seas. By C. WARREN STODDARD. Illustrated by WALLIS MACKAY.

Warner.—A Roundabout Journey. By CHARLES DUDLEY WARNER, Author of " My Summer in a Garden." Crown 8vo, cloth extra, 6s.

Warrants, &c. :—
Warrant to Execute Charles I. An exact Facsimile, with the Fifty-nine Signatures, and corresponding Seals. Carefully printed on paper to imitate the Original, 22 in. by 14 in. Price 2s.

Warrant to Execute Mary Queen of Scots. An exact Facsimile, including the Signature of Queen Elizabeth, and a Facsimile of the Great Seal. Beautifully printed on paper to imitate the Original MS. Price 2s.

Magna Charta. An exact Facsimile of the Original Document in the British Museum, printed on fine plate paper, nearly 3 feet long by 2 feet wide, with the Arms and Seals emblazoned in Gold and Colours. Price 5s.

The Roll of Battle Abbey; or, A List of the Principal Warriors who came over from Normandy with William the Conqueror, and Settled in this Country, A.D. 1066-7. With the principal Arms emblazoned in Gold and Colours. Price 5s.

Weather, How to Foretell the, with the Pocket Spectroscope. By F. W. CORY, M.R.C.S. Eng., F.R.Met. Soc., &c. With 10 Illustrations. Crown 8vo, 1s. ; cloth, 1s. 6d.

Westropp.—Handbook of Pottery and Porcelain; or, History of those Arts from the Earliest Period. By HODDER M. WESTROPP. With numerous Illustrations, and a List of Marks. Crown 8vo, cloth limp, 4s. 6d.

Whistler v. Ruskin: Art and Art Critics. By J. A. MACNEILL WHISTLER. 7th Edition, sq. 8vo, 1s.

White's Natural History of Selborne. Edited, with Additions, by THOMAS BROWN, F.L.S. Post 8vo, cloth limp, 2s

Williams (W. Mattieu, F.R.A.S.), Works by :
Science Notes. See the GENTLEMAN'S MAGAZINE. 1s. Monthly.
Science in Short Chapters. Crown 8vo, cloth extra, 7s. 6d.
A Simple Treatise on Heat. Crown 8vo, cloth limp, with Illusts., 2s. 6d.
The Chemistry of Cookery. Crown 8vo, cloth extra, 6s.   [*In the press.*

Wilson (Dr. Andrew, F.R.S.E.), Works by :
Chapters on Evolution: A Popular History of the Darwinian and Allied Theories of Development. Second Edition. Crown 8vo, cloth extra, with 259 Illustrations, 7s 6d.
Leaves from a Naturalist's Notebook. Post 8vo, cloth limp, 2s. 6d.
Leisure-Time Studies, chiefly Biological. Third Edition, with a New Preface. Crown 8vo, cloth extra, with Illustrations, 6s.

Winter (J. S.), Stories by :
Crown 8vo, cloth extra, 3s. 6d. each. post 8vo, illustrated boards, 2s. each.
Cavalry Life. | Regimental Legends.

Women of the Day: A Biographical Dictionary. By FRANCES HAYS. Crown 8vo, cloth extra, 6s. [*In the press.*

Wood.—Sabina: A Novel. By Lady WOOD. Post 8vo, illust. bds., 2s.

Words, Facts, and Phrases: A Dictionary of Curious, Quaint, and Out-of-the-Way Matters. By ELIEZER EDWARDS. New and cheaper issue, cr. 8vo, cl ex., 7s. 6d. ; half-bound, 9s.

Wright (Thomas), Works by :
Caricature History of the Georges. (The House of Hanover.) With 400 Pictures, Caricatures, Squibs, Broadsides, Window Pictures, &c. Crown 8vo, cloth extra, 7s. 6d.
History of Caricature and of the Grotesque in Art, Literature, Sculpture, and Painting. Profusely Illustrated by F. W. FAIRHOLT, F.S.A. Large post 8vo, cl. ex., 7s.6d.

Yates (Edmund), Novels by :
Post 8vo, illustrated boards, 2s. each.
Castaway. | The Forlorn Hope.
Land at Last.

NOVELS BY THE BEST AUTHORS.
Now in the press.

WILKIE COLLINS'S NEW NOVEL.
"I Say No." By WILKIE COLLINS.
Three Vols., crown 8vo.

Mrs. CASHEL HOEY'S NEW NOVEL
The Lover's Creed. By Mrs. CASHEL HOEY, Author of "The Blossoming of an Aloe," &c. With 12 Illustrations by P. MACNAB. Three Vols., crown 8vo.

SARAH TYTLER'S NEW NOVEL.
Beauty and the Beast. By SARAH TYTLER, Author of "The Bride's Pass," "Saint Mungo's City," "Citoyenne Jacqueline," &c. Three Vols., cr. 8vo.

CHARLES GIBBON'S NEW NOVEL.
By Mead and Stream. By CHARLES GIBBON, Author of "Robin Gray," "The Golden Shaft," "Queen of the Meadow," &c. Three Vols., cr. 8vo.

ROBT. BUCHANAN'S NEW NOVEL
Foxglove Manor. By ROBT. BUCHANAN, Author of "The Shadow of the Sword," "God and the Man," &c. Three Vols., crown 8vo.

BASIL'S NEW NOVEL.
"The Wearing of the Green." By BASIL, Author of "Love the Debt," "A Drawn Game," &c. Three Vols., crown 8vo.

JULIAN HAWTHORNE'S NEW STORIES.
Mercy Holland, and other Stories. By J. HAWTHORNE, Author of "Garth," "Beatrix Randolph," &c. Three Vols., crown 8vo.

NEW NOVEL BY CECIL POWER.
Philistia. By CECIL POWER. Three Vols., crown 8vo.

THE PICCADILLY NOVELS.
Popular Stories by the Best Authors. LIBRARY EDITIONS, many Illustrated, crown 8vo, cloth extra, 3s. 6d. each.

BY MRS. ALEXANDER.
Maid, Wife, or Widow?

BY W. BESANT & JAMES RICE.
Ready-Money Mortiboy.
My Little Girl.
The Case of Mr. Lucraft.
This Son of Vulcan.
With Harp and Crown.
The Golden Butterfly.
By Celia's Arbour.
The Monks of Thelema.
'Twas in Trafalgar's Bay.
The Seamy Side.
The Ten Years' Tenant.
The Chaplain of the Fleet.

BY WALTER BESANT.
All Sorts and Conditions of Men.
The Captains' Room.
All in a Garden Fair.
Dorothy Forster.

BY ROBERT BUCHANAN.
A Child of Nature.
God and the Man.
The Shadow of the Sword.
The Martyrdom of Madeline.
Love Me for Ever.
Annan Water.
The New Abelard.

BY MRS. H. LOVETT CAMERON.
Deceivers Ever. | Juliet's Guardian.

BY MORTIMER COLLINS.
Sweet Anne Page.
Transmigration.
From Midnight to Midnight.

MORTIMER & FRANCES COLLINS.
Blacksmith and Scholar.
The Village Comedy.
You Play me False.

BY WILKIE COLLINS.
Antonina.
Basil.
Hide and Seek.
The Dead Secret.
Queen of Hearts.
My Miscellanies.
Woman in White.
The Moonstone.
Man and Wife.
Poor Miss Finch.
Miss or Mrs.?
New Magdalen.
The Frozen Deep.
The Law and the Lady.
The Two Destinies.
Haunted Hotel.
The Fallen Leaves
Jezebel's Daughter
The Black Robe.
Heart and Science

BY DUTTON COOK.
Paul Foster's Daughter

BY WILLIAM CYPLES.
Hearts of Gold.

BY ALPHONSE DAUDET.
Port Salvation.

BY JAMES DE MILLE.
A Castle in Spain.

BY J. LEITH DERWENT.
Our Lady of Tears. | Circe's Lovers

PICCADILLY NOVELS, *continued—*

BY M. BETHAM-EDWARDS.
Felicia. | Kitty.

BY MRS. ANNIE EDWARDES.
Archie Lovell.

BY R. E. FRANCILLON.
Olympia. | One by One.
Queen Cophetua. | A Real Queen.

Prefaced by Sir BARTLE FRERE.
Pandurang Hari.

BY EDWARD GARRETT.
The Capel Girls.

BY CHARLES GIBBON.
Robin Gray.
For Lack of Gold.
In Love and War.
What will the World Say?
For the King.
In Honour Bound.
Queen of the Meadow.
In Pastures Green.
The Flower of the Forest.
A Heart's Problem.
The Braes of Yarrow.
The Golden Shaft.
Of High Degree.
Fancy Free.
Loving a Dream.

BY THOMAS HARDY.
Under the Greenwood Tree.

BY JULIAN HAWTHORNE.
Garth.
Ellice Quentin.
Sebastian Strome.
Prince Saroni's Wife.
Dust. | Fortune's Fool.
Beatrix Randolph.

BY SIR A. HELPS.
Ivan de Biron.

BY MRS. ALFRED HUNT.
Thornicroft's Model.
The Leaden Casket.
Self-Condemned.

BY JEAN INGELOW.
Fated to be Free.

BY HARRIETT JAY.
The Queen of Connaught.
The Dark Colleen.

BY HENRY KINGSLEY.
Number Seventeen.
Oakshott Castle.

PICCADILLY NOVELS, *continued—*

BY E. LYNN LINTON.
Patricia Kemball.
Atonement of Leam Dundas.
The World Well Lost.
Under which Lord?
With a Silken Thread.
The Rebel of the Family
"My Love!" | Ione.

BY HENRY W. LUCY.
Gideon Fleyce.

BY JUSTIN McCARTHY, M.P.
The Waterdale Neighbours.
My Enemy's Daughter.
Linley Rochford. | A Fair Saxon
Dear Lady Disdain.
Miss Misanthrope.
Donna Quixote.
The Comet of a Season.
Maid of Athens.

BY GEORGE MAC DONALD, LL.D.
Paul Faber, Surgeon.
Thomas Wingfold, Curate.

BY MRS. MACDONELL.
Quaker Cousins.

BY KATHARINE S. MACQUOID.
Lost Rose. | The Evil Eye.

BY FLORENCE MARRYAT.
Open! Sesame! | Written in Fire.

BY JEAN MIDDLEMASS.
Touch and Go.

BY D. CHRISTIE MURRAY.
Life's Atonement. | Coals of Fire.
Joseph's Coat. | Val Strange.
A Model Father. | Hearts.
By the Gate of the Sea.
The Way of the World.

BY MRS. OLIPHANT.
Whiteladies.

BY MARGARET A. PAUL.
Gentle and Simple.

BY JAMES PAYN.
Lost Sir Massing- | Carlyon's Year.
berd. | A Confidential
Best of Husbands | Agent.
Fallen Fortunes. | From Exile.
Halves. | A Grape from a
Walter's Word. | Thorn.
What He Cost Her | For Cash Only.
Less Black than | Some Private
We're Painted. | Views.
By Proxy. | Kit: A Memory.
High Spirits. | The Canon's
Under One Roof. | Ward.

PICCADILLY NOVELS, *continued—*

BY E. C. PRICE.
Valentina. | The Foreigners.
Mrs. Lancaster's Rival.

BY CHARLES READE, D.C.L.
It is Never Too Late to Mend.
Hard Cash. | Peg Woffington.
Christie Johnstone.
Griffith Gaunt. | Foul Play.
The Double Marriage.
Love Me Little, Love Me Long.
The Cloister and the Hearth.
The Course of True Love.
The Autobiography of a Thief.
Put Yourself in His Place.
A Terrible Temptation.
The Wandering Heir. | A Simpleton.
A Woman-Hater. | Readiana.

BY MRS. J. H. RIDDELL.
Her Mother's Darling.
Prince of Wales's Garden-Party.
Weird Stories.

BY F. W. ROBINSON.
Women are Strange.
The Hands of Justice.

BY JOHN SAUNDERS.
Bound to the Wheel.
Guy Waterman. | Two Dreamers.
One Against the World.
The Lion in the Path.

BY KATHARINE SAUNDERS.
Joan Merryweather.
Margaret and Elizabeth.
Gideon's Rock. | The High Mills.

PICCADILLY NOVELS, *continued—*

BY T. W. SPEIGHT.
The Mysteries of Heron Dyke.

BY R. A. STERNDALE.
The Afghan Knife.

BY BERTHA THOMAS.
Proud Maisie. | Cressida.
The Violin-Player.

BY ANTHONY TROLLOPE.
The Way we Live Now.
The American Senator
Frau Frohmann. | Marion Fay.
Kept in the Dark.
Mr. Scarborough's Family.
The Land-Leaguers.

BY FRANCES E. TROLLOPE.
Like Ships upon the Sea.
Anne Furness.
Mabel's Progress.

BY T. A. TROLLOPE.
Diamond Cut Diamond

By IVAN TURGENIEFF and Others
Stories from Foreign Novelists.

BY SARAH TYTLER.
What She Came Through.
The Bride's Pass.
Saint Mungo's City.

BY C. C. FRASER-TYTLER.
Mistress Judith.

BY J. S. WINTER.
Cavalry Life.
Regimental Legends.

CHEAP EDITIONS OF POPULAR NOVELS.
Post 8vo, illustrated boards, 2s. each.

BY EDMOND ABOUT.
The Fellah.

BY HAMILTON AÏDÉ.
Carr of Carrlyon. | Confidences.

BY MRS. ALEXANDER.
Maid, Wife, or Widow?

BY SHELSLEY BEAUCHAMP.
Grantley Grange.

BY W. BESANT & JAMES RICE.
Ready-Money Mortiboy.
With Harp and Crown.
This Son of Vulcan. | My Little Girl.
The Case of Mr. Lucraft.
The Golden Butterfly.
By Celia's Arbour.

BY BESANT AND RICE, *continued—*
The Monks of Thelema.
'Twas in Trafalgar's Bay.
The Seamy Side.
The Ten Years' Tenant.
The Chaplain of the Fleet.

BY WALTER BESANT.
All Sorts and Conditions of
The Captains' Room.

BY FREDERICK BOYLE.
Camp Notes. | Savage Life.

BY BRET HARTE.
An Heiress of Red Dog.
The Luck of Roaring Camp.
Californian Stories.
Gabriel Conroy. | Flip.

CHEAP POPULAR NOVELS, *continued—*

BY ROBERT BUCHANAN.
The Shadow of the Sword.
A Child of Nature.
God and the Man.
The Martyrdom of Madeline.
Love Me for Ever.

BY MRS. BURNETT.
Surly Tim.

BY MRS. LOVETT CAMERON.
Deceivers Ever. | Juliet's Guardian.

BY MACLAREN COBBAN.
The Cure of Souls.

BY C. ALLSTON COLLINS.
The Bar Sinister.

BY WILKIE COLLINS.

Antonina.	Miss or Mrs. ?
Basil.	The New Magda-
Hide and Seek.	len.
The Dead Secret.	The Frozen Deep.
Queen of Hearts.	Law and the Lady.
My Miscellanies.	TheTwoDestinies
Woman In White.	Haunted Hotel.
The Moonstone.	The Fallen Leaves.
Man and Wife.	Jezebel'sDaughter
Poor Miss Finch.	The Black Robe.

BY MORTIMER COLLINS.
Sweet Anne Page.
Transmigration.
From Midnight to Midnight.
A Fight with Fortune.

MORTIMER & FRANCES COLLINS.
Sweet and Twenty. | Frances.
Blacksmith and Scholar.
The Village Comedy.
You Play me False.

BY DUTTON COOK.
Leo. | Paul Foster's Daughter.

BY J. LEITH DERWENT.
Our Lady of Tears.

BY CHARLES DICKENS.
Sketches by Boz.
The Pickwick Papers.
Oliver Twist.
Nicholas Nickleby.

BY MRS. ANNIE EDWARDES.
A Point of Honour. | Archie Lovell.

BY M. BETHAM-EDWARDS.
Felicia. | Kitty.

BY EDWARD EGGLESTON.
Roxy.

CHEAP POPULAR NOVELS, *continued—*

BY PERCY FITZGERALD.
Bella Donna. | Never Forgotten.
The Second Mrs. Tillotson.
Polly.
Seventy-five Brooke Street.
The Lady of Brantome.

BY ALBANY DE FONBLANQUE.
Filthy Lucre.

BY R. E. FRANCILLON.
Olympia. | Queen Cophetua.
One by One.

Prefaced by Sir H. BARTLE FRERE.
Pandurang Hari.

BY HAIN FRISWELL.
One of Two.

BY EDWARD GARRETT
The Capel Girls.

BY CHARLES GIBBON.

Robin Gray.	Queen of the Mea-
For Lack of Gold.	dow.
What will the	In Pastures Green
World Say ?	The Flower of the
In Honour Bound.	Forest.
The Dead Heart.	A Heart's Problem
In Love and War.	The Braes of Yar-
For the King. .	row.

BY WILLIAM GILBERT.
Dr. Austin's Guests.
The Wizard of the Mountain.
James Duke.

BY JAMES GREENWOOD.
Dick Temple.

BY ANDREW HALLIDAY.
Every-Day Papers.

BY LADY DUFFUS HARDY.
Paul Wynter's Sacrifice.

BY THOMAS HARDY.
Under the Greenwood Tree.

BY JULIAN HAWTHORNE.
Garth. | Sebastian Strome
Ellice Quentin. | Dust.
Prince Saroni's Wife.

BY SIR ARTHUR HELPS.
Ivan de Biron.

BY TOM HOOD.
A Golden Heart.

BY MRS. GEORGE HOOPER.
The House of Raby.

BY VICTOR HUGO.
The Hunchback of Notre Dame.

CHEAP POPULAR NOVELS, *continued—*

BY MRS. ALFRED HUNT.
Thornicroft's Model.
The Leaden Casket.
Self-Condemned.

BY JEAN INGELOW.
Fated to be Free.

BY HARRIETT JAY.
The Dark Colleen.
The Queen of Connaught.

BY HENRY KINGSLEY.
Oakshott Castle. | Number Seventeen

BY E. LYNN LINTON.
Patricia Kemball.
The Atonement of Leam Dundas.
The World Well Lost.
Under which Lord?
With a Silken Thread.
The Rebel of the Family.
"My Love!"

BY HENRY W. LUCY.
Gideon Fleyce.

BY JUSTIN McCARTHY, M.P.
Dear Lady Disdain.
The Waterdale Neighbours.
My Enemy's Daughter.
A Fair Saxon.
Linley Rochford.
Miss Misanthrope.
Donna Quixote.
The Comet of a Season.

BY GEORGE MACDONALD.
Paul Faber, Surgeon.
Thomas Wingfold, Curate.

BY MRS. MACDONELL.
Quaker Cousins.

BY KATHARINE S. MACQUOID.
The Evil Eye. | Lost Rose.

BY W. H. MALLOCK.
The New Republic.

BY FLORENCE MARRYAT.
Open! Sesame! | A Little Stepson.
A Harvest of Wild | Fighting the Air.
Oats. | Written In Fire.

BY J. MASTERMAN.
Half-a-dozen Daughters.

BY JEAN MIDDLEMASS.
Touch and Go. | Mr. Dorillion.

CHEAP POPULAR NOVELS, *continued—*

BY D. CHRISTIE MURRAY.
A Life's Atonement.
A Model Father.
Joseph's Coat.
Coals of Fire.
By the Gate of the Sea.

BY MRS. OLIPHANT.
Whiteladies.

BY MRS. ROBERT O'REILLY.
Phœbe's Fortunes.

BY OUIDA.
Held In Bondage. | TwoLittleWooden
Strathmore. | Shoes.
Chandos. | Signa.
Under Two Flags. | In a Winter City.
Idalia. | Ariadne.
Cecil Castle- | Friendship.
maine. | Moths.
Tricotrin. | Pipistrello.
Puck. | A Village Com
Folle Farine. | mune.
A Dog of Flanders. | Bimbi.
Pascarel. | In Maremma.

BY MARGARET AGNES PAUL.
Gentle and Simple.

BY JAMES PAYN.
Lost Sir Massing- | Like Father, Like
berd. | Son.
A Perfect Trea- | A Marine Resi-
sure. | dence.
Bentinck's Tutor. | Married Beneath
Murphy's Master. | Him.
A County Family. | Mirk Abbey.
At Her Mercy. | Not Wooed, but
A Woman's Ven- | Won.
geance. | £200 Reward.
Cecil's Tryst. | Less Black than
Clyffards of Clyffe | We're Painted.
The Family Scape- | By Proxy.
grace. | Under One Roof.
Foster Brothers. | High Spirits.
Found Dead. | Carlyon's Year.
Best of Husbands | A Confidential
Walter's Word. | Agent.
Halves. | Some Private
Fallen Fortunes. | Views.
What He Cost Her | From Exile.
Humorous Stories | A Grape from a
Gwendoline's Har- | Thorn.
vest. | For Cash Only.

BY EDGAR A. POE.
The Mystery of Marie Roget.

CHEAP POPULAR NOVELS, *continued—*

BY E. C. PRICE.
Valentina.

BY CHARLES READE.
It Is Never Too Late to Mend.
Hard Cash.
Peg Woffington.
Christie Johnstone.
Griffith Gaunt.
Put Yourself In His Place.
The Double Marriage.
Love Me Little, Love Me Long.
Foul Play.
The Cloister and the Hearth.
The Course of True Love.
Autobiography of a Thief.
A Terrible Temptation.
The Wandering Heir.
A Simpleton.
A Woman-Hater.
Readiana.

BY MRS. J. H. RIDDELL.
Her Mother's Darling.
Prince of Wales's Garden Party.

BY F. W. ROBINSON.
Women are Strange.

BY BAYLE ST. JOHN.
A Levantine Family.

BY GEORGE AUGUSTUS SALA.
Gaslight and Daylight.

BY JOHN SAUNDERS.
Bound to the Wheel.
One Against the World.
Guy Waterman.
The Lion In the Path.
Two Dreamers.

BY ARTHUR SKETCHLEY.
A Match In the Dark.

BY T. W. SPEIGHT.
The Mysteries of Heron Dyke.

BY R. A. STERNDALE.
The Afghan Knife.

BY R. LOUIS STEVENSON.
New Arabian Nights.

BY BERTHA THOMAS.
Cressida. | Proud Maisie.
The Violin-Player.

BY W. MOY THOMAS.
A Fight for Life.

CHEAP POPULAR NOVELS, *continued—*

BY WALTER THORNBURY.
Tales for the Marines.

BY T. ADOLPHUS TROLLOPE.
Diamond Cut Diamond.

BY ANTHONY TROLLOPE.
The Way We Live Now.
The American Senator.
Frau Frohmann.
Marion Fay
Kept In the Dark.

By **FRANCES ELEANOR TROLLOPE**
Like Ships upon the Sea.

BY MARK TWAIN.
Tom Sawyer.
An Idle Excursion.
A Pleasure Trip on the Continent of Europe.
A Tramp Abroad.
The Stolen White Elephant.

BY SARAH TYTLER.
What She Came Through.
The Bride's Pass.

BY J. S. WINTER.
Cavalry Life. | Regimental Legends

BY LADY WOOD.
Sabina.

BY EDMUND YATES.
Castaway. | The Forlorn Hope.
Land at Last.

ANONYMOUS.
Paul Ferroll.
Why Paul Ferroll Killed his Wife.

Fcap. 8vo, picture covers, 1s. each.
Jeff Briggs's Love Story. By BRET HARTE.
The Twins of Table Mountain. By BRET HARTE.
Mrs. Gainsborough's Diamonds. By JULIAN HAWTHORNE.
Kathleen Mavourneen. By Author of "That Lass o' Lowrie's."
Lindsay's Luck. By the Author of "That Lass o' Lowrie's."
Pretty Polly Pemberton. By the Author of "That Lass o' Lowrie's."
Trooping with Crows. By Mrs. PIRKIS.
The Professor's Wife. By LEONARD GRAHAM.
A Double Bond. By LINDA VILLARI.
Esther's Glove. By R. E. FRANCILLON.
The Garden that Paid the Rent. By TOM JERROLD.

J. OGDEN AND CO., PRINTERS, 172, ST. JOHN STREET, E.C.

www.ingramcontent.com/pod-product-compliance
Lightning Source LLC
Chambersburg PA
CBHW060512030726
47498CB00004B/921